Blurred Attraction

RECKLESS BEAT BOOK ONE

EDEN SUMMERS

Blind Attraction
Copyright © 2013 by Eden Summers

Editing by Rachel Firasek
Copy Editing by Lori Whitwam
Cover Art by LM Creations
Formatting by Champagne Formats

This book is a work of fiction. The names, characters, places, and incidents are products of the writer's imagination or have been used fictitiously and are not to be construed as real. Any resemblance to persons, living or dead, actual events, locales or organizations is entirely coincidental.

All rights reserved. With the exception of quotes used in reviews, this book may not be reproduced or used in whole or in part by any means existing without written permission from the author.

The author acknowledges the trademarked status and trademark owners of various products referenced in this work of fiction, which have been used without permission. The publication/use of these trademarks is not authorized, associated with, or sponsored by the trademark owners.

Dedication

To my editor. This is the third piece we've worked on together and not once has your faith in me wavered. You've taught me so much and I hope you know how much I appreciate you.

To my crit partners, street team, family, and friends—Thank you. For everything. I'm blessed to be surrounded and supported by such great people. I couldn't have written Mitchell and Alana's story without you.

And to my hubby. You may not be able to sing…or dance…but you will always be my rock star.

Chapter One

ALANA SHELTON SUCKED in a deep breath and relaxed into her seat. An unfamiliar world drifted by the window as her plane taxied into the Richmond, Virginia airport.

This was it—life.

Finally, she was free, alone, and able to grasp independence with both hands, even though those betraying body parts trembled in her lap. Her heart pounded with the erratic beat of excitement, and her palms were sticky with sweat. She'd waited too long for today. Too damn long dreaming of what it would be like to breathe without restriction.

"You didn't enjoy the flight?"

She peered over her shoulder and smiled at the elderly man seated beside her. "You know what, I actually think I did."

Soaring above the clouds was invigorating. Everyone around her seemed to take the view for granted. They weren't in awe of tiny houses below or the unending curve of barely visible roads.

The man grinned at her, and the sight was so unfamiliar her chest tippy-tapped with the slightest case of arrhythmia. She shouldn't be talking to him, shouldn't be conversing like they were friends, but she'd become warmed by his conversation. He'd sprinkled light chatter into her first flight and helped her relax into unfamiliar surroundings. Which was profound, seeing as she'd been forbidden to speak to members of the opposite sex since she was born.

If her mother were here, chastisements would be flying from her lips. *Don't speak to him. Don't ever trust a man.* Actually, if her mother were here, the flight attendants would've had to prepare sedatives long ago. The woman who raised Alana in the quiet seclusion of a Monument, Colorado retreat didn't deal well with men. Alana was sure the local police station had a notice on their billboard that stated as much.

If you have a dick, avoid this woman.

It wasn't easy being the daughter of a man-hater. It wasn't fun being deprived of any sort of masculine guidance either. But there was no other choice. Not until now, when Alana was confident enough to make her own decisions and step into the world by herself.

"Do you need help with your luggage?" he asked.

"No, thank you." The plane pulled to a stop, ending the tiny glimpses of scenery that had flickered past like snapshots. "I have a friend waiting for me."

Her best friend, Kate, was the only woman who had the slightest understanding of Alana's restricted upbringing.

She unclasped her belt and wrung her hands together, fighting away the jitters. She was determined to spend her mini vacation without the dark taint of her mother's outlook. The slate was wiped clean. At least as much as her nervousness would allow.

She'd never wanted to shun men. She was dying to learn the intricacies of the opposite sex for herself. The good and the bad. The scary and the exhilarating. No matter how determined her mother was to verbally bash anyone without a set of ovaries, Alana had always held an open mind. Secretly, anyway.

It was the thrill of the unknown. The taboo of breaking the rules.

Minutes ticked by before the cabin door opened and passengers disembarked. It was surreal. Pandora's Box was opening. Finally, she had the opportunity to let her hair down without someone hovering over her shoulder. She'd hoped for this day since she was a little girl, and now that it was here she wasn't sure if she should scream, vomit, or rely on alcohol to kill the overwhelming mix of emotions.

"Thank you…" Her words trailed as the man beside her stood.

His brows pulled together. "For what?"

Good question. What was she thanking him for? The conversation? The enlightenment? All he'd done was be kind, and yet the sparse communication they shared had been monumental to her. All it took were a few words. A smile here and there. Then, *bam*, this man had cemented her opinion that the opposite sex wasn't to be feared.

At least not all of them.

She wasn't naïve. God knew how many times she'd been called into the living room to watch another news broadcast on violence against women. And her mother's experiences were the stuff of nightmares. She was merely willing to keep an open mind.

"For being you." She swallowed over the gratitude drying her throat and grabbed her bag from under the seat in front of her.

He chuckled. "I hope you have fun in Richmond, Alana."

Then he was gone, walking away from her like he hadn't just changed her life.

She slumped back into her chair and began her breathing ritual. Deep in, slow out. Unwelcomed emotions were overwhelming her, and guilt sat at the top of the list. Her mother was still back in Monument, probably popping Valium over the thought of her only child being alone in this big, scary world.

You can do this.

She shoved to her feet and followed the line of people banked down the aisle, vowing to enjoy every waking moment, no matter how drained she was from the adrenaline rush. Nothing could wipe the grin from her face as she read the signs through the airport leading her toward the baggage claim.

EDEN SUMMERS

People were everywhere. Men hauled suitcases, children ran from parents, women strutted in business suits or sexy clothing that was way out of Alana's league. There were shops too, with shiny lights and bright smiles from retail assistants. It was like Disneyland. To her, at least.

"Finally!" A familiar female voice came from behind her. "Three cheers for the escaped inmate."

Alana froze. Strangers stared, security stood taller, and the prickle of anxiety over a crowd of people watching her tickled the back of her neck. High and low. High and low. Her emotions were a whirlwind, and she was determined to ride the experience no matter where it led.

She ignored the heat burning her cheeks and swung around to face Kate. "Trust you to make me feel uncomfortable as soon as my plane landed."

Kate laughed and yanked Alana in for a hug that squeezed the air from her lungs.

"You need to celebrate your liberation." Kate pulled back to scrutinize Alana's face. "Prison life was tough for you."

Prison life? Alana scoffed. "This vacation is far from liberation. You know I can come and go as I please."

"Yet you never have."

True. It wasn't easy to leave a mother who skirted the boundary of mental illness. There would be repercussions to this trip away. The leash around her neck would be notched tighter once she returned. But she would endure it all for the love of the woman who raised her.

"No men, no parties, no excitement," Kate continued. "It's actually more like hell than prison."

"It's better than what a lot of people have."

"Keep telling yourself that."

Kate beamed at her as they walked to the conveyor belt displaying suitcases from the flight. Kate's smile was too big, too contagious, as if she truly had witnessed the liberation of a friend who'd been a prisoner of war.

Alana's upbringing wasn't bad. Not completely… OK, it was entirely dictatorial and full of scaremongering, but no biggie. She could handle whatever life threw at her now. Although inexperienced in almost every facet of life, it hadn't stopped her from becoming strong and open-minded.

She was able to explore her love of photography and dedicate all her time to shaping it into a promising career. Her mother had always supported and nurtured her. She wanted her daughter to succeed, just as long as it was done without a male in sight.

"Here, hold this." She shoved her handbag into Kate's arms. Her suitcase was circling, about to fly past as she grabbed the handle and yanked it to the ground. She'd packed her entire wardrobe, which wasn't a whole lot. There were no pretty dresses, no cleavage showing tops or butt hugging jeans. All she owned was similar to the black slacks and loose T-shirt she currently wore.

"Can we schedule a trip to a shopping mall?" She glanced at her clothes and compared them to the tight skirt and equally tight tank Kate had on. There wasn't a subtle bone in Kate's body.

"I'm all over it. We'll upgrade you from the Amish look in no time."

"Your honesty is cathartic," she mumbled.

Kate was the ultimate bad influence. One-hundred percent sexy confidence wrapped in a blonde bombshell package.

"I call it like I see it, and those clothes definitely won't do for tonight."

"Tonight?"

Kate grinned. "All in good time, my precious."

They made their way toward the exit, past the automatic doors, and out into the foreign Richmond air. Everything was unfamiliar—the people, the scenery, the exhilaration. She was stepping into the unknown, and the sensation was unlike anything she'd ever experienced.

Every man who walked by was treated to her appraisal. Not only the good-looking ones, but the gruff, unkempt ones too. She tried to read them, tried to determine if she could pick the good from the bad. One man smiled, and the wave of tingles that washed from her belly to her throat made her laugh in response.

"This is mine." Kate pointed to a red compact car and pulled keys from her pocket.

The trunk popped open, the suitcase was slid inside, and moments later Alana was peering through a windshield as they approached a city she had never seen before.

"Are you ready to party?"

Her heart fluttered like butterflies' wings. "So ready I'm likely to lose my breakfast."

She gripped her seatbelt tight, needing the slight sense of grounding. She didn't even know what defined partying. She was clueless. All she had to go by were the long-distance phone calls from Kate, who had a knack of explaining the fabulousness of her life in vivid detail. Anything from the buzz of alcohol, the euphoria of sex, and even the heartbreak of lost love had been experienced vicariously through her best friend for as long as Alana could remember. "What did you have in mind?"

Kate leaned over and opened the glove compartment. "Only this." She dropped an envelope in Alana's lap and turned her attention back to the road.

"What is it?"

"Tickets to the start of your life."

Alana frowned. "More specifically?"

"A chance to have your ovaries massaged by the vocal perfection of a sex god."

"*Kate.*" She opened the envelope and pulled out two tickets. The writing on the paper was clear. The event started tonight at 9 o'clock and in a hotel she wasn't familiar with. "Give me the details."

"OK, OK. I won two passes to the private performance held by

Reckless Beat tonight. *Here.* In Richmond. The place where it all began."

"Is that a good thing?"

Kate scoffed. "A good thing? *A good thing!* Girl, I would've sold your kidneys on the black market to get these tickets. Reckless Beat are the reason I'm always in need of AA batteries."

"TMI, much?" Alana clutched the tickets and tried not to let nervousness take hold. A performance. A real, live performance. By men who inspire the use of sex toys, no less. "I know who they are, I'm just not sure I'm ready for all that…interaction."

Kate waggled her brows. "You totally are. They're the type of men your mother warned you about, and you're not going to miss a minute of their brilliance."

Perfect. "That's exactly what I need." Sarcasm aside, this was probably the best start Alana could wish for. As daunting as the real world was, she wanted to grasp it with both hands. Not only that, she wanted to shake it, squish it, mold, and cherish it.

There was no more hiding behind the walls her mother had built around her.

Kate reached across the car and squeezed Alana's wrist. "I know you're panicking, but trust me, you're going to have a great time this weekend."

Panicking? Yes. Likely to vomit in Kate's lovely little car? Yes, that too. "Is this a sit-down performance?" One where she had her own personal space to cling to.

"Sweetie, you're going to be so tightly compacted against strangers that you'll lose your virginity all over again."

"Great." Her voice was breathy, betraying her concern. "It sounds as fun as the first time."

"Trust me." Kate squeezed her wrist again. "You'll have a night to remember."

"I don't doubt it." She exhaled all the air from her lungs and focused on the world outside. There was no chickening out now. This was exactly what she'd wanted. Exactly what she prayed for. "As long as any battery action you require is kept on the down low and I don't have to hear it."

Kate grinned. "Hopefully, I won't need toys tonight. I'm planning on enjoying the real thing."

Oh, Christ. "Well, I guess there's no time to waste." She swallowed to relieve the dryness in her throat. "We need to go shopping. Stat."

Mitchell Davies finished tuning the last guitar in the lineup for tonight's show and handed it back to the sound technician.

"Thanks, Tim."

The man jerked his head in acknowledgement. "Are you all set this time?"

"Yeah." *Hell, yeah.* He couldn't wait for the rush of adrenaline and the thunderous spike of his pulse. Tonight was going to be epic. "I'm good to go."

"You sure? I don't want your neurosis calling me back down here *again*."

"You say 'again' like I've been nagging you incessantly." What was up with that? There was a pre-performance ritual that couldn't be messed with. "And I'm not neurotic."

Blake, the Reckless Beat bass guitarist, snorted from a few feet away.

"Oh, come on. It was one final check," Mitch muttered.

Tim raised a brow. "One after another, after another."

Fine. They had already rehearsed last night and collectively nailed the sound for their new album. But for the sake of sanity, Mitch had to triple check his babies to make sure nobody had messed with their strings overnight. He was paranoid when it came to live shows, and this one seemed more important than the concerts in front of thousands of fans.

For the first time in Reckless Beat history, they were giving a live performance of their latest album in front of an intimate crowd of their most loyal fans. They weren't even in a stadium. The stage he currently stood on was at the far end of a hotel ballroom in the heart of Richmond, Virginia. He'd actually be able to see the faces of the women who threw their panties on stage. Not that he approved of them slingshotting underwear his way. He'd much prefer to trail them down the legs of a beautiful woman once they were backstage or in his hotel suite.

You wouldn't hear him protesting, though. Foreplay was foreplay, and he wouldn't disrespect a woman who was prepared to start the proceedings when she wasn't even sure if she was invited to the festivities. It took balls to throw dirty underwear at anyone, let alone a celebrity who could call you out in front of thousands of people.

"What is everyone else doing?" He glanced at Blake and received a shrug in response.

"Ryan was in before sunrise," Tim answered. "Said he couldn't sleep."

"More like his wife would've kicked him out of bed," Blake offered.

Mitch shot him a glare. The last thing Ryan needed was the wrong people overhearing about shit that shouldn't be discussed. Nobody understood what was going on in that messed up marriage, not even husband and wife.

And still, no matter how turbulent Ryan's marriage became, it still seemed more appealing than the lucky dip that came with being single. Some nights Mitch ended up with a five-star woman, the next he was wondering if his bed partner had been reincarnated from a praying mantis. He'd been screamed at, tied up, bitten—in unpleasurable places—and cursed at more times than he cared to recall.

"I'm sure they're fine." He turned to the back of the stage and sank into the euphoria of the pre-show buzz. Sean's drums were already set up, crosses were marked on the floor where each band member needed to stand, and the usual mass of leads were taped to the ground to lessen the chance of him landing on his face mid-performance.

Within hours, people would be crammed up against the metal railing standing in front of the small makeshift stage. Screams would vibrate the room, his chest too, and hopefully his in-ear monitors would save him from an early onset of hearing loss. Men would take advantage of the excitement and work their charms on already aroused groupies. And the weakest of the women would faint.

All this in a mere few hours.

If that wasn't god-like, he didn't know what was.

"Can we leave now?" Blake came up beside him. "I need to get out of here before the adrenaline kicks in."

"Yeah." Mitch turned back to the room and pictured the empty space filled with moshing bodies. "We should go chill out in the suite or lay down and catch some Zs or something."

Sleep would be perfect if it wasn't entirely unachievable due to excitement. The pressure of satisfying hundreds of people had a way of stealing any possibility of slumber. At least without the help of drugs or alcohol.

"Or something? Are you hitting on me, bro?" Blake waggled his brows.

"Do I look like I want your tiny dick up my ass?" He ignored his best friend's laughter and gave a farewell salute to Tim. "See you later."

"Hopefully, not before it's necessary."

"Hopefully," Mitch grated. How could they put a limit on preparation? Especially when it came to music. He hadn't become one of the most envied lead guitarists in the industry through luck. No, sir. The so-called neurotic checking was a part of his awesomeness.

He jumped off the stage and scaled the security railing to head for the entrance to the ballroom. "You coming?" he called to Blake.

"Yep."

They strode in silence to the far end of the room and paused at the door. He wished he had the luck of his other band members who were safely secured in the homes of loved ones. Every time they travelled to the place where the band began, Ryan, Mason, and Sean would bunk with family, while he had to deal with the sarcastic charm of Blake, his brother from another mother, for uninterrupted hours.

His best friend was an asshole. The best asshole on the face of the planet. But an asshole nonetheless. The tattooed, stereotypical bad boy was an A-grade panty dropper, which meant a ravenous group of sex-hungry women were always close by. Unlike Mitch, who could blend into the masses with a baseball cap and dark glasses, there was no way to hide the ink marking Blake's skin. When they were together, it meant a whole heap of television re-runs or unnecessary guitar practice while locked away in the hotel suite.

He pushed the ballroom door open a cautious inch and straightened with relief at the sight of one of their security team standing a foot away.

"We all clear?"

Steve jerked his head. "The bitches are banked up outside for now."

"Bitches?" Blake pushed the door wide and frowned at the newest member of their security. "You wouldn't want Leah to hear you talking like that. She'll kick your ass to next Tuesday."

True story. Leah, their band manager, would bust the balls of anyone who disrespected Reckless Beat fans. She was such a pretty little thing, yet behind the smiles and professionalism stood a vulture—claws, sharp beak, crazy eyes and all. The woman even had the ability to squash Mason's ego if she wanted, and that wasn't an easy feat.

"If it quacks like a duck, waddles like a duck, and shits like a duck, it's a fuckin' duck." Steve crossed his arms over his puffed out chest. "I'm just callin' 'em like I see 'em."

"Nice," Blake grated. "Where did we find this guy, again?"

Screams burst to life from outside the hotel doors. A cacophony of sound that made them all wince.

"Shit." Women were everywhere, body to body, banked behind a wall of security outside. There were signs. Pictures. Posters. Some just waved their hands wildly in an effort to attract attention.

"It looks like all my fans have arrived. I wonder where yours are." He nudged Blake in the ribs and quickly dodged the tattooed arm that came sailing toward him. All it did was make the women scream louder.

"You wouldn't know what a fan was, unless one bit you in the ass." Blake snickered. "Oh, that's right, the last one did, didn't she?"

That woman had been crazy. The type to fall into the trying-too-hard-to-impress-a-rocker category. "Apparently, it's foreplay," he mumbled.

"Apparently, it's fucking psychotic," Blake countered.

The collective hype over the two of them was nowhere near the unruly insanity of what it would resemble if Mason were to walk into the lobby. There wasn't a pair of ovaries that could withstand the charm of the Reckless Beat frontman. Men, too, as Mason learned the hard way.

"Tell me again why we're doing an intimate performance." Blake stared through the floor to ceiling windows, his brow etched in concern. The women were rocking the crowd barrier, shaking it with Hulk strength. "One that puts us in close proximity to starved women."

"Publicity, my friend." Mitch clapped his friend on the shoulder and started for the elevator. Publicity was the excuse for every crazy-ass, life threatening thing they'd ever done. And tonight would be no different.

Chapter Two

"Come on," Kate called, tugging Alana's arm. "Hurry."

A mass of people filled the space before them, most of them packed like sardines in the small area in front of the stage. She planted her feet, already saturated with social interaction from the hours of useless shopping. Apparently, revealing clothing wasn't a stage of her liberation. Not yet. But then again, Kate exposed enough skin for both of them.

"You don't want to stand back here?" Back where people weren't rubbing against each other like a Discovery channel mating ritual.

"No way." Kate tugged her wrist harder, demanding compliance, and led her through the claustrophobic restriction of tightly compacted bodies. She would bet the New York peak-hour subway had nothing on the personal space violations currently filling this room. It was chaotic and entirely out of her comfort zone.

In and out, in and out, they made their way through the human obstacles until they were close to their destination—front row of what she assumed would soon be a mosh pit.

She would've thought the trek to the barrier was impossible, and somehow Kate squeezed past everyone, leaving no hairy, sweaty man untouched. Her best friend was Moses, only instead of the sea, she had the power to part groupies with the flick of her hand.

"So this is it?" Alana yelled over the mass of conversation.

It would be easy to start wishing she was home, in the place where no one had ever made her feel like butt floss, but she wasn't going to give up on her adventure. Not yet.

She staggered with the pulse of the crowd, her hips smashed against the security barrier holding the fans back from the intimate hotel stage. The jolts of pain as her bones clashed with the metal railing kept her awake despite the long day of traveling and unending hours walking back and forth through a shopping mall. Her body ached like she was in her eighties instead of her late twenties, and her weary muscles throbbed to her core. If it weren't for the adrenaline coursing through her veins, she would've collapsed long ago.

"This is going to be awesome," Kate squealed from beside her, bouncing on her toes even though her feet were encased in gravity-defying high heels. With a voracious smile, her friend waggled her eyebrows and turned her attention back to the curtain hiding the stage.

Kate kept repeating how lucky they were to have tickets to Reckless Beat's first performance of their new album—an event people would apparently pay big dollars to attend, if the tickets were actually on sale. The band members, and no doubt their PR manager, had decided to share the major event with a small crowd of their most dedicated fans…or the biggest crazed loons, whichever way you wanted to define them. And Alana was caught in the middle, her body compacted between Kate, a man with a horrendous mullet, and a woman with a set of lungs that rivaled Mariah Carey's whistle-like soprano.

The thousand or so fans stared at the curtain, transfixed with matching goofy grins. She couldn't help smiling along with them. Not that the curtain held any charm. The room simply overflowed with contagious euphoria.

The two security guards, one at either end of the stage, were the only people with stern expressions. They stood tall, their arms crossed over their thick chests while they scanned the crowd. She couldn't blame them. With the mix of hard rock and passionate love songs, the emotions in the room would swing from one extreme to another.

Reckless Beat was famous for intense rhythms and emotional lyrics. The smooth, deeply penetrating sound of the lead singer had even captured her own heart on more than one occasion, and she'd only listened to them on the radio.

"Welcome, Reckless fans. Are you ready to rock?" The male announcer's voice boomed from innumerable speakers around the room.

Screams and shouts combined into a loud drone, which reverberated in her head. The sound vibrated in her chest, giving her goose bumps. She fought the urge to cover her ears and laughed uncontrollably while Kate grabbed her hand and squeezed tight. They jumped up and down as their bodies pushed harder against the railing, the eager fans behind them vying for a better position.

"I can't hear you," he taunted from his hiding position.

The cacophony grew, the excitement making her veins buzz to life. Maybe she would make it through the performance without falling asleep after all. Lights flashed with searing brightness, illuminating the curtain so four silhouettes shone from behind.

"Well, I won't keep you waiting any longer," the voice said with a chuckle.

The curtain rose, mere feet from Alana's hands, and crept higher to reveal the members of Reckless Beat in all their tanned and muscled glory. The four of them stood close, almost within reach. The lead singer held the microphone stand in the center of the stage, with two guitarists standing to his left and one to his right. If she leaned against Mariah Carey beside her, she could see the drummer in the back, his talented fingers twirling those magic sticks in the air.

She had no clue what their names were. She only knew disjointed verses of a few of their top hits. But when the seductively sexy, lead guitarist kicked off with a delicate caress of the strings, her heart melted. He eyed the crowd from under thick lashes. His lips tilted with a wicked grin as he held his cherry-red instrument with confidence.

The first song drowned under fan hysteria. Lyrics filtered through. A song of love, or loss, she couldn't determine, and she didn't mind. Her heartbeat echoed with the drums, her body thrummed with the bass guitar, and the lead singer's voice traveled over her skin like warm honey.

As a teenager, her mother hadn't allowed her to go to concerts. She couldn't even leave the property without receiving a lecture and a glare of disapproval. It hurt and, being a stubborn teenager, she rebelled as often as possible. Over time she learned to accept her isolation and grew to understand why it was necessary. She was now content with what she had. A retreat for women recovering from abuse was her home. A quiet, and at times, highly emotional environment, her mother had opened when Alana was a child.

She closed her eyes, tilting her head back to let the music sink into her soul. The words cleared as one by one the fans decided to enjoy what they were here for.

"Kiss me one last time. Let me taste the love on your lips…"

A shove from behind made her eyes open and she clutched the rail for support. If she came any closer to the railing, she'd be riding it. Ignoring the constant nudge at her back, she glanced up at the stage and found the lead guitarist peering down in her direction. His fingers slid over the strings, moving in intricate patterns, and yet his intense gaze never wavered from where she stood.

Her heart skipped a beat while he stared at her. Then reality slammed to the forefront. He had to be focused on someone else. Either Kate, with her beautiful, blonde hair and barely concealed breasts, or one of the numerous stunners gyrating against her. She was foolish to think his attention rested on her.

Who knew? Maybe he loved a good mullet and liked playing the back nine. It would be a damn shame, though. All the drool-worthy sensuality claimed by his own sex wouldn't be fair. For a fleeting moment she beamed back, wishing those gorgeous hazel eyes devoured her, not someone else.

To keep from falling into a daydream involving his skilled fingers teasing her body, she turned to the lead singer. His forehead held lines of concentration, his hands delicately molding the microphone in the stand. She could see why he made females swoon. He was pleasure personified—blonde, spiky hair which curled at the ends, rough stubble women would kill to brush against their skin, and handsome features that defied the wicked voice belting from his mouth.

She heard every heartfelt word he sang, yet her mind lingered on the image of the guitarist. The memory of his seductive mouth teased her to take another look. After a few moments of wavering restraint, her gaze drifted back to him. His head was lowered, his concentration on the beautiful instrument in his hands. His jean-clad legs tapped to the beat and she had the sense he not only played the music, he lived it. Breathed it.

His hair rested against his shoulders in true rock star fashion, the dark brown shade gleaming in the bright lights. The material of his black shirt strained against his chest and pulled tight over his muscles. He had a bare hint of dark stubble covering his chin, and although he grasped his guitar with sculpted, masculine arms, his face held more of a boyish charm. A mix of soft features—kind lips, smooth skin, and gentle eyes.

Very, very, nice.

She didn't protest when her nipples tingled with the first sign of arousal. Yes, she fell into the sexually deprived category. She wasn't the first person getting on the giddy train for one of the band members, though. The women around her had departed the station long ago.

Her gaze skimmed up his lean waist, over the shirt with white, undecipherable writing, past the mouth that encouraged her to lick her own lips, and to the eyes now staring at her.

Time stopped. She froze in place, a blush heating her cheeks. She bit her lip to hold back the smile bursting to break free and failed miserably. Why not take pleasure in the sleep-deprived hallucination? She would never speak to him or get close enough to touch his hard body. She may as well release the fantasy reins and enjoy.

She swayed her hips, the smile never leaving her face, and danced for him. It wasn't much in the way of moves, but she pretended the focus in his eyes was because of her, not the people surrounding her. That maybe they were sharing a moment, her first of many innocent flirtations this weekend.

Kate jabbed her in the ribs. "Mitch is staring at you!"

Alana shook her head in denial. Unless she had something unnatural sticking to her face, he had no reason to be interested in her. On the other hand, her lack of hysterics probably made it obvious she shouldn't be here. The competition to win tickets had been for hardcore fans only. If Kate hadn't offered her a ticket, Alana would be sitting at home, still clueless to what the band members even looked like.

"Don't be stupid," Alana yelled back, giving her friend a good-natured hip bump.

Kate leaned closer. "Seems like it to me." She jerked her head in Mitchell's direction and Alana followed Kate's lead, her hungry gaze falling back on his face.

This time, she knew her dimples were making an appearance. Her throat dried, and she struggled to maintain eye contact. He was too damn desirable, his expression turning every inch of her skin to flames. Then one side of his lips lifted in the cutest grin she'd ever seen.

Before she burst into a fit of giggles, she distracted herself, looking at the drummer, the lead singer, and the stage lights. She needed to be careful or she'd leave in a daze without remembering any of the performance.

The last notes of the song sounded, and again the crowd burst into cheers. She laughed through the hysteria, dizzy, high on excitement.

"Thanks, guys. You rock!" The lead singer ended his appreciation in a yell. "Do you like the new album so far?"

Alana was deaf. Nothing but bells ringing in her ears.

"I guess that's a yes."

Glancing up at the stage, she found Mitchell staring at her again. She smiled and put her fingers to her ears. When he responded with a cringe of apology and a shrug, she almost squealed like the groupies beside her.

He was communicating with her. *With her*. She didn't understand why or how. Everyone else was vying for his attention and all she could do was blush, yet his gaze still remained on her.

The lead singer cleared his throat. Once. Twice. "OK, OK. We get the picture." He laughed, and the noise around her lessened. "We're going to take a small break and be back in twenty to show off the rest of the album."

Mitchell's lips tilted into a delicious curve, one that made her insides burn. He pulled the guitar strap over his head. She resisted fanning her heated face as he turned to hand his guitar to one of the stage crew. Even his back view was flawless. Strong shoulders, a lean waist, and the tightest ass she'd ever seen.

He pivoted the top half of his body around and raked his gaze along the front row with an impassive stare. When he reached the place where she stood, he stopped. One side of his lips lifted and he winked in her direction, then turned to leave the stage.

She blinked…and blinked again. The world faded away while she relived the moment, trying to determine if she'd won the hot guy lottery. She didn't even notice the curtain falling or that people had stopped dry humping her.

"Jesus Christ, Alana!" Kate grabbed her shoulder and gave her a shake. "Mitchell Davies winked at you!"

Alana swallowed. "I...I..."

What could she say? It sure seemed like he had. However, she had no experience with this sort of thing. Her intimate moments with men involved three isolated nights of fumbling, grinding, and stickiness she hoped to one day forget.

She still couldn't grasp the hype over sex. She'd tried, and the third time wasn't a charm. Since then, things had been drier than the Sahara. She'd even grown accustomed to her monkish lifestyle because the thrill of getting naked with another man wasn't an enjoyable contemplation. It hadn't even been worth the stress of sneaking away from the retreat.

"He totally winked at you," Kate continued, bouncing on her toes. "Crap, I gotta pee. Can you mind our spot?"

Alana nodded and gripped the rail for support. Wow. A guy crush sure did make you giddy. Kate had tried to explain the thrill of flirtation to her in an email when they were teenagers, but Alana had only experienced the emotion vicariously through movies or books. Real life didn't compare. She missed many things by being homeschooled.

Leaning against the railing, she bowed her head and took long, deep breaths to calm herself.

"Excuse me, miss." Alana raised her gaze from the floor, expecting the male voice to be addressing another woman nearby.

Two men stood on the other side of the barrier facing her. One was a security guard who'd been standing at the front of the stage. The other was unfamiliar, dressed in jeans, a baseball cap, and a white T-shirt which read "Reckless Beat Crew."

The guard didn't pay her any attention. He gazed over the crowd, skimming back and forth. The other man leaned close, the tip of his cap coming within inches of her face. She kept one eye on the burly man with the sullen temperament while she leaned back from the guy who continued to creep closer to her.

"Meet me backstage later?"

The deep voice whispered along her skin, and her body hummed in appreciation. She turned her focus to the eyes shaded under the cap and stopped breathing.

Mitchell Davies.

Her mouth opened to release a ragged sigh, and her brain refused to function beyond sending the instruction to stare. His face brightened with a smile and tiny laugh wrinkles appeared around his deep hazel eyes. On stage, under the bright lights, he was gorgeous. Up close he made her throat dry and her palms sweat. His smell even had her hooked, a mix of jasmine and sandalwood.

"Is that a yes?" He grinned.

Mitch leaned into the chocolate-haired beauty and inhaled her floral scent. He turned his face to hers, hiding himself from curious onlookers. So far, so good. Nobody had noticed the rock star standing amongst them.

It wasn't uncommon for him or the other band members to invite groupies backstage after the show. Up until the last twelve or so months, it had been the norm. Now, they'd grown tired of easy women. Unfortunately, their lifestyles didn't allow for much else, and none of them were monks.

He preferred to get sex the old-fashioned way, by flirtation and seduction. Though sometimes, like now, an itch needed to be scratched. Well, what he felt wasn't really an itch, it was more like a compulsion, an unyielding desire to touch the delicate skin of the woman in front of him.

The stage crew usually had the job of approaching fans. Placing himself in close proximity to a horde of screaming women wasn't his brightest idea. He knew from experience that the first appendage they grabbed for was *not* your arm, and they didn't grasp lightly. Tonight, his curiosity was almost suffocating, having the better of him.

The woman standing before him had stolen his attention from the first strum of his guitar. She stood out like a beacon, her wide eyes and shy smile destroying his focus. He could tell she wasn't a show-your-assets-to-get-a-backstage-pass kind of girl. In fact, he didn't think she was a hardcore fan at all. There'd been no screaming, no flashing, and no panties flying at the stage when he smiled at her. Instead of the typical seductive glances he'd grown accustomed to, she gave him a glimpse of her gorgeous dimples and broke eye contact. The angelic sight grabbed him by the balls and still hadn't let go.

His excursion to the security barrier had been in an effort to assure himself she wasn't the stunner the stage lights made her out to be. Those eyes couldn't be that bright, and her smile wouldn't be as hypnotizing up close. Once he confirmed his suspicions, he'd be able to concentrate on the second half of the show.

Only problem? Each approaching step made her beauty more apparent.

She was the most stunning woman he'd ever seen. And he'd seen a shitload of women. With clothes and without.

It wasn't her gleaming green irises, her flawless skin, or the lush lips he already imagined kissing. Her beauty came from the emotion in her features, and the way she presented herself. The shyness set amongst a throng of extroversion.

Her eyes were huge, like a virgin on her wedding night. He read her shock, her excitement, and even a little fear in the light depths. Her clothes were modest—faded jeans and a loose purple T-shirt, hiding what he fantasized would be a great figure. And black knee high boots. Non-slutty boots. Not like the needle thin stilettos the friendlier fans wore. These were sturdy, classy boots from a woman whose focus didn't lay on getting a piece of rock star ass in bed.

He couldn't even see her cleavage, for Christ's sake. After the years spent peering down at a crowd of half dressed women, their assets bouncing around for the entire world to behold, he'd thought he'd grown out of being a breast man. Nope. Apparently not.

He wanted a glimpse under this woman's shirt. He wanted to run his hands up her stomach, cup her flesh in his palms, and tweak her nipples until they were hard and aching. He wanted to saturate her innocence and make her beg to be taken.

Fucking hell. His pants tightened just thinking about it.

"I…" The one letter escaped her lips on a breath.

He itched to move his mouth over hers, to determine if she tasted as sweet on the inside as she appeared on the outside.

She cleared her throat and tilted her head to gaze back into his eyes. "I'm not sure—"

Steve bumped into his shoulder, and Mitch frowned. He realized trouble was brewing before a word was spoken and didn't appreciate the physical contact.

"We better head back. You've got a lot of eyes on you at the moment."

Mitch nodded at the bodyguard and placed his hand over the delicate feminine fingers resting on the railing. "I'll send Steve to get you after the show. We can have a drink. Get to know one another." He said the same line he told his crew to use when offering backstage passes. Only this time, it didn't work. Instead of her staring back at him with excitement, her eyes grew to the size of saucers.

She shook her head and her throat convulsed with a deep swallow. "I don't think—"

"Oh my god. Mitch, I love you!" Like a flock of seagulls, fans started to cram forward, pushing the beauty harder and harder against the railing.

Her face contorted in pain, and no matter how much he ached to hear her name, he had to leave. For her sake. Steve grabbed his shoulder and pushed him sideways. Green eyes didn't glance his way as he retreated. Her focus remained on the railing, her arms tense, her muscles straining to push herself backward.

"Shit." He continued to walk away in long strides and finally broke into a jog. The sooner he disappeared from fan view, the sooner she would be safe. With a wave to the crowd he moved around the corner of the stage and entered the private room where the rest of the band relaxed.

Before Steve followed, Mitch turned and blocked the entry. "Go check if she's hurt."

The bodyguard glowered. "I'm sure she's fine."

"That's great. Your psychic abilities leave me feeling reassured." Mitch gave a far from friendly smile. "But you're going back to check anyway."

Steve's top lip curled. Without a word, he pivoted on his heels and stormed away.

"Arrogant asshole." Mitch slammed the door and spun around to a room full of people staring back at him. "What? We've gotta get rid of him. I've had enough."

Their manager, Leah Gorman, picked up his black T-shirt off the sofa and threw it at him. "I know. I was just informing the guys about a complaint made against him from earlier tonight. A woman claims he manhandled her and she's threatening to sue."

He groaned and removed the spare crew shirt before yanking his own back on.

"I'll speak to him after the performance," Leah continued. "Don't worry, he won't work with you again."

"He shouldn't work with *anyone* ever again. The guy's a tool," Sean added from a chair in the corner while scratching his buzz cut with one of his drumsticks.

"So, was she still a hottie up close?" Mason raised a brow in his direction. "She seemed a little too cutesy from my position at the mic."

Mitch shrugged and strolled to the coffee table for a bottle of water. "She's all right." He didn't want them to know how perfect she appeared up close. All that would achieve was the entire band staring at her for the second half of the performance. "I might buy her a drink after the show, if she's lucky."

The four men laughed at him, and Leah smiled.

Fuck 'em. He could play the egotistical role just as well as Mason. Although, with the lead singer it wasn't a role, more like a personality trait built into his DNA.

"You're as transparent as Britney Spears' underwear." Ryan continued to chuckle.

Cracking the top to his bottle, Mitch glared at the rhythm guitarist. "She doesn't wear underwear, dickhead." He took a chug of his water and resigned himself to more humiliation.

"Exactly." Mason and Sean replied in unison.

He continued to down his water while he gave them the bird.

"All right guys, five minutes. Let's get this show on the road." Leah strode into the middle of the room. "I'll deal with the Steve issue. You just continue to hit this performance out of the ballpark. The fans love it."

Thirty minutes later, he was back on stage, halfway through the second part of the performance. His body buzzed from the heightened state of awareness that always came with performing in front of a live crowd. Right here, right now was what he lived for, what he loved more than life—the euphoria from holding an audience in the palm of his hand.

Tonight was better than normal. They were up close and personal with their biggest fans. Something they didn't get to experience with a packed stadium. He was mere feet from the people who made Reckless Beat into a worldwide sensation. Only he couldn't drag his attention away from one face in particular. He was stuck with half his mind on the music and the other half on a fantasy involving the hotel spa and a lot less clothing.

He glanced back in her direction, like he had every two minutes, hoping to glimpse the faint hint of her dimples. Yep, there they were. He was determined to lick the deep grooves, to make her moan and call his name.

He envisioned the way her eyes would glitter when he broke down her defenses. The way her breath would hitch and her fingers would cling to him. He wouldn't sleep again until he had her. He wouldn't be able to relieve the weight bearing down on his ribs.

The chesty blonde standing beside her waved her arms in front of the beauty's face, gaining his attention. He frowned while she pointed to his woman, nodded her head vigorously, and pointed to the exit.

He might not be proficient in sign language, but he assumed her actions meant he'd have a hot date later. Jerking his head in understanding, he concentrated on the lead up to his favorite solo. When Mason's voice fell away, he stepped forward, positioning himself in front of his future conquest and played to her. For her.

His fingers slid over the strings, hitting each note with ease while Sean hammered the drums and Blake and Ryan backed him up with their guitars. When the last chord sounded, he stepped back and caught her gaze. Her face was alight with an angelic glow, and an impressed smile tilted her lips. His blood thickened knowing he'd caused that mesmerizing reaction.

By the time the final song started, his palms were sweating and he'd deliberately stopped looking in the woman's direction. He wanted her. Bad. He blamed his monstrous surge in libido on the thrill of the hunt. He knew she wouldn't be an easy catch.

Panties and bras lined the stage, and not one of them hers. She'd watched them sail past, her mouth agape as if Reckless Beat fans were sex crazed deviants. Maybe they were.

His woman was straight-laced all the way. The thought of seducing the look of innocence from her, nice and slow, made his cock stir to life. The vision of taking her hard and fast against the elevator wall made him bite the inside of his mouth to beat off the enthusiasm.

He'd never felt this way about a groupie before. The crowd before him always seemed easily obtainable, like picking an apple from a tree. They were there because they thought they loved the band members, or craved the thrill of screwing someone famous. He couldn't imagine this woman acting the same. She may even turn him down.

A grin pulled at his lips. He was up for the chase.

When the final song ended in a flash of light, Mitch pulled the guitar strap over his head and strode straight toward his guitar tech. He handed his baby into the man's capable hands and walked to the rest of the band members, now hidden behind the lowered curtain. They shoulder bumped and clapped each other on the back to mark the perfect performance.

"Are you guys clearing out right away?" Mitch raised his voice over the continued screams from the crowd and focused his attention on Mason, Sean, and Ryan, who would soon leave to stay with their families.

"Yeah, Leah said she'd have security on stand-by and the cars waiting." Mason wiped the sweat from his forehead. "You ready to make a run for your room?"

Mitch glanced at Blake and raised a brow. Months ago, they all decided to remain in town for a few days after the show. They wanted to create hype over the album release, and what better place to start their promotional tour but Richmond, Virginia, the city where Reckless Beat originated?

"I'm ready to go." Blake ran his fingers through his spiky black hair and winced. "I need a shower."

"Let's get going, then. I plan on eating a shit load of my momma's cookin' before I go to sleep." Sean pushed out his non-existent belly and gave it a rub. "Nobody beat's my momma's cookin'."

"Sounds good to me," Ryan added. "I plan on groveling until my wife lets me sleep in the bed beside her."

Sean snorted and tapped his drumsticks on Ryan's ass. "Good luck, buddy. I think you'll need it."

"Fuck you." Ryan slapped the sticks away. "Watch your back,

Sean. If she ends up kicking me out, you might wake up with me lying beside you."

Ryan's relationship with his wife had deteriorated over the years. A marriage that was once filled with love and passion had died from the constant pressure of being in the public eye. Smiles and laughter had turned into snide comments and sexual starvation.

"With my dry run lately, I probably wouldn't kick you out either," Sean nudged Ryan's shoulder and headed toward the steps leading to the private area backstage.

"Are you still meeting up with the hottie?" Mason asked with a bump to Mitch's arm.

"Yeah. I asked Steve to get her after the show."

"Steve?" Mason frowned. "Leah gave him the axe, remember?"

Fuck. Mitch totally forgot.

He turned back to the curtain hiding the crowd. There was no way he could go out there. He enjoyed his limbs intact and his skin unmarred by cougar claws.

"Get one of the crew to find her," Mason offered. "Hey, Tim."

The guitar tech lifted his gaze from one of the stage speakers and gave a jerk of his head in question.

"Can you do Mitch a favor?" Mason continued, as if Mitch needed his hand held.

"Sure." Tim dusted off his hands and strode toward them. "What do you need?"

"There was a woman," Mitch said in a rush, then cleared his throat to try to hide his eagerness. "In the front row. Big, light green eyes, long brown hair. Dressed in jeans and knee-high boots."

Tim stared at him with a blank expression.

"She was next to a blonde with big tits," Mason added.

"Ahh." Tim nodded. "I remember the tits."

Mitch frowned. "Yeah, OK. Well can you go find the chick with the tits and bring her and her friend up to my suite?"

Tim smirked and gave a salute. "My pleasure." Without another word, he moved toward the curtain and disappeared behind it.

"Great." He was relying whole-heartedly on a guy who craved the second-hand attention he received from the Reckless Beat fans. Mitch fully expected Tim to saunter straight into the foyer and start posing for photos instead of finding the woman. Hell, it wouldn't be a first if he was caught selling clothing with fake Reckless signatures, either.

"I wouldn't pin your hopes on that one." Blake patted him on the shoulder. "He's a bit of a loose cannon."

Mitch's throat constricted a little. He had a snowball's chance in hell.

Making a conscious effort not to slump his shoulders, he followed Mason and Blake into the backstage room. They were greeted by a smiling Leah and a swarm of security guards all packed into the small space.

"Great job, guys." She moved forward and gave them each a kiss on the cheek as they passed. "Eww. You all need a shower."

"I'm pretty sure you do that after every performance." Blake chuckled and pulled her in for a bear hug.

Mitch watched the display of affection in a daze and tapped his foot. They still had to go through the drill of getting away from the fans with all their bits intact. He just wanted to be somewhere else… anywhere else, with his wide-eyed hottie beside him.

"Oh, gross, Blake!" Leah pushed at his chest.

Blake lifted her tiny frame off the ground and twirled her in a circle before placing her on her feet. When his hands dropped, she stepped back and shook her head in mock disgust.

"Let's get you boys home." She straightened her suit and glanced around the room. "OK, Ryan, Mason, and Sean, you'll be escorted to the cars waiting at the back of the building. Just be warned there are people everywhere. The function may have only held a thousand fans, but I think every other person in Richmond is outside waiting to get a glimpse of you. So be prepared for bedlam."

Her attention turned to Mitch, then Blake. "I have four men waiting to take you upstairs and anywhere else you need, until morning. There will also be additional hotel security around if you need them."

When they were led from the room, he scanned the hall, trying to spy a familiar face in the mass of people banked around the exit of the function room.

"You see her?" Blake asked, stopping beside him in the middle of the lobby.

Mitch cringed. He felt like an obsessive fan waiting for one special glimpse. She was only a woman. A wide-eyed, flawless woman, but a woman nonetheless. He needed to get a grip. "Nah. Maybe she's at the bar."

He played it cool even though his throat tightened. The blonde and her friend were nowhere in sight. All he could do was hope Tim found her.

Turning on his heel, they made their way to the shared suite upstairs. Mitch hightailed it to the shower to scrub the sweat from his body. He didn't give himself a chance to descend from the adrenaline high. Once his heart rate settled, the half-hard part of his anatomy would perk up and want to play. And he had no intention of performing alone tonight.

His shower lasted minutes. Enough time to wash and get out. He yanked on his boxers, pulled up cream cargo pants, and buttoned up a navy blue collared shirt. As he walked from the bathroom, he towel dried his hair, secretly hoping Tim might be in the suite with the woman.

He needed to find out her damn name.

"I gather from your disappointed expression, I'm not the only person you expected to see sitting here?" Blake asked from the sofa, his laptop resting on his thighs. The bass guitarist didn't go anywhere without it.

"Yeah. I thought Tim might've brought her up here. Maybe he

couldn't find her. Or she wasn't interested." He shrugged through the disappointment.

"Well, I guess it's me and you tonight, buddy." Blake lifted the laptop from his thighs and stood. "Let me get some decent clothes on, and I'll go downstairs with you. No harm in checking." He closed the device and placed it on the coffee table. "Unless we get molested by an over-enthusiastic bunch of groupies."

Mitch gave a halfhearted snort. The thought of mindless sex with a giddy fangirl turned his stomach. His mind was already set on a particular conquest. He just didn't want Blake to know how eager he was. "Sounds like a good fallback plan to me."

Chapter Three

Alana's legs shook as she paced the cement walkway in front of the hotel.

"It's only one drink, Al." Kate stood on the edge of the grass, staring at her while she went back and forth, back and forth. "If you don't go in there and see him, you'll regret it for the rest of your life."

True. Tonight had already been the most exhilarating night of her existence. The opportunity to meet with one of the world's most famous guitarists would never come around again, especially if she continued to live in seclusion on her mother's property.

"But what if…" There were too many "what ifs" coursing through her mind. What if he expected more than a drink? What if he didn't take no for an answer? What if the whole band was there and they wanted to share her around like a bottle of soda at a kid's birthday party?

She'd lost count of how many pieces of teeny, tiny panties had been thrown on stage during the performance. At one point Alana worried the entire crowd would be naked by the end of the show. And none of the band members paid them any attention. Being gifted with used female underwear must be a common occurrence.

"What if *what*?" Kate tapped her foot. "I'll be there with you. It's not like he can make you do anything you don't want to do. Your mother's brainwashed you into thinking men are douche bags. And for the most part, she's right, but you can't go through life hiding behind her bad experiences."

Alana growled in frustration and clenched her fists. Kate was right. She needed to toughen up. Her friend wasn't bullying her, she was trying to beat away the uncertainty and insecurities Alana's mother had crammed into her since birth. Christ. She already knew how to kick an attacker's ass. Her pepper spray was firmly in her jeans pocket next to her cell phone, and they would be in a highly populated hotel in the middle of the city. What could go wrong?

"Fine." She breathed out a sigh. "Let's do this."

"About time," Kate mumbled and turned to walk toward the hotel entrance.

Alana was going to do this. She would walk into the lobby, search for a celebrity who appeared far more stunning than any other man she'd seen in real life, and try like hell not to vomit on his shoes. "What if he doesn't want to see me?"

"Oh, for the love of god." Kate turned and placed her hands on her hips. "Are you fucking serious?"

"He told me earlier the security guard would come get me, and he never showed. Maybe he changed his mind."

Kate breathed out a calming breath. "Mitchell Davies is a rock legend." She raised her eyebrows. "He is sex on a stick. He makes my ovaries sigh. And you've stood here bitching like a fifth grader for the last twenty minutes. All this anxiety over a man any sensible woman would be inside dry humping right now." Kate gave her a forced smile. "You're going to go in there. You're going to blow his mind, and you won't be coming back out unless I say so."

At least she kept the blowing part above the belt.

Alana gave a slow nod. "Ohh kay."

They walked side-by-side into the glamorous lobby, around the closed coffee shop, and past the small groups of fans yet to leave the hotel. There was no sign of Mitchell or any of the other band members. With each passing moment, she grew more eager to find him, if only to see his flirty smile one last time—and his eyes. He had the sweetest eyes.

After fifteen minutes of searching, Alana sighed and came to a stop yards from the entrance doors. "He's gone, and so has the security guard from earlier." She gave one last visual sweep of the room before focusing back on Kate. "I think it's time to call it a night."

Kate glanced at her watch and shrugged. "Yeah. It's already one. Let's go home so I can get a few hours' sleep before I have to get up for work."

Alana hadn't taken more than two steps toward the exit when the hairs on the back of her neck lifted.

"Hey!" The male shout came from the other side of the lobby.

She knew who the voice belonged to before she glanced over her shoulder. The tone was unmistakable, even though they'd only previously shared a few words. Her feet rooted in place while Kate turned back around. The enthusiastic smile that crossed her friend's face made Alana's body shut down. She was entirely numb. Frozen.

"It's him," Kate whispered, her lips barely moving.

Alana gave a slow nod, and swallowed down the nausea pooling in her throat. She could act cool. She didn't have a lot of experience talking to men. In fact, she'd only spoken to five people of the opposite sex in the last twelve months. But she could do this.

"Start breathing before you pass out…and smile. You'll do great." Kate squeezed her shoulder and encouraged her to face him with a little push.

Alana pivoted on her toes while time passed in excruciating seconds. He walked toward her wearing the same cap from earlier and a fresh change of clothes. All laidback confidence and wordless charm. Their gazes met. Locked. He stared at her with gleaming hazel eyes and a cheeky grin that made her insides melt.

And he wasn't alone.

Another band member walked beside him, the guitarist with the raven, spiky hair and tattoos marking both arms. His eyes were blacker than night, dark and ensnaring, yet he had a cocky smirk that made her smile.

"It's Blake and Mitch!" The scream came from a group of five females hovering near the hall to the function room.

Neither man flinched at the attention. It wasn't until then she realized four more men strolled behind them, protecting the rock stars from a distance.

Blake gave a wave to the hyperventilating women who were being encouraged to stay back by hotel security. He leaned into Mitchell, spoke something in his ear, then changed direction and strode toward the growing crowd.

Alana glanced back at the man who stole her breath, his presence now only feet away, and swallowed at the intensity in his gaze. His eyes devoured her, caressing her body from her hair to her toes. She wasn't sure how he did it, but she could feel his gaze raking over her, sending every nerve into hyperawareness.

"Hey." His smooth tone made her breasts tingle—and places much lower too.

"Hi, Mitch." Kate's voice was bubbly and off pitch.

Alana looked at her and wondered if her friend realized she was bouncing on her toes like a child on a sugar high. She frowned at her and received a glare in return. Kate jerked her head toward Mitchell, wordlessly instructing Alana to greet the world famous musician.

"Hello," she offered and reached out her hand before thinking better of it. Did people still shake hands?

He glanced at her offering and grasped it in his own. His fingers were large, making hers appear childlike. Instead of greeting her in the way she expected, he raised her hand to his lips and kissed her knuckles. Fire sliced through her chest, and a moan echoed between them. More than three seconds passed before she realized Kate had been the one to make the noise.

"Can I buy you both a drink?" He didn't let go of her hand, just continued to stare into her eyes.

She glanced at Kate to break the connection and breathed through her anxiety. She hoped he couldn't sense the way her palm began to sweat.

Kate raised her brows. "It's up to you, Al."

"Al." Her name came from his lips in a barely audible whisper, and she couldn't fight the need to turn her gaze back to him. "Sorry. I've been wondering what your name was all night."

She pressed her lips together to hide her elation. Mitchell Davies, a man better designed than seemed humanly fair, had been thinking about her name. All night long.

Her insides tingled in a mix of excitement and apprehension. Her mother had taught her not to trust a gorgeous face, yet she easily melted into his touch. She was a slave to his testosterone. A novice who was looking up to a master. "Alana Shelton," she corrected, and cheered inwardly when her voice didn't waver.

He squeezed her hand before letting it go. "Nice to properly meet you, Alana."

"Let's get that drink." Mitch needed to concentrate on something other than the lightest green eyes he'd ever seen. They were more than stunning. They were intoxicating. He felt drugged by their gentle hold, unable to look away.

"Hey, Mitch." Blake called out, and jogged toward them. "Ladies," he greeted with a wave.

Jealousy washed over him, thick and rich, when Alana flashed her dimples at his best friend.

"Hi," she offered in the sweetest, most endearing tone.

He closed his eyes for a brief moment at the saccharine sound. He was in trouble. Big. Huge. Fucking gargantuan trouble. Had it really been that long since he'd been infatuated with a woman? He glanced at Alana and continued to wonder if there'd ever been a female to gain his interest so fast, or so thoroughly.

"Oh, my gosh. Blake Kennedy. Hi…I'm Kate."

Blake chuckled at Alana's friend. She was the typical star-struck groupie. They'd both become accustomed to this response from people. They'd learned how to react and kept their mouths shut on any information they didn't want made public. The best course of action was to convince themselves the fans were infatuated with the music, not the band members themselves, even though they both knew it was a lie.

He still hadn't been able to classify Alana into the star-struck category yet. He couldn't determine if her timid nature came from being excited to meet him or something else entirely. He was hoping for the latter. Hoping so hard it made his stomach churn.

"Alana, this is Blake, the bass guitarist for Reckless Beat."

"Nice to meet you." Alana offered her hand and Blake gave it a firm shake.

"You too, Alana. I'd kiss your knuckles like my boy Mitch did, but I think he might castrate me in my sleep."

Blake winked at him, and Mitch glared in return. Smart-ass mother trucker had been watching him while signing autographs with his pack of fangirls.

Alana lowered those gleaming eyes with a smile, and he caught sight of her dimples. Damn, she was cute. He stepped closer, ran his hand along her shoulders, and pulled her into his side. She stiffened, her back snapping ramrod straight, poised on the brink of doing a runner. His heart stopped. Maybe he shouldn't have touched her again. He peered down at her and hoped for the best. "Time for a drink?"

She gave a jerky nod and kept her gaze lowered.

"I'm going to head upstairs." Blake gave them a wave.

Mitch bit his lip to keep from laughing at Kate. The poor woman's face changed from cartoonish elation to utter grief. He suppressed a laugh and turned to his best friend, covertly tilting his head toward the grieving woman, hoping he would get the hint.

"Ahh." Blake stared back at him with a frown, and then glanced toward the third wheel. "Umm." He raised his palms in question. "You wanna come upstairs and…" He shrugged at Kate with a confounded expression.

Blake didn't drink. So apart from getting naked or watching television, there wouldn't be much else for them to do. Although Mitch was certain she wouldn't protest if asked to take her clothes off.

Alana sucked in a breath, and he tried not to grip her tighter in comfort.

"Yes." Blake's new friend nodded with enthusiasm. "Will you be all right, Al?"

Mitch's heart stopped for the seconds it took her to give a soft nod. "I won't bite," he whispered in her ear.

His words didn't have the effect he'd hoped for. Instead of receiving a smile or catching another glimpse of her dimples, she swallowed hard and gave a jerky nod.

He didn't understand her, couldn't put her puzzle pieces together to make the picture fit.

They stood in the middle of the foyer, two bodyguards hovering feet away, while Blake and Kate strolled to the elevator. When they pressed the button and the doors opened, Alana sighed and glanced up at him with a wavering smile. "I'm going to need that drink."

He chuckled and continued to stare at her. Loose strands of warm brown hair cupped her face, and her deep pink lips demanded to be kissed. Rather than fulfilling his body's need to taste her, he dropped his arm from her shoulder, grabbed her hand, and led her toward the hotel bar.

"Davies, you asshole!" a voice yelled from behind them.

Mitch turned. Steve stalked toward them, his chest heaving. The two bodyguards cut off his approach, forcibly pushing at his shoulders to get him to back off.

"You got me fired, you arrogant prick."

Alana gasped. The defenseless sound punched his protective nature to the forefront, and he stepped forward to block her from view.

"Go home, Steve." He didn't trust the glazed look in the man's eyes.

"Fuck you." Steve spat on the floor and gave him the double bird.

Mitch shook his head in disgust and turned his back, cupping Alana's shoulder to encourage her inside the bar.

Before they stepped through the entryway, a shout from the guards made him tense. "Mitch!"

On instinct, he shielded Alana's back and propelled them forward. A large glass vase flew past the side of his head, into the wall in front of them, hitting with a loud thwack. He jerked back as pieces of glass peppered his face, leaving tiny bites of pain. His grip on Alana loosened, and she dropped to the floor. She whimpered, the soft sound dissolving his shock and sharpening his focus.

"Alana, are you hurt?" He glanced down at her crumpled on her knees, her hair, shoulders, and back now covered with glistening shards of the shattered vase.

His lungs tightened with each passing second that she didn't respond. He dropped down behind her and winced at the stab of glass through his cargo pants. Hovering over her, he covered her body and glanced over his shoulder. His bodyguards were dragging Steve to the floor, their knees in his back.

When the threat to their safety vanished, he moved in front of her, the broken glass crunching under his feet. He stared at the shaking hands covering her eyes, and his chest started to throb. The visible skin around her cheeks held tiny scratches with bright red blood. "Alana?"

Still no response.

He placed a hand on her forearm, and she jerked at the touch.

Damn, what the hell should he do?

"Sweetheart, tell me what's wrong." He picked pieces of glass from her hair and wiped them from her shoulders. Relief flooded him when she didn't continue to flinch. He needed to keep himself busy, otherwise the fractures in his panic would deepen, and he'd cause a bigger scene.

Her breathing came in ragged pants. She pulled her hands an inch away from her face and lifted her gaze to look straight through him with rapidly blinking eyes. He supported her shoulders and tried to blow away the glitter of glass particles from her cheeks. The brush of his breath pulled another cry of pain from her throat, and she covered her hands over her face again.

"Christ." He was useless, with no concept of what to do. "Alana, please, sweetheart. Tell me what's wrong." He'd tried to protect her and failed.

"My eyes." Her voice broke.

"Is she all right?" Mitch glanced at one of the male hotel staff who knelt beside them.

She let out a sob. "I can't see."

Chapter Four

Pain slashed through Alana's vision. Her reaction had come too slow when the heavy vase hit the wall mere inches in front of her. Glass had sliced her face and flown into her eyes. And her worst mistake had been rubbing them to try and dislodge the fragments.

"She needs an ambulance." Mitchell's voice came from beside her, firm and demanding.

She kept her eyes squeezed shut and reached out a hand to grasp his shirt. He responded immediately, pulling her into the protective warmth of his embrace. She needed the grounding his arms provided. The comfort. For the first time in her life, she was truly scared, and the majority of her fear stemmed from the inevitable call she'd have to make to her mother.

Mom, I can't see.

Whenever she opened her eyes, the burn greeted her, and everything came into view in a kaleidoscope of blurred images. Even the soft breeze of the air conditioner made her snap her lids shut again. If this was permanent, she wouldn't be able to work, and she'd lose the limited independence she had fought to achieve.

Everything would be ruined. Her life. Her future. Her happiness.

A snap of bright light came through the darkness. Once, twice, three times. She flinched with each burst of illumination.

"Get those assholes out of here. And I want every photo destroyed!" Mitchell's ferocious bark made her wince. "Sorry, sweetheart. I'll get you out of here in a sec." Both his arms cuddled her close, and she sank further into the embrace. "Has someone called an ambulance?"

"Umm, excuse me, Mr. Davies. If her eyes are the problem, she would be best to see an optometrist." The man's voice was young and filled with unease. "The hospitals aren't equipped to handle complicated sight problems and usually only give the bare minimum care."

"Somehow I don't think any optometrists will be open at—" Mitchell released his grip with one arm "—one-thirty in the morning."

Alana listened to the exchange in silence, trying to slow her rampant breathing so she could think straight.

"My mother's an optometrist. I'm sure she'd be happy to meet with you, no matter the time." The young man's voice grew in strength, the confidence he held in his mother clearly shining through.

Alana shook her head and clutched at Mitch's shirt. She needed someone familiar to help her, someone she wouldn't be ashamed to cry in front of, or apprehensive about clinging to.

"I need Kate," she whispered and cleared her dry throat. "Can you take me to her? She can help me wash my eyes. It might dislodge whatever is blurring my vision."

"Would washing them help?" Mitchell hadn't directed the question to her.

"I don't think so. Not with tap water anyway." The young stranger replied.

Mitchell's other arm came around to hold her again, pulling her tight. His concern vibrated from him, increasing her alarm.

"Get her away from the gawking people and take her to find her friend. I'll call my mom."

Mitchell's head rubbed against her hair, as if he nodded in reply. "We'll be in my suite. Call the room as soon as you find out."

His arms moved from around her back, and the warmth from his chest faded. Strong hands encased her shoulders, supporting her on more than a physical level. "Are you all right with that, sweetheart?"

She continued to squeeze her eyes shut, trying not to flutter her lids and aggravate the debris still in there. "Yes. Kate will be able to look after me."

The grip on her shoulders tightened. "I'll take care of you."

She sucked in a breath, overwhelmed with…everything. His scent, his touch, his comfort. He placed a tender kiss on her forehead, and her control shattered. She let out a sob and squeezed her lids tighter. The burn of tears was excruciating. His kindness was too much.

Men weren't meant to be like this. They weren't kindhearted or gentle or protective. Especially not strangers…or so her mother had led her to believe.

"I'm sorry. This is my fault. I knew seeing you again was too good to be true."

His anguish gave her the determination to be strong. Lifting her chin, she smiled and placed a hand on his chest, pressing against the hard muscle beneath. "It's not your fault. At least I'll have a great story to tell my friends back home."

Was it morally acceptable to tell a lie if part of the statement was true?

She honestly didn't believe the situation was his fault, but she would never tell her friends back home. If her mother found out, she would worry herself into a stroke. It didn't matter how old Alana became, her mom never stopped treating her like a fragile piece of porcelain waiting to be broken by a man.

Mitchell leaned in close and brushed his cheek against hers. "I hope by the time I let you go, you'll have a far better story to tell."

Anticipation skittered over her skin, leaving a trail of goose bumps, which distracted her from the pain. She was falling for a man she didn't know and couldn't even see.

He stepped back, and a slight sense of vertigo hit her mind. She wavered, wobbling in space. Within seconds his hands were back on her body, lifting her off the ground. She squealed as her arms flailed for something to grip. "What are you doing?"

He began to walk, sure and certain, her weight not hindering him in the least. "I'm getting you upstairs."

Whispers passed her ears from people in the lobby while he cradled her in his arms, against his hard chest. He ignored her protests, and by the time they reached the elevator, she had relaxed and rested her hands around his neck.

Slowly, she opened her lids, hoping for some improvement to the coarse scratching in her eyes, but the discomfort and lack of vision hadn't changed. Fear bubbled in her belly, and she silently let out a long breath, needing to calm the anxiety that tried to regain hold.

"I had an uncle whose eyes were damaged by hot metal shavings. He burned his eyelids and singed his brows as well." His voice came soft and sweet while the elevator ascended. "The damage seemed horrific at the time. I remember overhearing my parents say he would probably lose an eye or go blind."

Alana rubbed away the stray hair tickling her cheek. She didn't want to become engrossed in a story that may have an ending that would break her heart.

"A few weeks later he was fine."

She sighed in relief.

"I was young at the time, but I'm pretty sure he didn't have surgery either. So I'm sure you have nothing to worry about."

"I hope so," she whispered and rested her head against his shoulder. Apart from helping out on her mother's retreat, Alana captured breathtaking landscape images with her camera and sold them to a local art gallery. If she couldn't see, there would be no way for her to make extra money. She didn't think there'd be much of a market for blind photographers.

The elevator dinged its arrival, and she heard the soft swoosh of the doors opening. Mitchell walked forward, not once needing to reposition her in his arms. His strength astounded her.

"You know my legs are still entirely functional, right?"

He chuckled, and the deep masculine sound made her smile. "Yeah, I know. But how cool was it to act like the macho hero in front of everyone in the lobby when I gallantly rushed you into my arms?"

She let out a bark of laughter and whacked him on the chest.

"I've always wanted to be a gentleman. I've just never had the opportunity."

Alana couldn't imagine him being anything but a chivalrous. In the little time they'd spent together, he seemed genuine. Open. Trustworthy. All the traits her mother tried to convince her didn't exist in a man.

"Who knows, I might knock Lynch off the popularity pedestal for a little while."

"Lynch?" She frowned, wishing she could see his eyes while they spoke.

Another chuckle sounded. "You're not a fan of Reckless Beat, are you?"

She bit her lip, unsure if her honesty would upset him.

"Yeah, I didn't think so. You weren't the screaming groupie type." He wriggled his fingers against her ribcage, and she gasped at the tickling sensation shooting through her body. Before tonight, she would've agreed that she wasn't the screaming groupie type. However, right now her lungs burned with something hot and needy, pleading to be released.

"Lynch is the lead singer. Mason Lynch. Blake, who I introduced you to before, is the bass guitarist. The guy on stage with the shoulder length wavy hair is Ryan. He plays rhythm guitar. Then there's Sean on drums. But for the love of god, if you ever meet the guy, don't tell him I mentioned his name last. He has an inferiority complex."

He came to a stop, held her tighter in his arms, and kicked out his leg. His shoe thudded against what she assumed was the suite door.

"Mitchell!" She wriggled, trying to get him to put her down even though she didn't want to be out of his arms. "Let me go so you can knock on the door."

"I'm fine. Blake will answer the door in a sec…as long as he isn't in the middle of increasing the band's popularity with your friend."

"What do you… Oh." Her cheeks heated. "Sorry. I'm a bit slow." She was an idiot. It wasn't as if she expected Kate to be in there playing solitaire. Alana had been savoring the joys of living vicariously through her friend for years.

He booted the door again.

"Oh, for Christ's sake. Put me—"

She heard the door handle turn and the sound of the door scraping over the carpet.

"Al." Kate's voice held a note of panic.

Alana tried to open her eyes, only to close them seconds later when the scratching and blurred vision became too much. "I'm fine."

Mitchell strode forward, and the light behind her lids darkened. "She's not fine," he growled, suddenly sounding more protective and territorial. "Where's Blake?"

"He's on the hotel phone. It started to ring a few seconds before you knocked on the door."

Alana pivoted and turned through the darkness until Mitchell lowered her. The back of her legs hit something firm but soft, and she settled down into the sofa. Large hands squeezed her knees, and she pressed her lips together, holding back a sigh. They were Mitchell's hands. His warm, strong, talented hands.

"Will you be all right for a minute? Can I get you a drink or something?"

She shook her head and hoped her voice wouldn't come out raspy. "I'm fine."

"I'm going to see what's happening with the phone call. I'll be straight back."

She nodded and let out a deep breath when his presence slipped away. It was stupid and crazy and foolish, and yet she already missed his strength. She craved his comfort.

"What the hell happened?" Kate's voice came from beside her as the sofa dipped.

Clenching her lids tighter with the abrupt slip into vertigo, Alana leaned back in the seat. "Slight altercation downstairs."

"Slight altercation?"

She sensed Kate hovering close to her face, peering down at her. Blake's voice came soft from the other side of the room, along with Mitchell's frantic whispers. Their conversation was too quiet for her to make out, so she passed the lonely minutes reciting what happened downstairs.

"Can I have a look?" Kate's breath brushed along her cheek.

Taking a deep breath, Alana tried to open her eyes again. When she lifted her lids, the scratching sensation caused her to blink rapidly, which only made the discomfort worse. All she could see were different shades of shadow lingering close to her face.

"Sorry," Kate whispered. "I thought I might be able to see something."

A cupboard squeaked from the other side of the room, and moments later a familiar hand cupped hers. "Here's a drink of water. Can you grab it for me?"

Their fingers brushed when she grasped the glass. Hyper-awareness rushed through her veins at the mere connection. It was stupid. Naïve. And still, all she wanted was his chest to snuggle against and the hope that he would make everything OK.

"The optometrist will be ready to see us in around twenty minutes."

Fate was cruel. Earlier, she'd been reluctant to meet him, now she didn't want to leave. Alana ran a finger up and down the glass, procrastinating, buying a few more moments in his presence. She had to say goodbye. A famous musician had better things to do with his time.

"Kate can take me." The words sounded reluctant even to her ears.

"Yea—" Kate stopped mid-word.

Alana turned her head toward Kate, then to Mitchell, and back again. They were silently communicating, and Alana didn't like it.

"No, I'll take you." Mitchell clutched her knee, and she fought the urge to squeeze her thighs together. Surely there had to be a hierarchy of priorities in a situation like this, and sexual desires shouldn't be at the top of the list. "I already have a driver waiting."

Another uncomfortable silence followed, broken only by Blake clearing his throat in the distance. She wanted to growl in frustration, even blinked her eyes open to try to see what they were doing, but it was no use.

"Maybe I can stay here and have a quick nap while Mitch takes you. It won't be long until I have to get up for work, and I could use some sleep."

Alana faced Kate. She felt like a burden to everyone and didn't know who to intrude upon. Should she trust her instincts and go with the intense stranger who wanted to take care of her, or beg her friend to give her the safer option?

"Sorry, I forgot you have to work in the morning."

"Technically, it's today, but I'm not too worried. I can run on a few hours sleep." A tender hand rested on her shoulder and squeezed.

Alana mentally pulled up her big girl panties and raised her chin. She trusted Kate to help lead her into the right decision, and if Mitchell was determined to take her, it would be stupid to protest. "All right."

She held out her glass and someone took it. Mitchell's hand supported her elbow as she moved to her feet, and his heady scent filled her nostrils. "I guess that means you'll be helping me wash my face and use the facilities too."

He chuckled. "Sweetheart, I'll help you do whatever the hell you like."

Chapter Five

MITCH LED ALANA from the car with one arm around her back, and his other hand entwined with hers. He'd dug himself into a hole simply fighting for the opportunity to take her to the optometrist.

When Kate had begun to agree to drive Alana herself, he'd fixed her with a frown and shook his head. She stared at him in question, but didn't say a word. Not until Alana was in the bathroom. That's when the fangirl antics started.

"You feel obligated to help her, don't you?"

A few tired seconds passed before he understood what the hell she was talking about.

"I watched the interview you did with Sandra Waters a few years ago. You helped resuscitate the groupie who overdosed on your tour bus."

Mitch clenched his jaw and raised an eyebrow while she continued. This was one of the many things he hated about his celebrity status. People thought they knew him. They believed everything they read and judged him on the innumerable lies that were put to print.

"I remember your offhanded comment about always wanting to help people. You said you felt obligated to stick around until things were resolved. You mentioned you learned it from your mother, who's a charity volunteer."

Oh, Mitch remembered too. The whole situation had been a publicity stunt. Well, to a degree, anyway. One of their groupies had come close to permanently checking out on the bus.

Instead of leaving the media's focus on the bad influence of musicians using drugs, they fudged the facts. With his mom being a long-serving supporter and volunteer for numerous charities, they used him as the scapegoat and turned the story around to an uplifting piece on how he saved the life of a fan.

At the time of the nationally broadcasted interview, he'd still been in shock at watching a woman almost choke to death on her own vomit. None of them was aware of the drug use. He'd been so traumatized that he repeated exactly what his PR manager suggested. In the end, it made him appear to be a man who went above and beyond to be a Good Samaritan, instead of the freak under pressure that he was.

But he couldn't tell Kate it was a load of B.S., so he nodded.

Technically, it wasn't a lie. For starters, he did feel obligated to help Alana. He also needed to figure out why she seemed important to him. Why he didn't want to watch her leave. The fact that he yearned to get her naked and hear her sigh his name in pleasure came in a close third.

The optometrist's lights glowed in the darkness of early morning, and a slim woman with gray hair walked toward the sliding doors to meet them.

"You must be Mr. Davies and Ms. Shelton. I'm Louise Pierce."

He smiled at her. "Please call me Mitch. And this is Alana." He would've offered his hand, but he had no intention of letting go of the warm bundle in his arms anytime soon.

"Nice to meet you, Mitch." She indicated for them to move inside and locked the door behind them. "So, how are you, Alana?"

He squeezed Alana tight around the waist, offering his support.

"I'm all right. A little worried. I'm hoping the damage isn't permanent."

Louise strode alongside them, helping lead Alana to the back of the building. "Well, let's take a look. You can wait out here, Mitch."

He dropped his arms from around Alana's body, and a sudden chill swept over him. The women walked away, heading to the first door down the hall. Muffled words brushed his ears as he inspected the display cases filled with glasses, each step bringing him closer to where Alana and Louise spoke.

"These drops will help to show any damage to your cornea. They may sting a little."

Mitch paused, waiting for a gasp, an oath, a whimper. When nothing came, he relaxed a little, still inching further down the hall.

"Now, I'm going to turn the light off and take a look."

He moved closer, making sure his footsteps were silent.

"Ouch. Yes, you have done a bit of damage, haven't you?"

"What does that mean?" The panic in Alana's voice put him on edge. Even closer than he already was. He wished he could be in there beside her, holding her hand, but that was ridiculous, right? He didn't even know her.

"Oh, honey, it isn't anything to be concerned about. There are scratches in both eyes, but none of them are deep enough to cause permanent damage."

Mitch hovered at the side of the doorway.

"Are there any glass splinters in there? It feels horrible, and I can't keep my eyes open."

His heart ached at her discomfort, and still, he had no idea why. Those fleeting moments when he peered down at her from the stage had crawled under his skin and settled uncomfortably in his chest. He wanted to help her. Comfort her. Make love to her. And his soul demanded he do it now.

"No, there's no debris. The pain comes from moving your eyelids over the abrasions when you open and close your eyes. It's temporary. Corneas heal rapidly."

The light flicked on, and Mitch slid back out of view.

"Now, I'm going to get you to wear some bandage contacts. They will cover the scratches so it doesn't hurt to blink your eyes. They also speed up the recovery time and lessen the risk of infection."

"All right." Alana's voice came soft and hesitant.

"Have you worn contacts before?"

Cupboards opened and closed, followed by the tear of cardboard and the squeak of ripped plastic.

"No. I've never had problems with my sight."

"OK, rest your head back and try to keep both eyes open as long as you can…There, the first one is done…and…the second one too. You're a pro."

Alana chuckled. "That feels better already. Didn't help with the sight, though."

"No it won't help with that at all." A chair creaked. "You're going to need someone to take care of you for at least a day or two. Until the damage begins to heal and you can see again."

Deafening silence filled the air. He peeked his head around the doorframe to take another look. Alana sat in the hydraulic chair, her forehead wrinkled in concern, her eyes open and staring straight ahead. He'd almost forgotten how gorgeous those light green irises were.

Louise stopped scribbling on a piece of paper at her desk and glanced over her shoulder. "Is everything all right, honey?"

Alana shook her head and raked her fingers through the loose strands of her hair. "I'm not from Richmond, and the friend I'm staying with is working tomorrow." She lowered her voice. "I'm not sure how I'm going to cope on my own."

Mitch pressed a clenched fist against his mouth to hold in his offer to help. For starters, he wasn't meant to be hovering in the doorway, and he was likely to become involved in something far from temporary if he spoke up.

"How about your boyfriend? I'm sure Mitch or one of his family members wouldn't mind having you around for a while."

A grin pulled at his lips when the tops of Alana's cheeks darkened.

"He's not my boyfriend," she whispered. "He's…" She bit her bottom lip. "He can't take care of me."

Like hell he couldn't. There was no way he could remain silent, not with her entirely vulnerable, and gorgeous to boot.

"You can stay with me." He stepped into the middle of the doorway, and Louise turned to smile at him. Alana shook her head, and he now noticed the dark smudges of fatigue under her eyes.

"We can discuss it back at the hotel." He reached for the piece of paper Louise held out and read the name of the eye drops he needed to arrange for the concierge to buy. "It's already past three o'clock. We need sleep."

Alana rubbed her eyelids and began to stand. "Thank you so much for seeing me in the middle of the night, Louise."

Mitch rushed to grab her arm, steadying her while she stepped from the chair's platform.

"Not a problem at all. My son was thrilled I could help one of his idols."

"I'll make sure the band sends him something as a thank you." He glanced at Louise, who beamed a bright smile and led Alana from the room. He stopped at the front counter, made sure Alana was stable, and pulled out his wallet. He grabbed some bills, more than enough to cover a call out at this insane hour, and placed it down. "Thanks for everything."

Louise glanced at the money, then back up at him, and shook her head with wide eyes.

Before she protested, he grabbed Alana's elbow and led her into the cool spring night. The driver started the car on their approach and climbed out to open the back door.

"Everything go well, Mr. Davies?"

Mitch placed his hand on top of Alana's head to ensure she didn't hit her forehead when climbing into the car. "In a few days she will be back to normal." A few days in which he planned to sate his desire for her and get the cloying need to protect a fragile stranger out of his system.

Alana's eyes no longer burned with every brush of her eyelids, yet she still couldn't stand to have them open. Her vision was like an out of focus image. She could distinguish light and dark and shades of color, but nothing else. Each object bled into the next, up close or far away, it didn't matter. Nothing was clear. And it made her dizzy.

Closing her eyes, she nestled further into Mitchell's shoulder. His arm rested behind her neck. The side of his body pressed up against hers, providing warmth and comfort. She inhaled his scent, pulled it deep into her lungs, and sighed. He was a fairytale. A handsome and strong and protective fairytale, and she wasn't ready for it to end.

The soft, chilled leather of the back seat reminded her of cool sheets on a nice clean bed. Or maybe her thoughts were in the bedroom because of the gorgeous man beside her. She wanted to see him naked. To learn his body, to touch and stroke and claw. She wanted his lips on her mouth, not her forehead. His fingers on her breasts, not her shoulders.

A smile pulled at her lips, one of unfamiliar seduction and sexual confidence. With newly found bravery, she wrapped her arms around his waist and relaxed when he didn't lean away. Her reality of men was warping. Everything she'd been told was being exposed as a lie with each additional minute Mitch held her close.

The dark of sleep tugged her harder, making consciousness waver. She whimpered once, twice, trying to fight the pull of slumber. There had never been a more comfortable place to rest her head, or a better fantasy to fall asleep to. Images of his smile played behind her eyelids, vivid and arousing. She relaxed into his touch as his hands moved around her back, underneath her knees, and she finally jerked to awareness.

"Shh," he said close to her ear. "Let me carry you upstairs, and you can fall back asleep in my arms."

His words were fuzzy and tickled her neck. She must be dreaming.

She relaxed into the pull of his arms and settled into his chest once he stood. This morning she awoke with the fear of the unknown. Tonight she would sleep with heavenly dreams of a stranger's embrace.

"No," she mumbled and blinked her eyes. "I have to wake up. Kate needs to drive us home, and I don't want to be half asleep when she does."

"You're not leaving tonight, sweetheart." His words were soft, yet brooked no argument. "It's only a few hours until dawn. You already said Kate has to work today. Let her sleep, and first thing in the morning we can sort everything out."

She didn't argue. She didn't want to. It was only common courtesy that nudged her to leave in the first place. Better to abandon the arms of a rock star on a good note, than be remembered as the blind woman who wouldn't let go.

She remained quiet until they reached his suite. "Please put me down."

He squeezed her tight before letting the arm underneath her legs fall. A click sounded, then a buzz, followed by a slide of the door. His fingers came to rest on the low of her back, and he grasped her other hand, leading her forward.

"The lights are out," he whispered. "Kate isn't on the couch. She must be in Blake's room."

Alana envied her friend's free spirit and the way she enjoyed herself with men. Kate wasn't easy with her body, she just wasn't afraid to share herself in the name of pleasure. More importantly,

Kate loved sex.

Alana thought the whole intimacy thing was a bit of an anti-climax. Maybe things were different in a committed relationship. Over time, a man would learn a woman's wants and desires. But at her age, she still hadn't experience the big O with a partner.

"This is my room."

She sucked in a breath before she could suppress her shock.

"Don't worry." His soft voice caused goose bumps to form over her skin. "I'll sleep on the sofa."

Sofa? Her mood changed from a frenzy of anticipation, to increasing disappointment. Anger at herself, and the way her mother had brought her up to be on the defensive around such a gentle man, bubbled low in her belly. She clenched her fists at her sides and hoped the room was dark enough for Mitchell not to notice.

Any other woman would've straddled him by now, or bared her breasts and laid herself out like a platter to be devoured. She needed to get over herself, over the insecurities her mother had heaped on her shoulders, and experience life for herself. Mistakes and all.

"What will I sleep in?" she asked, striving for a seductive tone. There had to be a way for her to show her interest without looking like a fool.

"Umm. Shit." His footsteps retreated. Bright light illuminated the back of her eyelids. "I think I've got a spare T-shirt and boxers you can wear. That is, if you don't mind wearing my clothes."

At the moment, she wouldn't mind being under his skin, let alone his clothes.

"That sounds nice." Damn, she had no clue how to flirt. Her palms moistened, and she discreetly wiped them on her jeans.

Who was she kidding? Mitchell wouldn't be attracted to her in her current state of disarray. Blind, scratched up, raccoon–ish eyes no doubt. She didn't even want to think about what had happened to the light swipe of mascara she put on earlier. Definitely not one of her most appealing moments.

Oh, god, why was she even here?

"What's wrong?" His hands grasped hers. "You're frowning."

She cleared the frustration from her face and smiled. "I'm tired." And confused. And needy. And wanton.

"Do you want me to help you get dressed?"

Her nipples hardened and a spark of arousal ignited in her womb. "A little help would be nice." She could've dressed by herself—she was a grown woman, after all—but the offer to have his hands on her body couldn't be declined.

She wanted to feel all the things Kate had told her about. All the things her mother had warned her of. And she didn't want to feel them with anyone other than Mitchell.

He released a deep breath, and she worried it came out of annoyance. Taking her hand, he led her to the foot of the bed and helped her sit. He tugged at her left boot, once, twice, then must've realized there was a zipper and began pulling one down, then the other.

"I like your boots."

"You do?" She didn't own a lot of clothes or footwear. Variety wasn't necessary when living on her mom's property.

"They're sexy, without being slutty."

She laughed, but covered her mouth to quiet the noise. "You like sexy but not slutty?"

"I'm sick of slutty. I've dealt with slutty for far too long."

She gave a solemn nod. "Well, I'm *definitely* not the slutty type." If only he knew to what extent. He would laugh in her face.

"I know." He removed one boot, and the next. "I think that's what attracted me to you in the first place."

Her heart stuttered, chugging like a car out of gas before it took off at super speed. He ran his hands up her calves, over her knees, and she inhaled sharply when he reached her thighs.

"I like your belt, too." He gave a soft yank on the waistband of her pants.

Her chest expanded and small doses of panic slid into her

bloodstream. She was on a stranger's bed, unable to see, and completely clueless. Holy hell, what was she supposed to do?

No. Toughen up. Live a little.

She was on a *rock star's* bed, unable to see his captivating eyes and handsome smile, and, for once, she had an excuse to fumble. She should be cheering. Well, maybe not about the lack of sight, but the situation was definitely a keeper.

Before she lost confidence, she fumbled for the bottom of her shirt and yanked it over her head. Alana anticipated a compliment, nothing outlandish, just something sweet, like men always said in the movies.

Nothing came.

She sat on the edge of the mattress, in nothing but her jeans and bra, and he offered silence. Mortification weighed her down, and she wrapped her arms around her stomach to ward it off. "Can you hand me your shirt?"

Mitchell slept with glamorous women, gorgeous women, women who had a reason to be confident. She was stupid to think her figure would be anything worth complimenting. Just because she was proud of her all-natural, perky, full breasts didn't mean he would be.

His grip released from her waistband, and she raised her chin, masking her disappointment. Light fingers trailed along her abdomen, tracing the material of her jeans, and delicately moved up to circle her belly. She bit her lip and swallowed.

Please, god, don't let him stop.

"You have the most beautiful body." His voice was low, a rumble of noise over her skin.

Large, warm hands ran up her ribs and hovered at the bottom of her bra. She'd never been touched so delicately—with reverence and desire. Yes, she'd had lovers, but none had bothered to treasure her.

She let her head fall back, sinking into the pleasure.

Her thighs were nudged apart, his heavy weight coming to rest in between as one hand ran between her breasts. He glided his touch to her chest, her neck, and held her jaw. His breath brushed her lips, yet he continued to hover, killing her slowly with the pain of waiting.

"You guys should close the door, unless you want people to join in."

She gasped at the sound of another man's voice.

Mitchell swore.

"Get outta here, Blake." Mitchell stepped away, leaving her half-naked and vulnerable on the bed.

"The light was on. I thought I'd check on Alana. It's not my damn fault you left the door open, you grumpy fucker."

"I'm fine—"

The door slammed, startling the life out of her.

"Sorry. I didn't think." He huffed out a breath. "I didn't even contemplate them waking up. I should've—"

"Only goes to show how sex-starved you are, brother." Blake teased through the door. "Seducing a chick who can't even see your ugly face."

Alana pressed her lips together, holding in the laughter that wanted to break free.

"Go fuck yourself, Blake." Mitchell's leg leaned against hers.

"Will do." Blake's voice was distant. "Night, Alana."

"Night," she called out, smiling.

Something touched her head, and she jerked back.

"It's my shirt." He pulled it down over her face, and with numb limbs she lifted her arms into the holes.

What was with the clothes? Weren't they about to… Christ, she was confused.

"I'm going to set up a bed on the sofa."

She tilted her face in the direction of his voice and frowned. "Mitchell?" Surely he couldn't take Blake's comment seriously.

He ignored her. "The boxer shorts are on the bed beside you. Do you think you're able to get them on by yourself?"

Her throat dried. She reached out her arm and felt around until she found the silk material. "Sure."

"I'll be back to turn out the light in a few minutes." Without another word, he left, the soft clasp of the door announcing his departure.

Trying to ignore what happened, she stood and yanked off her jeans. She threw them to the floor, along with her socks and bra, then pulled on his boxers. The clothes were way too big and smelled like him, alluring and masculine, and way too annoying when she knew he wouldn't be sleeping anywhere near her.

She was sitting back on the corner of the bed when a light rap came at the door.

"I'm decent." Although she didn't want to be.

The door opened, and she clasped her hands in her lap, her eyes still closed. She waited for her confidence to build, for her opportunity to ask him to stay or even to lie beside her for a little while. She refused to be remembered as the woman who made the famous rock star sleep on the sofa.

"All right, I'll turn off the light so you can go to sleep."

"There's no need to sleep on the sofa. I'm sure the bed is big enough for both of us."

The door latch clicked.

"We're both tired, Allie. Your eyes need rest to recover, and I don't want to risk disturbing you."

Brushed. Off.

She'd never played the needy card before. Unfortunately, tonight she had the best hand. "But what if I need something before morning? What if I wake up and have to go to the bathroom or get a glass of water?"

Silence.

"I don't want to yell out and wake everyone."

He cleared his throat. "I can sleep on the floor in here, then."

"No." She shook her head with a huff. "You can sleep in the bed. If you're worried about me groping you, or sniffing your hair during the night, you can rest assured I'll stay on my side."

He laughed, long and loud, the sound growing closer with each passing second. His weight came back between her thighs, his breath back on her skin.

"It's not you I'm worried about." His fingers ran through her hair, and she leaned into his caress. "You're probably still in shock. And Blake's right. You don't know me, can't even see me. I don't want you to regret anything when you wake up."

"Nothing needs to happen." She found the sides of his thighs and moved her hands up to rest at his waist. "Just sleep."

His lips brushed her cheek. "If I stay, *you* can rest assured I won't get a lick of sleep because all I want to do is grope you and sniff your hair."

Chapter Six

Mitch punched his pillow and changed his position for the eighty-fifth time. The temptation to kiss her not only made him restless, it made his cock hard. There'd never been a more inviting pair of lips. He could see them clearly in his mind, luscious and full, still glossy from the last swipe of her tongue. He'd done well to refrain. And holy fuck, if he didn't get a ticket into heaven for doing it, he'd be pissed.

Every time he looked at her, he became entranced by her long brown hair, her mouth, her dimples. Then his gaze would focus on her eyes and he'd cringe. Blake was right. He needed to back off.

Alana wasn't a hussy. He remembered the way she startled at his touch when they first met. She'd been wary, not slutty—coy, not cocky. He couldn't ignore that. If he kissed her now and she did melt in his arms, he wouldn't be sure where her consent came from—desire, exhaustion, or even delirium.

His unwelcomed change into a Boy Scout didn't mean he'd stop wanting to sleep with her. He only needed to refrain from seducing her until she could see who she was sleeping with. Or at least get enough rest to ensure her best judgment.

"You're not comfortable?" Her voice was soft and tired.

He pushed out a breath. "I'm comfortable enough."

"You can't sleep because you want to grope me and sniff my hair, right?" She snorted, and he wanted to smother himself.

He reached under the covers and poked her in the ribs. "You're blind and in a predator's bed. I'd stop tormenting the bear if I were you."

She sniggered, and he smiled at the sound. Her beauty had him in awe. Not only the defining facial features that made her appear angelic, but her attitude, her innocence, the way she made him chuckle. She didn't fawn over him or treat him like a god. And he liked it.

"You…don't scare me." She sounded confused.

"And that surprises you?"

She let out a long sigh, paused a moment, then gave a derisive scoff. "I'm different, Mitchell. I'm not used to…people. I'm not familiar with the real world."

He frowned. "What do you mean?" He turned to face her, using the opportunity to move a little closer before leaning up on one elbow.

"I live on a retreat outside of Monument, Colorado. My upbringing was…different. I didn't get the chance to travel into town often, and my interaction with people only came from those who stayed on the property, or the occasional delivery driver. So I thought I'd be more…nervous and uncomfortable in a foreign place, surrounded by strangers. And yeah, it surprises me that I'm not."

Mitch couldn't contemplate the solitude. He grew up in Brooklyn, New York, and when Reckless Beat hit the big time, he moved to Manhattan to be closer to the other band members and their studio. He wouldn't know the first thing about nature or serenity or isolation. "Do you like it?"

Seconds passed.

"For most of my life it was all I knew. I was homeschooled, so there weren't many children for me to play with. When I graduated, I did a photography course online, and the few times I left the property to go into Monument or Colorado Springs, I didn't stay long."

He felt the bed shift with her shrug. "But now I'm beginning to think that lifestyle won't be enough for me."

She fell silent, and his mind drifted from the beauty of nature to the beauty of her body. He bickered with his libido and tried to convince himself to roll over. At the moment, Alana lay right in front of him, her features shadowed, her hair aglow from the red digits from the alarm clock. He stared at her, his gaze roaming the sheet clinging to her breasts and thighs and back to her face. Her breathing changed, each exhale coming longer, each inhale deeper until there was no mistaking the sound of slumber.

Damn it.

He fell onto his back, waiting, wondering when his cock would take the hint and stop its salute to perfection. With a huff, he rolled over, gave his pillow a covert uppercut, and resigned himself to reciting chords, lyrics, or baseball scores until his mind and body numbed to the point of unconsciousness.

Mitch opened his eyes with a start, and he leaned up on an elbow to determine what woke him. Alana lay peaceful beside him, resting on her belly, hugging her pillow.

"Sorry." Kate's voice drew his attention. She had her head poked inside the door, her body out of view. "I need to wake Alana so I can go home and get ready for work."

He placed a finger to his lips and slid from the bed. When he reached her, he jerked his head toward the lounge room. She frowned, turned on her toes, and walked ahead.

"I'll look after her today," he whispered, his voice groggy from sleep.

Kate glanced at him over her shoulder.

He held his hands up to halt her reply. "She can't take care of herself, and I don't have any plans. Just give her a call when you finish work, and we can go from there."

She turned to him and narrowed her gaze. "She's not a groupie. She won't enjoy being treated like one."

He raised his chin, annoyed at her assumption. More so in the fact she would've been right if they were discussing the treatment of any other woman in his past. "I know."

Kate opened her mouth and closed it again.

"Look, I like Alana and don't mind spending time with her while you're at work." He shrugged, acting blasé when he felt far from it. "She's safe here with me."

She gave a flirtatious smile. "I doubt it."

Yeah. So did he. He wouldn't admit it, though.

"Fine." She opened her handbag, rummaged through the contents, and pulled out a business card. "Here's my number. If there's any problems, call me, and I'll try and get someone to cover me at work."

He reached for the girlie pink card, but she held tight. "Promise me you'll treat her with respect."

He yawned, scrubbed a hand through his hair, and pulled his tired gaze up to meet hers. "No problem."

Kate scrutinized him, her brows deepening with each passing second until she released the card and turned with a sigh. "Make sure you text me later so I have your number."

Yeah, that was at the top of his to-do list. He was practically jumping out of his skin at the opportunity to give a crazed fan his personal contact details.

He watched her leave, trying not to fall asleep in the middle of the entryway. After he locked the security latch behind her, he grabbed a glass of water, used the bathroom, and tiptoed into the bedroom. His angel still lay peacefully, her body now on its side, curled into the pillow. The scratches on her face had lost their bite, no longer standing out on her beautiful skin.

Making sure not to wake her, he climbed onto the bed. He stared at her, watching her eyelids flicker, her chest rise and fall. He'd promised to be respectful, and he had no intention of reneging. However, it wasn't his fault if Kate's definition varied from his.

With a kiss goodbye to his inner Boy Scout, he shuffled forward, breathing in her floral scent as he approached. He curved his body into hers, thigh to thigh, her back to his chest.

There was nothing disrespectful about spooning. They both had clothes on; there was no sexual interest. Well, fine. His hardening cock disagreed, but he had the big man under control. He just wanted to be close to her. To appreciate her delicate skin and the soft curves of her body. And her smell. That sweet and innocent scent did unthinkable things to his senses.

Once she woke, he would blame his proximity on his movements during sleep. Until then, he would nuzzle the back of her neck and hope to hell he received another opportunity to be this close to her. Respectfully, of course.

Alana gradually woke from a deep sleep, climbing layer upon layer of drowsiness until consciousness greeted her. A delicious warmth coaxed her back into slumber, but her pillow was hard as stone and made her jaw ache.

She blinked open her eyes to bright light and blurred vision. Panic stole her breath. She couldn't see. Why couldn't she see? She pushed from the hardness below her, blinking in quick succession to alleviate the dryness while her heartbeat thundered in her chest.

"Sweetheart, it's OK."

Large hands gripped her wrists.

"It's Mitch."

Her heart stuttered, and then slowed as the memories of yesterday began to clear.

Mitchell Davies.

Shattered glass.

Warm breath and sweetly whispered words.

She squinted at where her hands rested. Oh. No. She'd mauled his chest.

"Human pillow, at your service."

She groaned and jerked away, wanting to dive under the covers to hide the heat warming her cheeks.

"Oh, no you don't." Strong arms encased her waist and pulled her into his embrace.

Another groan escaped as she rested her face on his hard pecs again. "I bet I'm making a lasting impression."

His chest convulsed with laughter. "I didn't mind the cuddling. I wasn't a fan of the drool, though."

A gasp burst from her lips and she sat up straight. "No way." There would be a lot of comfort food in her near future if she'd drooled all over the chest of a celebrity.

His laughter grew. "I'm joking…I'm joking. You should see the expression on your face."

Alana whacked him, hard, and smiled when his mirth died with an "umph." The next second, she was on her back, his body on top of her, his thighs straddling one of hers. His weight made her breath catch, not because he was too heavy, but because he was too delicious. Too damn inviting. Strong and powerful, yet gentle in the way he clasped her wrists above her head.

She wanted to grind into him, to get the slightest friction on the parts of her body that craved attention. The desire to see if a man could bring her pleasure made her ache.

"That wasn't nice," he growled, and her nipples tightened in response.

His face was a blur of color, a mix of light and dark, which confused her, so she closed her eyes and pictured him the way she remembered. His hazel eyes filled her mind, his shoulder length hair falling down to frame his cheeks.

"You shouldn't tease the blind girl."

Something soft grazed her skin, then something rough. His

cheek? His stubble?

"How 'bout I make it up to you?" he whispered in her ear.

She opened her mouth, but excitement stole her reply. Unfortunately, her stomach had no problems with being vocal. It started out as a low grumbled and turned into the call of the wild.

"Holy shit. Did you swallow a lion?"

She let out a sob and turned her head away.

"I'm sorry," he whispered and placed a kiss at the base of her neck. "No more teasing the gorgeous blind chick."

Alana swallowed down the burst of pleasure threatening to explode inside her. He was seducing her. This thing between them wasn't about love or emotion or commitment. It was about gratification and passion and lust. There could be no future with Mitchell, yet her heart had already started to attach itself to him, drawing strength from his every touch and seductive word.

"I'll go order us some breakfast…or lunch. What would you prefer?"

She opened her eyes, not that it helped to answer her questions. "What time is it?"

He moved from her body, and she suppressed a whine of disappointment.

"Twelve twenty-five on the bedside clock."

Damn! "Where's Kate?" She sat up, brushed the hair from her face, and scooted to the side of the bed.

"There's no point getting up. She left hours ago." The mattress bounced, then stilled, and she followed his dark shadow around the room. "I'm going to take care of you until she finishes work. So lie down and rest. I'll be back in a minute."

She dropped back onto her pillow and listened to his departing footsteps. Lunchtime meant she still had hours until Kate finished work. Almost half a day to spend with the man beyond her dreams.

She stared at the ceiling and fought to hold back her smile. Even the plain white paint appeared fuzzy in her mangled vision, but at least the dry scratching had subsided. There was no pain, only a mild discomfort she'd be happy to ignore when in Mitchell's company.

His deep voice whispered through the suite, and her belly filled with eager butterflies. He'd kissed her. And she couldn't wait for him to do it again. On the lips this time. She wanted to drown in his arms, devour his mouth, and lose her breath to him.

Feeling the need to use the ladies' room, she scooted from the bed and felt her way along the mattress. From there, she held out her arms until she reached the wall. She ran her hand along the smooth plaster and found the entry to the bathroom Mitchell had led her to last night.

Getting back to the bed wasn't as easy. She hadn't bothered to flick on the light when she entered the bathroom, knowing the hues clouding her vision would become more confusing. So she didn't notice the counter before she rammed into it with her hip.

"Argh. Shit!" Pain radiated through her waist. She clutched her hip and sank her teeth into her bottom lip.

"Allie, are you all right?"

The sweet, familiar way he spoke her name made her smile through the discomfort. Not many people called her Allie, and she loved the way it sounded on his lips.

"Yeah. Peachy," she chuckled. "I decided to give myself a hip reconstruction." She ran her fingertips along the counter and stopped at the basin to wash her hands.

"Can I come in?"

She splashed water on her face and rinsed her mouth out. "I'm—"

The door opened, the bright light causing her to blink.

"I'm fine, Mitchell."

His shadow moved into the tiny room, and she turned her focus back to the cool water, trying not to hyperventilate. He stood behind her, the warmth of his body seeping into her backside. Strong hands landed on her thighs and trailed up to her hipbones.

"Does it still hurt?"

She swallowed, unsure whether to laugh away her excitement or remain silent. "I said I'm fine." Her voice came in gasps.

He massaged her hips, his touch seeping through the thin material of the silk boxers, causing an electrical current to shoot through her womb. Her head fell back to rest on his chest and she closed her eyes.

"So you want me to stop?" Fingers ran along the waistband of her boxers, teasing her with excruciating strokes.

She chuckled softly. "I didn't say that."

"Mmm," he murmured into her neck, the vibrations making her breasts ache.

"You're very thorough with your patient care."

One hand slid from her hip, over her stomach and up to brush the side of her breast. A groan escaped her lips, and she clutched the counter for strength. The fingers of his other hand delved below her waistband, slowly searching, stroking.

He leaned his erection into her ass and nipped at her neck. "You wouldn't be the first to compliment me on it."

Alana stiffened and fought to control the jealousy tightening her lungs. He froze. After long seconds of thick silence, he rested his forehead against her shoulder. "I'm sorry. That was tacky." He pulled his hand from her boxers and sighed. "I can't think around you."

She reached her hand behind her neck and ran her fingers through the long strands of his hair. "No biggie. I was eighty-nine percent positive you weren't a virgin." She smiled, trying to break the discomfort. "At least I'm clued in now."

He gave a derisive laugh. "Yeah, I'm definitely not a saint. Being slutty goes with the job, I suppose."

Dropping her hand, she turned in his arms and peered up to the dark blur of his face. "Don't say that." She felt her way along the hard contours of muscle on his chest, until she cupped his cheeks. "Don't be ashamed of who you are or what you choose to do in your spare time."

His head shook slightly. "I haven't been, or I wasn't until…"

Her heart stilled, waiting for him to finish the sentence. She wanted to hear him say "you," no matter how foolish it would sound after the short amount of time they had spent together.

"…recently."

She released her breath slowly, disguising her disappointment. His hands gripped her hips and she moved closer into his body. She brushed his hair behind his ears, and the pressure of his forehead rested against hers. Her cheeks heated with the need to kiss him. She yearned for the press of his lips, for the swipe of his tongue. If only she could see.

She ran her fingers around to the back of his neck. "I want you to kiss me."

Her chest pounded, the fury of each heartbeat echoing in her ears as she waited for his response. When nothing came, she closed her eyes and began to silently pray.

His hands lowered to her ass, lightly cupping. Time stood still as his head tilted down, and she swallowed hard in the seconds it took for his mouth to descend upon hers. The pressure was delicate, like silk against her lips. He kissed her once, twice, his force growing with each caress as he tilted her head back for better access.

She teased the hair at his nape with tender strokes and scraped her nails over his skin. She wanted more. Taste, touch, passion. She wanted to be consumed by him and driven to the brink of insanity with the ferocity of his worship.

Grinding her hips into his, she rubbed against his erection, arching her back at the hardness she longed to take in her hand. He growled into her mouth, gripping her ass with force, and crushed his body into hers. She gasped, all the air escaping her lungs.

He deepened the kiss, their tongues clashing as he lifted her off the ground and placed her on the counter. His weight pushed between her thighs, his erection nudging against the thin material covering her sex. She gyrated her hips and tugged at his hair, her body demanding more. He answered her silent pleas by thrusting into her again, letting the delicious friction of his cock rub against her clit.

Each sensation was new. The pleasurable sex, the passionate intimacy. There were no nerves, no apprehension. She craved more. She wanted to learn everything Mitchell could teach her, no matter how little time they would have together.

The ache in her core infiltrated her entire body, driving her to kiss him deeper, to grind back into his thrusts. His hand left her ass, traveling down the front of her boxers, past the waistband, into her panties. She whimpered at the brush of his fingers against her sensitive bundle of nerves and jolted when they delved deeper, penetrating her pussy.

She broke the kiss, panting for breath, and rocked herself against his digits. "Please, Mitchell. I want you inside me."

He didn't respond, only planted his lips back on hers and stole the air from her lungs. Her sex pulled at him, tugging his fingers deeper until the pleasure became too much.

She pushed at his chest. "Stop. I want you inside me."

She'd never wanted anything this much. Not even freedom. Mitchell coaxed pleasure from her effortlessly when other men had failed completely.

"Not this time," he whispered and brushed his mouth against hers.

She wanted to break away, to plea for him to fill her. He wouldn't allow it, his lips demanding more from their kiss. His fingers stroked in and out, his thumb flicking her nub at every insertion. Her breasts screamed for friction. Her core convulsed with the first signs of orgasm. She whimpered, so close, on the edge and about to soar.

A faraway knock sounded, and she jerked back, bracing one hand on the counter and the other on his chest.

"Shh." He soothed, his fingers continuing their torment. "It's only room service. They can wait." He leaned into her, his cheek brushing hers, his lips at her ear. "I'm not answering the door until you come."

She moaned, believing his declaration. She closed her eyes, blocking out the smudged picture and concentrated on the memory of his cheeky grin peering down at her from the stage. He had the best facial features, boyish yet charming, devilish yet seductive.

His lips pressed against the side of her neck, and she tilted her head to allow him better access. He nipped her, the bite of pain adding to the pleasure beating between her thighs. She had to press her lips together to hold back a scream.

The pace of his fingers increased, his strokes coming harder, his thumb now a constant rub against her clit. Her abdomen filled with heat, her orgasm forming and growing until it took over.

She gasped. Her core convulsed in time with his rhythm, and she rocked her hips against his hand. She ignored the world, bowed her head into his shoulder, and let ecstasy conquer. Gradually the euphoria died down, leaving her in a panting, heaving mess on the counter.

The knock sounded again, for the second time or the tenth, she had no clue.

"I better get the door." His fingers withdrew, along with his warmth. A rush of tap water sounded followed by a kiss on her cheek. Two seconds later she was alone with only her rampant heartbeat and wild thoughts to keep her company.

She was rooted to the spot, her eyes blinking at nothingness while her brain struggled to process her emotions. Over the years, she'd contemplated her sexuality, never really knowing if she was heterosexual, homosexual, or merely non-sexual. She'd always found men attractive, had fantasized and lusted over them in magazines and on the television. There just hadn't been a physical spark when it came to sex.

Nobody had been able to touch her and bring pleasure.

Until now… Now she couldn't wipe the relief from her expression. Mitchell had touched her with skill and confidence. She acknowledged his expertise would've come from an overly healthy amount of experience. He knew how to stroke, how to kiss, how to caress…and she didn't care where his expertise came from.

She wasn't broken, and that was all that mattered.

A tear fell down her cheek, and she wiped it away with a relieved breath. Years of brainwashing from her mother hadn't crippled her. She'd begun to worry the trauma from being surrounded by abused women had sunk in. She'd never held the hatred or deeply scarring fear for men like her mother clung to, but still, Alana thought the aversion might have settled into her subconscious.

Her interaction with the opposite sex was limited, her experiences tainted. Yet she'd grown into a woman who learned not to be frightened of things because of other people's nightmares. She still held apprehension and a healthy dose of wary caution, but her stomach filled with butterflies knowing her upbringing hadn't scarred her ability to be with a man.

She was growing increasingly attached to Mitchell as the minutes passed. He showered her with attention, fought to protect her, went out of his way to take care of her. And now, he'd given her the one gift no other man had been able to.

Heat consumed her eyes and her nose tingled. She sniffed and shook her head. She wasn't going to cry a river of tears over her first outsourced orgasm. Nope. That was ridiculous.

She lifted her chin and breathed deep. She'd been raised covered in a blanket of fear, and each day away from home showed how much she needed to break free and live her own life. Releasing the breath, she scooted from the counter, righted her clothing, and took her first step into a new life that was bright and shiny…even if she couldn't see it.

Chapter Seven

MITCH TIPPED THE waiter and showed him to the door. His stomach growled. He was starving, not only for food, but for his voracious hunger for Alana. As he walked into the bedroom, she shuffled from the bathroom, her hands up while she took cautious steps.

"There's nothing in front of you. If you take three small steps forward, you'll hit the mattress."

She smiled. "Thank you."

He stared at her as she approached the bed. She looked perfect in his clothes, casual with her long hair resting over her shoulders, and damn sexy with the way the oversized shirt hung from her breasts. He'd never get the picture out of his head. Or be able to pull his boxers on again without thinking of her.

"Something smells nice."

His inner slut replied *it's you*, but instead of voicing the flirtation, he said, "I hope you're hungry. I think I ordered enough to feed a football team."

She strolled along her side of the mattress and sat when she reached her pillow. "I can't believe how quick it came. I've only stayed at a few hotels, but whenever I've ordered room service, it took forever."

"Yeah. Another perk of the celebrity lifestyle. People usually go out of their way to make us happy." He pushed the trolley closer to the bed and sat in front of her. One by one he placed the plates on the bed and removed their lids. When he glanced up at her, a deep frown etched her brow. "What's wrong?"

"Umm…" She rubbed the back of her neck. "Just trying to figure out how I'm going to eat."

Score one for Mitch Davies. "I'll feed you."

She cringed and sank her teeth into her bottom lip.

"What?" He chuckled. "Being hand fed by my skillful fingers isn't appealing?" He'd been referring to his guitar skills, but the ruby red that darkened Alana's cheeks implied she took his statement another way.

"As much as I like to be completely dependent on a total stranger, who happens to be extremely wealthy and famous, no, I'm not looking forward to being baby fed." She lifted her gaze from the quilt cover and stared straight through him. "I can think of much better ways to embarrass myself."

He grabbed a pancake off the nearest plate, tore a bite-sized piece off, and held it in front of her lips. Her nostrils flared slightly and she closed her eyes with a soft moan.

"Those smell divine."

Almost as good as you.

Her tongue snaked out, enticing him to place something entirely different against her mouth. He could already feel the slide of her tongue over his shaft, the way she'd suck him deep, making him groan.

"You ready?" He cleared the gravel from his throat and placed the pancake against her lips.

With ladylike politeness, she opened slightly and allowed him to feed her. He watched her chew and had to swallow over the lump in his throat. She had the sexiest lips, both full and made for pleasure. He couldn't pull his gaze away.

Needing a distraction, he grabbed a piece of bacon from one of the plates and put it in his mouth. Not even the salty goodness made his mind wander. Every thought was firmly placed on her. On getting her naked. On making her wet.

He moved to his knees and shuffled toward her, letting their legs brush when he sat. He needed to taste her, one last time to get her out of his system. Then he would eat.

He leaned into her, and she tilted her head toward him, sensing his approach. He dismissed the soft and slow advance, his hunger too strong, and went straight in to lick the sweetness from her lips. She jerked in surprise and her hands came to land on his shoulders.

He should back off. Retreat. Instead, he parted her lips with his tongue and breathed in her feminine mewls. She yielded to his hunger, kissing him back with pleasure that made his cock hard as stone. He cupped the back of her neck and leaned further into her, the soft flesh of her breasts rubbing against his chest. The ache to be inside her grew, the pressure on his balls becoming insistent.

"Thought I could smell food." The bed bounced with Blake's weight.

Fuck. Mitch broke the kiss and growled. "Great timing, bro."

Blake bit off a large piece of bacon and chewed. "We discussed this last night. If you leave the door open, I'm going to invite myself to the party," he finished with a wink.

Mitch feigned a stern expression as he struggled not to chuckle.

"Just remember that the next time you two want to get funky." Blake continued. "If the door isn't shut, I'll be taking it as an open invitation to join the festivities."

Alana's jaw gaped, and he gave a warning shake of his head to Blake, who frowned back in confusion.

"He's joking, Allie." Mitch placed his hand on hers and gave a squeeze.

She kept her gaze downcast and smiled. "Morning, Blake."

"Morning, sweet cheeks," he said around another bite of bacon.

Her dimples came out in a gorgeous show of angelic perfection, and Mitch shot Blake a glare. "Don't you have something better to do?"

"Than eat?" Blake raised a brow. "Nope. I don't have any plans until the interview later. So, I'm all yours."

Interview? "Shit! I completely forgot about the radio station. What time do we have to be there?"

"Four-thirty."

Fuck. He'd planned to spend the day in the suite seducing Alana. He didn't want to place her out of her comfort zone, and he couldn't leave her here to fend for herself either.

Her gaze lifted to focus straight past him in concern.

"It's fine." He gave her hand another squeeze. "I'll work something out. They don't need me anyway. The focus is usually on Mason."

"No." She shook her head in disgust. "You're not missing out on an interview because of me."

"I'll stay back and look after her." Blake smirked at him. "You're the important lead guitarist, remember. I'm sure I can find something we can both do to pass the time."

Mitch clenched his jaw. Why the hell was Blake pushing him?

"I'd be happy to do that, as long as you don't have to be there, Blake." Alana held her head high, and Mitch's heart plummeted to the base of his stomach. Had she turned into a groupie already? Did she now want to see what Blake had to offer? "I think I'd be comfortable staying here with him."

Her eyes focused closer to his face and her lips tilted up in a grin. "You said he was gay, right?"

Blake choked and held his hand to his mouth while he reached for a glass of juice from the trolley. Mitch's veins flooded with relief and he threw his head back and laughed. His girl was a little tease.

"You told her I was gay?" Blake blurted.

"No, he didn't." Alana's dimples deepened with her widening smile. "I was just trying to put you back in your place."

Mitch's laughter grew, echoing off the walls. Blake sat in silence, blinking at him with a gaping mouth. His girl was a tease, *and* a hard-ass. He leaned over, placed a kiss on her cheek, and gave a cocky wink back to Blake.

"Right. I guess there's always a first for everything. I can't remember a groupie ever knocking back a three-way—"

"She isn't a groupie," Mitch growled, and the temperature in the room dropped. What was up with Blake? He wasn't usually a troublemaker, and yet he wouldn't quit with the comebacks this morning.

"I think that's my cue to leave." Blake grabbed a pancake and began to lift off the bed.

"No!" Alana shook her head. Her brow furrowed and she reached out to stay him. "I was only joking. Please don't go."

Mitch stared at where her hand lay on Blake's crotch and appreciated that his friend didn't comment.

Nobody spoke. Nobody moved. The only change in the room was the unmistakable awkwardness that settled around them.

"Please tell me I don't have my hand someplace inappropriate." Alana's voice broke.

"You wouldn't be the first woman we've shared, if that's what you're after," Blake purred.

She yanked her hand back and snapped her eyes shut as she tilted her face away. "Excuse me for a minute." She scooted from the bed and felt her way along the mattress.

"Alana, wait."

She shook her head, the color now drained from her face. The women they were accustomed to would've loved the threesome invitation. Yet her hands shook when they reached for the wall, and her face had lightened to a paler shade than white.

He went after her, but the bathroom door closed before he got there.

"Is she OK?" Blake asked in concern.

Mitch had no idea. He wasn't used to women like Alana, fragile and unpredictable. He'd grown to loathe the easy females who found a way to their hotel suites, but at least he knew what to expect from them.

"I don't know. She's been through a lot in the last twenty-four hours." He stood at the bathroom door and knocked softly.

"Just give me a minute," her voice wavered.

Instead of waiting, he turned the handle, giving her time to protest if she was using the facilities. When nothing came, he pushed the door open and went inside, closing it behind him. She sat on the counter, in the same position he'd pleasured her earlier. He tried to clear the image from his mind, to concentrate on the here and now, but he couldn't dislodge the vision of her back arched in delight or her lips wide as she panted in release.

She sat in silence, her legs dangling above the floor, her hands gripping the edge. There were no tears, yet her eyes held undeniable sadness.

"What's wrong?"

She shook her head and kept her lips clamped shut.

"Sweetheart, I don't think Blake minded that you grabbed his johnson." He stepped closer, moving between her legs.

She let out a defeated laugh, but didn't speak.

He wiped the stray hair from her face. "Tell me what's wrong."

"I don't know… Everything. Anything. I'm out of my element. I don't know what I'm doing, and I'm sick of trying."

"Trying?" He peered into her eyes and wished he could read her thoughts.

"I'm trying not to be anxious and apprehensive. I'm trying not to feel vulnerable and needy. And I'm trying damn hard not to be a burden, but I can't see a thing, and I don't want to annoy you." She wiped her hands over her face and looked in his direction. "But most of all, I'm trying to appear indifferent and act like every second with you doesn't scare the hell out of me."

His breath caught in his throat, and he wiped away the lone tear paving a glistening trail down her cheek.

"I'm not used to this, Mitchell. I'm not like you. I'm probably not like anyone you've ever met. My life is different…solitary." Her gaze fell and she hung her head. "I think I should call Kate to come and get me."

He clutched her to his chest and hushed her words, trying to calm her down. He'd find out what she meant later. Right now he had to stop her thoughts of leaving.

"Do you really want to go?"

Silence.

He placed a finger under her chin and peered into her unfocused eyes.

"Allie?"

She shook her head and swallowed. "No."

A flicker of hope ignited in his chest, one he'd never experienced before. He held her close for long, silent moments, enjoying the smell of her hair and the pliancy of her body.

"I don't even have clothes to wear. Or a toothbrush." She sighed and relaxed into him. "I'm used to taking care of myself. I don't like being dependent on anyone, especially you."

He pushed back, gripping her shoulders. "Especially me?"

"You're famous, and I'm a no-name country girl with issues beyond your imagination. You don't need me here wasting your time."

"And what if I *want* you here? What if I enjoy having you around?"

Her gaze dropped. "Like I said, I'm different. You're used to spending time with women and forgetting about them the moment you leave. It won't be the same for me. If I stay, I'll become attached, and that's the last thing we both want."

Having a permanent woman in his life had never been an option. Right now, though, he wanted nothing more than to spend a few more days with Alana. She reached up to lightly stroke his chest, her fingers outlining the different rows of muscles in his pecs and stomach.

Mitch mimicked the simple way her fingers traced around his body, doing the same to her legs. "Why do you keep saying you're different? You seem normal to me."

She let out a derisive laugh. "I've been cocooned from the world for most of my life." She spoke slowly, as if choosing her words carefully. "My mother has issues from her past and hasn't been able to overcome them." Her fingers dipped to his waist, teasing his hips, making his cock pulse. "She wanted her own world, so I suppose she kind of created one."

He trailed his fingers higher, to the tops of her thighs. "And this makes you different, how? Lots of people live on farms and rarely get to socialize." His hands dipped between her thighs, spreading them further apart, and she sucked in a breath.

She let her head fall to his chest and slowly exhaled. "You're the fourth man to ever touch me." Her voice was a whisper. "Ever."

He paused, waiting for an explanation.

"And I'm not just talking about sexually."

He stopped breathing.

"There've been no uncles to play football with, no cousins to chase around the yard, no teachers or coaches to tap me on the shoulder for a job well done. You're the fourth, Mitchell, and the only man who has ever given me pleasure."

His heartbeat echoed in his ears, loud enough for the world to hear. He didn't understand. She had flawless beauty, a natural allure that didn't need make-up or fancy clothes. Shit, even sleep-deprived and dressed in his baggy T-shirt, she still made him harder than set cement. And yet he was the first man to bring her pleasure? "I don't get it."

She slid her hands around his waist, and drew patterns with her fingers on his lower back. "My mother used to live here in Richmond, that's how I know Kate. Our moms grew up together. And when my mom was in her early twenties she was…" Her fingers paused. "She was attacked by a man."

Mitch removed his hands from her legs, a sudden wash of disgust pouring over him. He ran his arms around her and held her close, wishing he could take away her pain.

"After it happened, she couldn't live here anymore and moved to Colorado. She purchased a property with my late grandparents' money and set up a type of retreat for women recovering from abuse." Allie hugged him back, resting her cheek against his heart. "Apart from the occasional trip into the city, I haven't been around other men at all."

His mind spun. "What about…" He had so many questions and didn't know where to start. "You said I was the fourth. Who were the others?"

"Experiments." She chuckled against his chest, and he winced at the sting of jealousy. "By the time I turned twenty-one, I had a lot of questions I wanted answered. Against my mother's wishes, I went into Colorado Springs a few times and searched for what I thought I was looking for." She shrugged. "Turns out those men lacked your finesse."

He clenched his jaw, unable to speak. This woman deserved the world, yet she'd never experienced it? It was unacceptable. Abhorrent.

"It's not as bad as it sounds."

He shook his head and wondered how she could say that. She wouldn't have experienced a childhood crush, a high school dance, or even dating.

"I had contact with the outside world via the phone and internet. I watched movies, read books, surfed the web, and talked in chat rooms. I live a relatively normal life, I suppose. I'm just not used to interaction with men."

He stepped back, unable to hold her close any longer when the anger at himself had grown into a consuming ball in his chest. She sat up straight, her gaze almost focused directly on his.

"Christ. I'm sorry. You didn't want to meet me after the gig last night, did you?" He relived the past twelve hours in his mind while he scratched his fingers through his hair. "Fuck. You didn't want to have that drink with me, and then when I wanted to take you to the optometrist you tried to refuse, and I pressured you."

"Mitchell, it's not that—"

"Damn it. I wondered why you flinched at my touch when we first met and why you didn't want to hang around. All this time I assumed you were shy." He scrubbed a hand over his forehead, pissed as hell that he'd been narrow-minded to her objections. "Kate even tried warning me this morning, but I didn't fucking listen."

"Mitchell." She pushed from the bench and stumbled forward. He caught her before she corrected herself, and then dropped his hands from her arms, not wanting to make the situation worse.

She stepped into him, grabbed onto his shoulders, and stared at his throat. "Yes, I was scared. But never of you. The thing that alarmed me was how much I enjoyed your touch." A soft kiss peppered his chin and he closed his eyes. "My mother brought me up believing all men are…" She sighed. "You weren't what I was expecting. I like you, and those three words are something I never thought I'd have the opportunity to say to a man. So when I tell you I'm trying to fit in and trying not to feel vulnerable and needy and scared, that's what I mean."

He gazed down at her, hating himself for pushing her into something she wasn't prepared for. He couldn't even find the words to apologize.

"Please touch me, Mitchell. One last time before I leave."

Squeezing his eyes shut, he fought for control. Fear gripped him by the balls and held tight. Disgust churned in his belly. He wanted to cocoon her in his arms and protect her from the world, just like her mother had done her entire life.

Her hands ran down his sides and under his shirt, her tiny nails scouring a trail up his chest. *Christ.* He needed to think. His blood burned in his veins, urging him to lift her in his arms and carry her to the bed, but how could he? How could he sink himself into this fragile woman and ignore the fear that he might break her?

"Don't think. Don't judge. Just pretend I'm not damaged and make love to me before I go. Please."

Delicate fingers found his nipples, tweaking, rubbing until he needed to bite his tongue to stay in control. His erection jerked between them, begging for attention. The need to take her built inside him, growing and morphing until he wanted to fall to his knees in surrender.

"Mitchell?" She kissed his neck, trailing her fingers down his chest, over his stomach. Lower. When she gripped his cock, he hissed in a breath and everything inside him snapped.

His lips found hers and one hand cupped her face. He opened the door and shuffled her backward into the bedroom. He devoured her, tasted every part of her mouth, and held her tight to his chest so she couldn't let go. She whimpered, mewled, the tiny, needy sounds sinking into his soul, her dainty fingers gripping his waist.

He lifted her, hauling her ass into his hands while her legs wrapped around his hips. The heat of her pussy burned through his boxers. Her hands framed his face, keeping their lips meshed as he walked her to the bed.

When his knees hit the side of the mattress, he dropped her, letting her fall back on the soft quilt. Plates clanged and cutlery collided from the other side of the bed. Their breakfast feast still lay there, the food now teetering at odd angles with the weight. And Blake nowhere in sight.

Not taking any chances, Mitch stalked to the bedroom door and found his friend sitting on the sofa, laptop in hand. "I'm closing the fucking door. You so much as touch the handle, and I'll break your fingers."

Blake grinned. "No problem. I'll just put my ear against the wall and listen."

Mitch clenched his fist and took a threatening step forward.

"I'm joking." Blake chuckled. "Geez, lighten up."

Mitch continued to glare as he slammed the door.

In three steps he was on the bed, walking on his knees toward Alana. She rested on her elbows, her eyes gazing unfocused on the quilt beside her. He'd regretted not being able to save her from harm yesterday, but right now his desire to have her looking at him made his chest ache. He needed her to see the emotion in his expression because the thought of putting his feelings into words scared the shit out of him.

His palms began to sweat, and his throat constricted. There was no time to breathe. No time to think. He wanted inside her, and his world would end if he didn't get there soon. He gripped the waist of his shirt, pulled it off, and threw it to the floor.

Her head turned, following the noise, and when he sat back on his haunches, simply staring at her face, she frowned and blinked back at him.

"Mitchell?"

He moved closer, hating the confusion in her voice. "Yeah, sweetheart?"

"I…I can't see." She swallowed and sat up. "I need you to tell me what to do. *Show me* what to do."

He shuffled closer until they were an inch apart. "Just touch me."

Anywhere.

Everywhere.

He picked up her hands and placed them on his chest, one over his heart. Leaning in, he nipped her chin, kissed her neck. "I want you to touch every inch of me."

Her head fell to the side giving him better access to lick and nip and nuzzle. The tender stroke of her fingers fell down his pecs, waving over each of his ribs, and stopped at the waist of his boxers. His mind screamed for her to go lower, to grip him again and relieve some of his suffering.

"Allie, are you sure you want to do this?" He licked a trail along her collarbone.

"Yes," she panted. "It's all I want." The elastic at his waist lowered. "Just you."

He helped her remove his boxers, the plates on the bed colliding as he pulled first one leg, then the other free. He sat naked before her, and breathed slowly through the uncertainty. Women usually devoured him with their eyes, their lips, their tongues. He wasn't used to going without the looks of admiration. He'd never realized the boost they gave his ego.

Alana reached for the bottom of her T-shirt—his T-shirt—and pulled it over her head. He shut his mouth to stop himself from gaping and simply gazed at her, taking in her beauty. She had the most perfect body, just like he expected. Round, pert breasts with dark pink nipples, and a slim waist he couldn't wait to get his hands on.

"I hope you're not staring." She grinned at him as she started to lower the loose boxers and her panties at the same time.

"I'm sorry to disappoint." His voice went hoarse.

Alana licked her lips, a nervous gesture that had him gripping his cock in an effort to beat back his arousal.

"You're beautiful."

Her gaze lowered and her hands came up to run over his shoulders, around his neck. "Kiss me."

He didn't need to be told twice. His lips claimed hers, soft at first, then the pressure changed into an uncontrollable urgency. They gripped at one another, their hands roaming each other's bodies in a frenzy he couldn't understand and didn't contemplate. He leaned into her and hugged her close while he lowered her to the pillows.

She lay in his arms, her gaze unfocused around his chin. Her hips pressed into his, the tiny gyrations making his erection rub against her sex. He growled and ran his hand over breasts that begged to be cupped and a waist that yearned to be trailed in kisses. Her fingers rested on his shoulders, their grip becoming tighter the further south he traveled.

When he reached the mound of curls between her thighs, she sucked in a breath. The musk of her arousal lay heady and hypnotic in the air. Later he would taste her, suck her pussy lips into his mouth and feast on her. But now he wanted to touch. He trailed lower, brushed her clit, and smiled to himself when she bucked.

"You mentioned before that no man had ever brought you pleasure."

She nodded. "Except you."

"So tell me now, do I make you feel good?"

He ran his index finger through the wet juices of her slit, and she responded with a gasp. He didn't need her answer to know the truth. She was responsive to his touch. So responsive. Unlike any other woman he'd been with.

"Yes," she panted, swallowed. "I love how you touch me."

With teasing slowness he nudged two fingers inside her core, then retreated. He repeated the movement over and over and over again, each time sinking a little deeper until her hands clung to the headboard and she whimpered in need.

He lowered himself down her body, licking a path down her stomach, tasting the salt of her skin. One of her hands clutched his hair, and her fingers gripped the strands tight enough to make his cock jerk. He kissed her curls and swiped her clit with his tongue.

"Oh, god, Mitchell." Her hips rocked with his strokes, each motion sinking them deeper. The sound of her cries, the suction of her pussy, the heat of her body, drove him wild. He needed to take her. To sink into her. To spend himself in the most enticing woman he'd ever seen.

He twisted and turned his fingers with each withdrawal, hoping to find her sweet spot. At the same time, he sucked her clit into his mouth. Two strokes later he was rewarded with the first spasm of her core.

"Mitchell." She cried his name and pulled at his hair. He didn't stop. He worked her harder, flicking and licking the bundle of nerves until her back arched off the bed and she gasped with pleasure. Watching her writhe in orgasm filled him with overpowering emotion. His heart palpitated, his stomach turned, and his throat tightened. He clenched his eyes closed, silently thanking her for the trust she'd gifted him.

Gradually, her body stilled, the only sound between them coming from their frantic breaths.

"Ready for round two?"

She chuckled as he made his way up her body, biting and licking her soft flesh. He couldn't look into her eyes, not now. Even though she couldn't see him, he still felt exposed, his heart on his sleeve ready to give to her.

"I don't think I'll ever want to stop."

The woman was complete brilliance. Every time she opened her mouth shocked him. "Don't tell me that or I'll never let you go." He grazed his teeth over her breast.

Her lips pressed together in a bashful smile. He reached for the bedside table and retrieved a condom. As he sheathed himself in quick jerks, she ran her nails down his waist, sending goose bumps on a burning trail around his body.

"Mitchell?"

He rested himself between her thighs, nuzzled the base of her neck, and inhaled the lingering scent of her perfume. "Mmm?"

"Can we do this differently?"

He leaned back on his arms and peered down at her. "What do you mean?"

Her throat convulsed with a swallow. "Can I be on top?"

He blinked. Were there twenty-four hours in a day? Hell yes. "I think I can accommodate that."

Clutching her around the waist, he switched their positions, rolling them to the edge of the king-size bed and away from the clattering plates. She pushed to her knees and hovered the heat of her sex above his erection.

"I've never—"

"I know." He gripped her hips and ground his length along her slit. "It's OK."

She rose higher allowing him to position the head of his cock at her entrance. Slowly, she lowered onto him, taking him inch after agonizing inch into her tight pussy. He groaned, gripped the headboard, and closed his eyes. He was done for, completely lost to her perfection.

Her hands rested on his pecs as she began to rise and fall. He ground his teeth together, trying not to let the snug grasp on his shaft drive him over the edge. Each undulation tortured him with undiluted pleasure, inching him closer and closer to completion.

"You're quiet… Am I doing it wrong?"

Fuck. He was Marcel Marceau, unable to get a word out for fear of losing control. He clenched the headboard tighter, sucked in a breath, and went to his happy place. "So good, Allie. Don't stop."

He needed to touch her, to concentrate on what she needed before he blew the whole ballgame. Releasing his talon grip, he opened his eyes and rested his hands on her thighs. Her hips rocked faster at his touch. He slid his hands up her hips, over her waist, and cupped her breasts, teasing her nipples between his fingers.

"Oh, yes." She ground harder, sharper. Her hands reached up to hold his in place, and she groaned, her pussy milking him, clenching tighter. Plates clattered, bowls tipped, but he didn't care.

Her teeth bore into her lower lip, and she leaned her head back, riding him like a prized pony. He bucked into her, increasing their pace. "Oh, god, you feel good." Like fire and silk and heaven.

She touched herself, and he closed his eyes at the erotic image she made. He jerked when her fingers brushed his sac, not expecting the sudden shot of awesome. "Sweetheart, don't… I'm…I'm almost there."

A smile tilted her lips but she ignored him and lightly massaged his balls, while the other hand dipped lower to play with her clit.

"Tease."

She grinned at him, her dimples showing. Damn he wanted that mouth. He sat up, caught her gasp with his lips and sent his tongue in search of hers.

"Ride me," he demanded with a thrust of his pelvis. The plates on the bed punctuated his movements with a clang.

Her legs moved around his waist and her hands to his face. She sucked on his tongue and complied, her hips retreating then sliding home, retreating then sliding home. He closed his eyes, focusing on nothing but the way her slick heat glided over his cock. When she broke the kiss, panting into his neck, he gripped her ass in both hands and thrust hard.

Her cry filled the room and her back arched, lifting her breasts close to his face. His balls began to tighten with an impending climax he had no hope of controlling. He lowered his head to her chest, drew a nipple into his mouth, and sucked hard.

"Mitchell," she cried out with release.

His name was the last straw. He groaned, long and loud, jerking up into her body. He ignored the clash of plates and concentrated on Alana. She sank her teeth into his shoulder, and with each pulse of her pussy, the suction from her lips tightened. He rode out the bursts of rapture, holding her against him, sinking his fingers into her hair.

Gradually the pleasure faded, dissipating until his muscles were heavy and lax. She sighed in his arms, the heaving of their chests slowing. He ran his fingers through her hair and kissed her head, surveying the wreckage covering the other side of the bed. "I think we may have ruined breakfast."

Chapter Eight

"Your hair is smooth like silk."

Alana closed her eyes and leaned her head back. Mitchell sat behind her on the bed, his fingers stroking through her hair, untangling what she knew would be an unruly mess.

"Should I use the brush?" His breath whispered over her neck, and she shivered.

She'd been breathless and wordless and mindless all day. She could only nod.

The brush smoothed her hair in soft, caressing strokes. Occasionally, Mitchell would hit a snag, suck in a breath, then treat her like she had tiny strands of glass growing from her scalp.

"Don't worry about being gentle. You'll be sitting there for hours trying to get the knots out if you do."

"I don't want to hurt you." He pulled her hair to the side and placed a scorching kiss at the base of her neck.

"You won't," she whispered.

Not physically, anyway.

The only way he would hurt her was emotionally, and the more time they spent together, the more she knew she wouldn't be left unscathed.

He'd doted on her since they made love. First, he'd charmed one of the maids into cleaning up the mess in the bedroom, tipping her with an amount that made the lady gush. He then ordered a second breakfast and fed Alana by hand, teasing and seducing her all over again with bites of food in between soft kisses. With her limited sight, she hadn't known what would come next, the pancakes that melted in her mouth, or the hot lips of a man she was starting to fall for.

"You guys ready to go?"

Alana glanced toward Blake's voice and smiled.

"Ahh, I think so," Mitchell answered. "Does her hair look good?"

Blake sniggered. "She looks hot."

"Not the answer I was looking for," Mitchell muttered.

She raised her hand for the brush. "I'm sure it's fine. I'm not going to be center of attention anyway."

She still didn't know how Mitchell had talked her into going along to the interview. Actually, that was a lie. He'd seduced the agreement from her. When their second breakfast arrived, so had a pile of clothes, underwear, her necessary eye drops, and hygiene products. All for her. All from him. Tears had stung her eyes at his thoughtfulness. But it was the way he paid delicate attention to her in the shower that convinced her to go along with him to the radio station.

No matter how much she protested the ability to wash herself, he didn't listen. He'd led her into the warmth of the water and caressed her skin with soap, his large palms traveling over every inch of her body. On more than one occasion her thigh rubbed against the hardness of his erection, yet he never acknowledged his arousal. He devoted himself to taking care of her, and her heart attached a little more to him with each stroke against her flesh.

"Let's get going, then." Mitchell grasped her hand and led her from the suite.

A flurry of excitement met them in the lobby. People greeted Mitchell and Blake, fans screamed in the distance—too far away to be inside the hotel—and security guards mumbled instructions on where to walk.

The noise hammered at her, making her chest throb, her palms sweat. "Mitchell, I can't do this."

He squeezed her hand. "I've got you, sweetheart. We're almost there."

They walked fast, and she struggled to keep up. Dark shadows blurred her vision, making her cling onto his waist for support. Any moment she expected to trip on someone or something and slide gracelessly along the lobby floor on her face.

"The coast is clear, sugar. You've got nothing to worry about." Blake patted her on the shoulder, his support giving her a needed dose of comfort.

The room became brighter with each step, the shadows standing out against the glow. Footsteps surrounded them, sliding doors opened and closed, the hum of an engine, and still the guards instructed them. *Let me lead the way. The car is just outside. You take the passenger seat, Mitch and the woman in the back.*

Her blood thickened with each beat, cutting off her oxygen, making it hard to breathe.

"Lower your head, Allie, and climb in."

She did as instructed, following Mitchell into the vehicle and sliding along the back seat to sit beside him.

Nobody spoke during the ride. The soft murmur of the radio and the occasional *click, click, click* of the indicator was the only noise to break the silence. She leaned into him, catching her breath, and tried not to rub her leg against Tony, the bodyguard, who sat on the other side of her.

"Not long and we'll be there," Mitchell whispered, nuzzling behind her ear.

She smiled and squeezed his hand.

"Are you still happy to have a coffee downstairs by yourself?"

"Yes. I'll be fine." Alana refused to be a distraction, stating she would remain in the car if need be. The compromise, suggested by Tony, was for her to wait in the coffee shop on the ground floor until the fifteen-minute interview had concluded.

Mitchell, and even Blake, had protested, but Alana wouldn't agree to come otherwise. She could sit by herself, drink a coffee, and listen to the chatter of mingling people for the short amount of time. If she encountered a problem, she'd ask a waitress for help.

"I'll get out first." Tony's deep voice startled her, kicking her heart rate back into unwelcomed territory.

"No arguments here," Blake replied. "When it comes to fans, I'd much prefer to have them groping you than me."

"Do they really grope?" Alana murmured into Mitchell's shoulder.

He chuckled. "Unfortunately, they grab anything they can get their hands on."

She cringed. "Maybe I'll stay in the car until Tony can come back and get me."

He released her hand and stroked her shoulders, pulling her closer into his body. "I won't let anything happen to you…again." The regret in his voice was palpable.

"OK, here we go." The car came to a stop and Tony climbed out, letting in a wave of screams before he slammed the door shut.

"There's nothing to worry about, sugar," Blake reassured her. "We're at the back entrance to the building, and there are only a few people at the doors. Security already has it under control."

A few people? She wasn't deaf. Instead of alerting him to the fact she heard half of Richmond releasing their siren calls at the car, she nodded and swallowed the bile rising in her throat. "All right."

Blake's door opened, then Mitchell's. "I've got you." He gripped her hand and led her from the car. "Once we get inside and meet the rest of the guys, Tony will get you settled in the coffee shop."

She tripped up the curb, once again along the path, and sighed in relief once they passed the wailing crowd and entered the relative safety of the building.

"Easy as groupies on a gig night, wasn't it, Al?"

She cringed at the analogy, but couldn't help smiling. "Yeah. As easy as I assume groupies are on those types of occasions, I would have to agree."

"Mitch?" A female voice called, and Alana swallowed involuntarily. "Are you guys ready to head upstairs?"

"Yeah, but first I want you to meet someone. Leah, this is Alana. Allie, this is our awesomely talented band manager, Leah."

"Nice to meet you." Alana raised her hand to the shadow in front of her and hoped for the best. There was an uncomfortable pause that caused the hair on the back of her neck to rise, and a soft hand gripped hers in a firm shake. They were communicating behind her back…well probably right in front of her eyes. She sensed it.

"You…too, Alana." Leah's words were stilted.

"There was a problem last night with the ass cake you fired. He threw a glass vase that shattered in Alana's face. At the moment, she can't see."

"What?" Leah gasped. "Why wasn't I told? I need to be informed of these things, Mitch."

"It's fine. Settle down. She's here so I can keep an eye on her. I've been taking care of her to make up for the position I put her in."

Alana hid her disappointment behind a smile as the two of them spoke. His words ripped the happiness from her lungs. Was that what he'd been doing? Taking care of her to make up for what happened? If that was the case, he needn't have worried.

"I've gotta go." Mitchell kissed her temple.

She pressed her lips together to contain her emotion, even though her wounded pride urged her to jerk away. "Bye." She gave a half-hearted wave.

His heat continued to surround her moments later when the

blur of shadows around them faded into the background. Tight hands gripped her shoulders and the darkened haze of his face filled her vision. "What's wrong?"

She shook her head, not wanting to open her mouth. If she spoke, she would tell him to drop the knight in shining armor act and call Kate to pick her up.

"We met less than twenty-four hours ago, and yet I can already sense when something is wrong. Please tell me, otherwise I won't be able to concentrate in the interview, and I'll make a dick of myself."

For a second, her lips twitched in humor, but then she remembered why she'd been upset. "Has everything between us been about obligation? The sex, the clothes, the shower? Were you doing it because you thought you needed to?" Her voice broke on the final word, and she scrunched her nose, fighting back the unwelcome emotions determined to break free.

A quick, firm kiss landed on her lips, startling her. "I've told you before; I say stupid shit around you because you make me lose focus. I didn't mean it to sound that way." His mouth caressed hers again. This time softer, sweeter. "I'm sorry. Once this is over, I think everyone will be coming back to the hotel for a few drinks. Hopefully by then, I'll be able to relax a little and my foot won't be in my mouth as much."

Alana tilted her face to steal another kiss. "OK." She wasn't convinced, but she wouldn't be a drama queen and call him a liar either. At the moment, she had time up her sleeve, and spending a little more with Mitchell wouldn't be a chore. She just hoped for her heart's sake he was telling the truth.

"You ready to grab a coffee?" Tony's voice came from beside her, and Mitchell's heat left her body. A momentary wash of apprehension nudged her senses at the thought of being led around by another unfamiliar man, but she suppressed the judgments her mother had tried to instill in her. Mitchell, Blake, and even the optometrist's son had shown her only kindness. She would do her best to trust

Tony, too.

"Definitely." Coffee would be her savior. A great big bucket full.

A hand grabbed hers and laid it to rest at the crook of a large arm. "Don't worry. I'll make sure you get settled." Tony led her forward, taking slow steps so she could keep up.

"I'll see you later, sweetheart." Mitchell's voice drifted away along with the sound of his footsteps.

Tony walked her to the coffee shop in silence, only pausing for a moment to open the door. Inside, the noise spiked her anxiety. Voices melded together, some in hushed tones, others loud and obnoxious. The coffee machine hissed, cutlery clattered, footsteps sounded, and bells rang. She had to close her eyes and trust his guidance while she tried to calm herself with steadying breaths.

He patted her hand in reassurance. "Here, sugar, I've got a seat for you." He grabbed her fingers and draped them over the back of a chair.

"Thank you." She felt for the table, then the seat to gain her bearings before she sat down.

"You're right up against a wall, only a few rows back from the cashier."

She nodded. At least if she had any trouble, she knew where to turn for help. She would be fine, though. Once she had a coffee in hand, she could relax and simply sit and think. Maybe even relive some of the seductive memories from earlier.

"What would you like me to order for you?"

"A cappuccino with two sugars, please." She reached for the money in her pocket and pulled out a note.

"Are you sure that's all you want?" he asked, his voice gruff, but deeply caring. "Don't women usually want the skim, soy, caramel, mocha, double decaf crappa latte stuff?"

Alana chuckled. Tony was clearly not the chatty type. She appreciated his attempt to make her comfortable. "No. I'm not a crappa latte kind of girl."

He gave a huff of laughter and patted her hand resting on the table. "OK. A standard cappuccino it is. I'll go order it now, but I won't be able to wait around. I need to check the exit point and make sure my boys are all right."

"Not a problem." She raised the note in her hand.

"Don't worry, sugar, Mitch already gave me a big enough bonus to take care of it. I'm starting to think he might actually like you."

Her heart clenched, and she had no clue why. Maybe it had something to do with other people noticing his interest when she physically couldn't see it, or that she feared he would lose interest in her within any given heartbeat. Either way, her chest did funny things at the mere thought of Mitchell.

"I'll get them to bring the coffee to your table and ask them to keep an eye on you."

"Thank you."

He left without another word.

She drummed her fingers on the table, played with the saltshakers, fiddled with her hair. Time dragged. Keen vision had always been her strong suit. Not only for clarity, she also had the ability to behold things differently than other people. She found beauty in the blandest of settings. Her mother claimed it was the reason Alana's photos sold so well.

Losing her vision cut her to the core. She wanted to see the buildings, the skyline, the hills. She itched to capture moments in time with her camera and perfect them with special effects on her computer.

Instead of allowing the melancholy to take hold, she focused on her other senses. Freshly ground coffee clogged the air and her lungs craved every breath. At home, she lived on the store bought stuff. It was drinkable, but never held the delicious scent that currently filled the room.

The noise no longer unsettled her. An elderly couple chatted in whispers to her left, their voices holding the fragility of age. Eager women near the front of the store laughed, not minding that their conversation was easily overheard.

"A cappuccino with two sugars?" A female voice came from beside her.

"Yes, thank you." She heard the clatter of the saucer, the tinkle of the teaspoon, and then the footsteps as the woman retreated.

Alana felt for her cup and palmed the warm crockery in her hands. As she raised the mug to her lips, a shiver ran down her spine. Were people staring at her? Talking about her? She ignored the paranoia and took a sip of coffee. The hot liquid burned her tongue and scorched the back of her throat, and yet she savored every second of it. The taste was rich and creamy with a dash of sweet perfection. She didn't need double, caramel, mocha, decaf, or whatever Tony called it. Plain and simple was divine.

Time dripped by. At the end of her drink, she reached for the cell phone in her pocket, then thought better of it. No point going in search of a clock if she couldn't see. With a sigh, she started to fiddle. Mitchell couldn't be too much longer.

"Excuse me." The feminine voice came from the table to her left. Alana ignored it. "I'm sorry, miss, but my husband and I were just discussing how you look a lot like someone we used to know."

A person's shadow moved closer to her table and Alana sensed the words were directed at her.

"Are you from around here, dear?" It was the elderly woman who had sat at the nearby table.

"No, sorry. My mom lived here a long time ago, but this is my first visit to Richmond." She shook her head in dismissal and lifted her coffee cup to her lips, even though it was empty.

There was a pause, a few whispered words.

"I don't mean to pester you, but what is your mother's name?"

Alana smiled through the discomfort of not being able to make eye contact and kept her gaze lowered. "Susan Shelton."

A chair scraped along the floor, and a man close by cleared his throat.

She waited for a reply, stroking the sides of her coffee mug. The likelihood of anyone here knowing her mother was slim, yet her name seemed to be a conversation stopper.

"And how old are you, child?" The man's voice came now, fragile and filled with hints of anticipation.

"Umm." She frowned, and unease covered her skin. "I'm… twenty-seven."

She heard a gasp, and a heady sense of foreboding clogged her throat. "Why do you ask?"

Another chair scraped. One more darkened shadow approached her table, suffocating her, making her claustrophobic.

"Child, I think you're our granddaughter."

Mitch sat in one of the plush chairs in the radio station's boardroom, dodging questions about Alana as they waited to be taken into the studio. He glared at Blake, trying to think up the best retribution for the way he kept adding fuel to the fire.

"If she's blind, what the hell have you been doing with her for the last twelve hours?" Ryan asked.

"Praying," Blake replied with a chuckle.

Sean, Mason, Ryan, and even Leah focused on him with matching expressions of disbelief.

"Praying?" Leah's eyes widened.

"Yeah," Blake continued. "They had the bedroom door closed and Alana kept calling out to God and Jesus and any other spiritual leader who'd listen."

Snorts of laughter filled the room.

Mitch remained seated, arms crossed over his chest, eyebrows raised. The smart-ass comments wouldn't end for a while.

"I'm not sure what Mitch was doing, but their religion sounds like a lot of fun."

"I bet it beats jerking off to the porn stash on your laptop," Mitch shot back.

Blake smirked. "Now that you mention it, her moans of enthusiasm *were* a great soundtrack to my whack job."

"You're an ass," Mitch snarled and glanced away, trying to suppress his laughter. The fucker always had a comeback.

"Seriously, Mitch, I hope you didn't seduce the girl when she's in such a vulnerable position." Leah made it sound so sleazy. "She'll have a great story to spin to the media once the fun and games are over. It could turn into a PR nightmare."

Alana wasn't the attention-seeking type, but he'd been wrong before. Women had a way of messing with his mind, especially when his dick was involved. Only this time, he was sure he knew Alana's type. He was certain she wouldn't run to the tabloids at the first opportunity. "I trust her."

He did. For some strange, hormone-riddled reason, he trusted the shit out of her. "She won't cause any trouble."

Tony stalked past the windows of the boardroom and opened the door, breaking the fixation on Mitch's love life.

"How is she?" he asked before Tony said a word.

Mason groaned and Mitch ignored it. He wouldn't hide his worry over her wellbeing. He cared for her and had to admit he enjoyed her vulnerability and the way she relied on him. Her image still hadn't left his mind, her smile, her dimples, her gorgeous light green eyes. He couldn't wait to get downstairs to see her again.

"She was fine when I left her ten minutes ago." Tony shrugged. "I ordered her a coffee and she seemed happy to sit there and wait."

Mitch nodded in thanks.

"There were three guys down there checking her out. I'm sure they'll keep her company if she gets lonely."

Mitch pushed forward in his chair and sat up straight. "What?" He gripped the table, poised to raise to his feet when Tony's face brightened with a smirk.

"You really like her, don't you?" Mason asked with a chuckle. "Oh, this is going to be so much fun."

Mitch didn't agree. They'd all gone through it before. Ryan used to do the puppy love thing with his wife Julie. Sean still held resentment from the last woman who broke his heart, and Mitch was pretty sure the reason Blake spent a lot of time on the laptop was because of a woman too.

He didn't bother answering. They would only twist his words into something they found humorous. Unfortunately, it was their ritual, the way they bonded, and Mitch supposed he deserved a little payback for the years of shit he'd given.

A knock came at the door, and Jenny Jay, the local radio host, poked her head inside the room. "You guys ready?"

Leah moved beside him as he pushed from his chair. "I'm going to check on Alana while you guys do your thing. I'll try and convince her to come back up with me. That way we can leave straight after the interview and avoid any fan drama."

"Thanks." He ran both hands through his hair and breathed deep. "Let's get this shit over with."

The members of Reckless Beat followed Jenny down the hall and entered the small studio room while the bodyguards waited in the reception area. They'd done the radio gig so many times before that when Jenny ran through her spiel on how things would run on air, Mitch zoned out.

His attitude didn't change once they were live. Mason always handled the majority of the questions. Being the lead singer, he was the one the fans loved the most. The rest of them would indicate with hand gestures if they wanted to answer something specific, and they kept Leah happy as long as they all spoke at least once.

Today, Mitch hoped his "hello" to the listeners would suffice.

"So, Mitchell—" He cringed when Jenny Jay said his name. "—the newspaper tells of another heroic scene. Apparently you came to the rescue of one of your fans last night. How does it feel to be back in the spotlight saving another beautiful woman?"

He gave an uncomfortable laugh, uncomfortable because he had no idea what the hell to say. He hadn't seen the newspaper and could only imagine the way the assholes would've distorted the truth.

"Umm, good…I suppose." There, he'd done his quota.

"I've been told you spent the night taking care of the female in question, rushing her to get medical attention in the early hours of the morning. Is this another case of not being able to turn down a woman in need?"

Blake snorted softly beside him, and Mitch wanted to do the same. That damn interview would haunt him for the rest of his life.

"I think the majority of people would react the same way to a woman in need. Alana was powerless to stop her injuries and unable to take care of herself afterward. I merely did the right thing." He gave a firm nod, happy with his answer.

Jenny Jay smiled back at him before turning her next question to Ryan and the rumors of his failing marriage.

Halla-fucking-lujah. For once he hadn't dug the hole deeper for himself.

Blake leaned toward him and covered the mic in front of them. "Boy, is Leah gonna be pissed you didn't milk that PR opportunity for all it's worth."

Mitch nudged his best friend's shoulder away and ignored the comment. Leah still owed him for the last PR nightmare. He didn't care about their manager's reaction, anyway. His attention rested on how he would persuade Alana to spend another night with him.

A knot formed in his chest, and he rubbed it away. He needed to hold her a little longer, to memorize her features, and hopefully score a little more prayer time too. Only problem—he didn't think she would be easy to convince.

Chapter Nine

"Child, I think you're our granddaughter."

A hand came to rest on top of Alana's, and she flinched. "I'm sorry, but you're mistaken." She slid her hand out from underneath the weight. "My grandparents have passed away."

The elderly woman released a soft sob.

"Shh, shh," the man consoled. "What's your name?"

Alana frowned and glanced over her shoulder in the hope a waitress would rescue her. At home, she was exposed to emotionally fractured people every day. She recognized the tone of heartbreak and the fragility of loneliness. Her ability to provide comfort was taught at an early age. Only now was different. Without her sight, she didn't think it was possible to give these people what they needed. She wasn't in a position to soothe them. She was in a place of vulnerability, and each time they opened their mouths and addressed her as a child, the tension built inside her.

"Alana," she replied, rubbing the tiredness from her eyes. She wished she could help them, to ease their solitude or whatever else they were dealing with. But she wasn't the person they needed. Her mind was frazzled from the events of the last twenty-four hours. Her senses were already on high alert—from her lack of sight and the recent discovery of pleasure. Whatever they were looking for would be lost on her. She could cause more harm than good.

"What about your father, Alana?" The woman's voice broke.

She tensed. Time for the conversation to end. She grasped for the corner of the table with both hands and pushed herself to stand. She didn't know where she was going, or how she would get there, but she couldn't stay. "I'm sorry. I'm not the woman you're looking for. Now, if you would please excuse—"

The man grabbed her wrist. "Your father is our son."

Anger boiled her blood. He had no right to touch her. No right to use his masculinity to wordlessly threaten her.

Damn it. Her mother was pouring into her thoughts like a flash flood. Her nightmares were becoming reality.

She straightened and looked in the man's direction. She couldn't make out his features, could only see him standing with a woman to his side.

"My father is a rapist," she snapped and waited for the gasps.

None came.

"Child, please sit so we can discuss this," he pleaded.

Alana frowned and clung to the table as her hands trembled. Why weren't they shocked? Why weren't they appalled by her admission?

She shook her head, confused, and tried not to let the sinking sensation overwhelm her. "My grandparents are dead," she whispered. "My father was a rapist." Those two sentences had been repeated to her as a child, over and over and over again, until finally she stopped asking about her family.

"Our son has done some regrettable things, yes. But I assure you, Alana, we are your grandparents."

Bile rose up her throat. This couldn't be happening. It couldn't be real.

"I'm sorry." She blinked straight ahead, unable to believe a stranger's words over what her mother had preached to her all her life. On numb legs, she pushed her chair back and maneuvered around the table, bumping into them in her effort to flee.

"Please, Alana," the woman choked.

She didn't stop. With her fingers outstretched in front of her, Alana fumbled forward, colliding with tables and chairs, causing plates to rattle and people to curse. Her vision brightened with each step, leading her to the front of the store. To the sanctuary of the unknown.

"Where's the door?" she pleaded.

A gentle hand landed at the small of her back, jolting her heart. "It's a few feet ahead," the elderly man answered.

She jerked from his touch. They had to be con artists. Manipulators. And with her sight impairment, she made for an easy target.

"Leave me alone." She glared over her shoulder, hoping her gaze hit its mark.

The noise in the coffee shop lowered to hushed whispers before he spoke again. "Excuse me, sir, could you help this lady outside, please?"

Now he wanted to help her? None of this made sense.

Another chair scraped along the floor.

"No problem." The voice was younger, more comforting than the man who'd begun to truly frighten her. Maybe her mother's aversion was justified and all men were to be feared.

No. She shoved away the thought. Not Mitchell. Something inside her said she couldn't turn her back on what she experienced last night. She couldn't lessen the profound moments they'd shared.

A soft hand gripped her wrist, and she fought to hold back the terror at his touch. She'd never been so vulnerable or weak. Her mother had taught her to defend herself, how to attack an attacker. Yet right now, beside someone who sounded too old and frail to even break into a sweat, she was trembling.

"Watch your step." The younger man led her forward into the

warm breeze.

Cars zoomed by in the distance. The sound of women screaming Mason's name and echoing chants of "Reckless Beat" came from her left. Heels clicked, men spoke, phones rang. Disorientation made her knees weak. Her throat dried. Instead of faltering, she tilted her lips in a fake smile and inclined her head to her helper. "Thank you."

His grip dropped from her wrist. "Not a problem."

Then he was gone. And she was left alone.

She closed her eyes, took a deep breath, and tried to gain her bearings. The building stood tall behind her. She could take a step back, walk herself around to another entrance, and ask for help. Or she could do what she should've done in the first place.

No matter how monumental last night was, being Mitchell Davies' mistress wasn't a role she should be playing. The morning with him had served its purpose—she'd experienced something she would never forget—and now it was time to leave before she became too attached. Once she found somewhere quiet to rest, she would call Kate and get out of here. Out of the chaos and suffocation.

She let the air seep from her lungs, pivoted on her toes, and glanced up at the dark shadow of the wall. She inched closer to the building, taking small steps so she wouldn't trip. Reaching out, she touched the cold glass window and trailed her fingers forward. Slowly, she advanced until her hand slid off the edge and into air.

She suppressed a squeal as her steps faltered. "Goddamn it." Vertigo threatened to drag her to her knees, but she settled into the building, bowing her head until she caught her breath.

Once the threat of tears and the pulse of dizziness subsided, she moved around the corner. Her palms grated against something rough–cement or stone, no longer glass. When the noise around her lessened, she leaned her back against the wall and slid to the ground. Her ass hit the hard cement with a painful jolt, one that felt a lot like hitting rock bottom. She closed her eyes, rested her elbows on her knees, and covered her face to ward off the nervous breakdown.

Her chest heaved, the constriction tightening with each breath. Something wasn't right. Her mind kept going over the couple's reactions. How they didn't flinch when she mentioned the rape. How they remained adamant about the family connection.

What if he wasn't a con artist, and the words he spoke were true?

She shook her head, determined to stay strong. Dropping her hands, she leaned to the side and removed her cell from her pants pocket. Kate would cheer her up. She always did. There couldn't be much time before her friend finished work. Then they would go home together and relax over a few cocktails like they'd planned to do since last month.

She cupped the device in her hand, her heart beating harder with each second she stared at the black blur. Why hadn't she set up the voice recognition application? She could see the dark hues of her jeans, the cream fuzz of her arm, and only a big black spot where her phone should be.

Closing her eyes, she unlocked the screen by touch. That part was easy, she'd done it a thousand times before without thought or sight. The next step would be harder. There weren't many contacts in her address book, but she had no way of knowing where Kate's name sat or how far to scroll to get to it.

She placed her finger in the bottom left corner, where the book icon would take her to the numbers stored. With a deep breath she started to slowly scroll, trying to recount each person listed and what size each icon made. When she reached the position she thought would be close, she pressed her screen, and pressed again where she thought the connect button would be.

Raising the phone to her ear she waited for the ring tone.

Nothing.

She lowered the phone again, lifted the device right before her eyes, and tried to see where she needed to press, but it was no use. Her sight couldn't make out the letters. Again, she blindly pressed her screen and placed it to her ear.

She held her breath and sighed when the ringing started.

One ring, two.

"Alana."

Shit.

"Mom?"

So close. Kate's name sat directly above her mothers.

"What's going on?" A hint of panic came from the other end of the line. "I got off the phone to Kate's mom not long ago, and she told me you were on the second page of the Richmond newspaper."

Holy crap. She'd left a life where no one knew her existence, and now she was making newspaper headlines…ones she couldn't see.

"Umm…" Alana had nothing to say that her mom would approve of. There was no comfort, not one single word that would calm the storm that was her over-analytical mother.

"I promised you I wouldn't call and check up on you, so Patty looked it up on the internet. We've been listening to the Richmond radio station, and the man spoke about you on-air, Alana. He mentioned your name."

Mitch talked about her during his interview? Through the panic and vulnerability, her chest sparked with an emotion far more palpable than she'd ever experienced before. She wanted to ask her mother what he said, but staying on the topic wouldn't be safe.

"How did my grandparents die, mom?"

"What? Please, Alana, the man said you were hurt, and he'd taken care of you all night. What does that mean? Are you OK? Did he hurt you?"

She couldn't tell if her mother's panic increased from Alana not answering the questions or because she'd mentioned her deceased grandparents. "I met an elderly couple not long ago. They tried to convince me they were my father's parents."

Silence.

"Mom?"

"You should come home."

No. Apart from being visually impaired, she loved the freedom of being away from the retreat. She'd already learned a lot from her experiences. Men weren't horrible creatures. Well, most anyway. She realized she wasn't a lesbian, which was a bonus, and truth be told, she contemplated staying in Richmond for longer than her return flight date. Much longer.

"How did my grandparents die?" She clutched the device in her hand, praying for an honest answer.

"I don't want to discuss this over the phone. When you get home we can sit down and talk about it." Her mother was adamant, the previous panic overridden by determination.

"Mom…" Alana swallowed over the gravel in her throat. "Just tell me this. Are my grandparents still alive?"

She heard nothing but the rush of cars and people talking in the distance as she waited.

"I don't know," her mother whispered.

"You don't know?" All the years she'd hoped for family to connect with, something outside of the secluded life on the retreat, and she'd been told they were alone. That the only person she had in her life was her mother. "You don't know?" she repeated louder. "You told me they died. You told me since childhood that I had no family."

"Alana, please. Come home and we can discuss it."

Home? Home wasn't a place surrounded with lies and deceit. Home was somewhere filled with warmth and love and honesty. And apparently, it was a place she had never visited.

"No." She rubbed her forehead to ease the tension pounding in her head. "I don't think I'm coming home at all." She had her own money. Not a lot, but it would be enough to keep her in Richmond for a while and give her the opportunity to figure out what she wanted for her future. "I'll speak to you later."

"No! Wait."

Her mother didn't deserved a hearing. Alana had endured a lot because of her love for the woman who raised her. But she wouldn't abide this. Not now. Not ever. "Bye, Mom." She removed the phone from her ear and pressed at the screen numerous times hoping to hit the disconnect button. Now she had no way of getting in contact with Kate and didn't know how to find Mitchell.

Fantastic.

Pushing against the wall to her feet, she shook her hands, trying to dislodge the vulnerability that caused her limbs to shake. She could do this.

A male cleared his throat a few yards away, the closest sound she'd heard since hiding around this side of the building. On alert, she snapped her head in the direction it came from.

"Alana, I'm sorry."

She released the breath restricting her lungs. The elderly man had more determination than she anticipated.

"I didn't realize you were visually impaired when we first approached you in the coffee shop. I didn't mean to scare you into fleeing. I just followed you to make sure you were all right."

"It's fine." She tried to smile. The man who may very well be her grandfather was her only ally in finding Mitchell or getting in contact with Kate. Thank you, fate.

In the distance, the women screamed louder, more hysterical, chanting a mass of indecipherable words. Her panic returned. Reckless Beat's interview must be finished, and the band was probably in the lobby or leaving, causing the crowd to go wild.

"Can I help you get to where you need to be?" His voice approached.

She nodded and blindly stepped forward. Mitchell couldn't come outside to search for her. It would be suicide…by groping. His bodyguards may even encourage him to leave and go back to the hotel without her.

She knew he cared. He'd already made that obvious. He just wouldn't be able to roam the streets when there were screaming women and fans willing to push him to the ground in an effort to touch him.

"Yes. Please. I need to hurry."

"Mitch, I couldn't find her."

Leah's eyes held a hint of panic that seeped under his skin and kicked his heart into overdrive.

"What do you mean, you couldn't find her? She's in the coffee shop downstairs."

She swallowed and shook her head. "Alana's not there."

He increased his pace down the radio station's hall, and Leah struggled to keep up.

"What's going on?" Blake asked from behind.

"Alana's gone," he said over his shoulder, not stopping his momentum. "I'm going to find her."

"You can't just walk around unattended, Mitch." Leah grabbed his upper arm, trying to slow his progression, but he didn't stop until he reached the elevator. "There's a crowd outside. They'll eat you alive."

He smacked his fingers against the Down button and turned to face Blake's worried expression. In the background Mason, Sean, Ryan, and Tony strode toward them, meeting up with the other two bodyguards who had been waiting in the reception area.

"What's the rush?" Ryan stopped beside him.

"Alana's not in the coffee shop. I don't know where she is."

"Maybe she got a better offer." Mason chuckled, then wiped the smirk off his face when Mitch glared at him. "Sorry," he mumbled and broke eye contact.

"What are you going to do?" Sean asked.

"I'm going to find her." He turned back to the elevator and slammed his fingers into the Down button again, and again, and again.

"You can't." Leah's voice rose.

"Watch me," he snapped, and uncomfortable silence settled over them.

"Hold up, pussy-whipped." Mason broke the discomfort. "Why don't I get Dan and Pete—" he motioned to the two other bodyguards, "—to step outside with me, Sean, and Ryan. Building security is already out there, so the hype should be controllable." Mason glanced at Leah as she shook her head, but he didn't acknowledge her disapproval. "We'll chat with the fans, sign some autographs, and keep them occupied while you, Blake, and Tony go search for her. She couldn't have gone far walking around like Stevie Wonder."

The elevator dinged. Mitch didn't wait for the doors to fully open before he stepped forward and pushed them apart. "That'd help, but with or without you, I'm going to find her."

"Settle down, Maverick, this isn't the danger zone." Sean smirked as he followed everyone into the elevator. "She might still be in the building."

Mitch's finger would get a cramp if he gave the bird every time he felt the urge. Why did everyone have to be a smartass twenty-four-seven? And why did they have to be so good at it?

"Well, his safety will definitely be in jeopardy," Leah grumbled.

They descended in silence while his blood ran cold. Where was she? "Did you check the bathrooms?"

"Yes," Leah replied. "I checked the bathroom stalls. I glanced outside, I double checked the lobby."

Shit.

When the elevator dinged its arrival on ground level, he bit his lip waiting for everyone in front of him to move out.

"We'll go do our thing," Mason stated as a chorus of screams sounded outside. "Meet back inside in fifteen minutes."

"I won't be coming back until I find her," Mitch replied and pivoted from their makeshift circle to begin the search. A firm hand grabbed his upper arm.

"We'll meet back here in fifteen minutes and re-evaluate if you haven't found her." Mason looked at him in concern. "Don't do anything stupid, Mitch. She'll be fine."

Mitch inclined his head, and Mason's hand fell from his arm. "See you in fifteen minutes."

He jogged, keeping up the steady pace as he checked every inch of the lobby, peering out every window, trekking down every hall. The woman at the information desk hadn't seen Alana. The ladies in the female bathroom hadn't either, and didn't appreciate when he shoved open every stall door to double-check. Or maybe it was his presence, along with Blake and Tony, in a woman's bathroom that pissed them off.

He didn't care.

He had to find Alana.

Now.

The need to see her had his pulse increasing with each step. He had to make sure she was all right, that those gorgeous dimples would still greet the sound of his voice.

He pushed through the inside entrance to the coffee shop, his backup still in tow. Tony spoke to the barista while simultaneously giving death stares to anyone who came within a yard of him and Blake. Tony even held the gasping fans who begged for an autograph at bay with a firm shake of his head. The guy had a soft and gooey center, but on the outside he was one scary mo-fo.

"She left a while ago," the lady behind the counter said with a worried look on her face. "I think there was an issue—"

"Issue?" Mitch hadn't meant to yell. Really, he hadn't. It was the adrenaline and fear pushing him to over-express himself.

The woman's face fell. "I'm sorry, we were busy, and I didn't have the opportunity to check if she needed help. She walked out the front doors while telling an elderly gentleman to leave her alone. I haven't seen them since."

Panic-filled thoughts flashed through Mitch's mind. What would an old man want with Alana?

"He followed her?" Blake asked.

The woman nodded. "I think so." She wrung her hands. "Look, I'm sorry."

"It's not your fault," Mitch added and began to head for the front doors.

"*Wait.*"

He stopped and pivoted back around. Blake and Tony did the same. The woman stood on her tiptoes, glancing over their heads. "I think the lady over there was with him."

The three of them followed her gaze. In the third table back from the window sat a woman with gray hair, her head bowed, her hands resting in front of her.

Without a backward glance he headed for her, ignoring the excited stares that followed wherever he went.

"Excuse me." Mitch knelt beside the table, and her reddened eyes turned to face him. "Have you seen a young woman, chocolate brown hair, green eyes? She would've had trouble with her vision."

The woman's gaze became distracted with something behind him, outside the window. He began again. "I'm sorry to bother you, but—"

"Mitch." Tony tapped him on the shoulder.

He peered up at the bodyguard, who was staring in the same direction out the window. His heart skipped a beat as he turned and moved to his feet.

There she was, bathed in a halo of sunshine, her hand clasped around the crook of an elderly man's elbow as they walked past the coffee shop windows.

"Thank fuck for that," Blake muttered.

Mitch held back from running to her. He didn't mind being called pussy-whipped, or under the thumb, or whatever his friends wanted to classify him as. The thing that settled uncomfortably in his chest was the addiction clawing his insides. After only one night together, the thought of losing her had turned his limbs into shaking clumps of lead.

It wasn't normal.

Or natural.

"Why are you so happy?" he asked over his shoulder.

Blake shrugged. "I've been feeling spiritual today. Was hoping to listen in on another prayer session later."

"You're a dick." Mitch shook his head and took the first step forward to claim his girl. He ate up the distance, his pace quickening until finally he reached the door, yanked it open, and stood a yard before her. "Alana."

Her head turned in his direction, her focus aimed at his face, but not directly on his eyes. A smile tilted her lips. "Mitchell." Her voice was breathy, exactly the way he felt. She took a step away from the man at her arm and paused. "Mitchell?"

He went to her, grasped her in his arms, and held her to his chest. "Where the hell have you been?" he whispered into her hair.

She hugged his waist and squeezed tight. "There was a bit of… drama."

"It was entirely my fault," an aged voice informed him.

Mitch raised his gaze to the man standing directly behind her. After hearing about the issue in the coffee shop, he wanted to castrate the seemingly harmless stranger, no matter how much regret the man held in his eyes.

"No, it's not." Alana shook her head and pivoted from Mitch's chest. "I was just…stunned."

The old man's eyes glistened with unshed tears when he looked at Mitch.

"What's going on?" He rubbed his forehead, trying to hide his face and brush away some of his anxiety. He couldn't wait around in the wide open for hours. They needed to leave before women with no sense of respect swarmed them.

"I don't want to discuss it now. I'll tell you about it later. I just want to get out of here."

The man bowed his head in defeat.

"Mitchell, can you please get Mr. Bowen's phone number for me?"

Mitch glanced at Mr. Bowen, who now had a hopeful smile on his face, his hands shaking as he rifled through his wallet. "Sure, sweetheart."

"Here are my personal contact details." Mr. Bowen shuffled forward and handed the card to him, before turning to Alana. "Rose and I would love to hear from you. Please, don't hesitate to call at any time."

Alana inclined her head. "I'd like that. Hopefully we can meet up again before I leave Richmond."

Mr. Bowen reached for her hand and encased it in both of his. "We would love to, Alana. It would make us extremely happy."

Mitch stood back and watched, entirely confused as to why an elderly man would be eager to meet up with Alana again. How did they know each other when she'd never been in Richmond before? The whole situation was doing his head in.

"It would make me happy, too."

Her gaze lowered when the old man's shaking hand cupped her cheek. "I'm glad to have met you." And with that, he began to walk away, past Tony who stood a few paces behind on alert, toward the coffee shop door, which Blake held open.

Mitch stepped into her, this time raising her chin with a delicate finger so he could gaze into her eyes. "You scared me." He placed a fleeting kiss on her lips, denying his body the full devouring it craved. "Are you all right?"

She nodded, and he kissed her again. This time when he went to pull back, she snaked her hand around his neck and held him close, deepening the kiss. Her tongue sought his, her lips moving in a heated rhythm that would soon leave him unable to walk away without readjusting his cock.

"Oh, come on!" Blake shouted. "Enough, already. This shit's going to be all over Facebook."

Mitch wanted to growl. Unfortunately, Blake was right. There were too many eyes on them. "We better go."

"OK."

Something wasn't right in Alana's world. Her smiles weren't as bright, her expression less cheerful. He grabbed her arm and placed it at the crook of his elbow. "Tell me what's wrong, and I'll fix it."

She let out a breath of soft laughter, but her happiness quickly faded. "Just take me back to the hotel. I'm tired."

He supposed she would be exhausted after the excitement of the last twenty-four hours. Her body wouldn't be used to the late nights like his. "No problem." Once they were back in the suite he would give her time to rest. She would need it because he had no plans to let her go home with Kate tonight.

Chapter Ten

ALANA RESTED INTO Mitchell's chest as he hauled her down the suite hall. "You keep carrying me like a child."

He released a breath of laughter. "I keep carrying you like a man who can't keep his hands off you."

Her cheeks heated and warmth suffused her from head to toe. They hadn't spoken a word in the car, and neither had Tony or Blake. There had been an unending silence that spoke of the unnecessary annoyance she had dragged the band into as he lightly held her hand.

She should've felt remorse, but whenever his skin was on hers, she was whitewashed with arousal. It wasn't natural or explainable. It simply was. She couldn't even see him, yet his touch sparked her soul to life, and she wasn't sure if anything would ever feel the same once their time was up.

"Do you want to talk about it?" He carried her into a room bathed in light and placed her down on a familiar mattress.

"No. Nothing happened," she lied and kicked off her shoes. He didn't need to know her secrets. She didn't want him to. The reality of her conception, her upbringing, and her current situation with her so-called grandparents wasn't something she was proud of. And it definitely wasn't something she had any urge to discuss with a celebrity who had the perfect life.

"OK, I'll leave you to rest, then."

His figure retreated, taking the pounding beat of her heart with him as he moved to the opposite side of the room. Darkness descended when he pulled the curtains closed, and the dull illumination around the window wasn't enough for her to be able to see him through her blurred vision.

"Where are you going?" She climbed to the middle of the bed, her limbs heavy and exhausted, and hoped he would follow.

"Away. Far, far away, so I'm not tempted to wake you."

She chuckled and rested her head into the pillow. She'd never been more tired, and in the same breath she'd never wanted to stay awake more than she did right now. "Would it be needy if I asked you to stay?" She only needed a power nap. A mere few minutes of sleep to recharge.

"It would be torture." The bed dipped with his weight. "But I can deal with it." He snuggled in behind her, his body nestling into hers like it was coming home.

"Torture?"

"I want you, Allie."

She turned into him, her lips widening of their own accord. "What's stopping you?"

He pressed his mouth to hers, gentle, soft, so delicate it made her whimper. "You need to rest."

She needed a lot of things, and suddenly an orgasm had shot to the top of her list. After the slightest taste of sexuality, she now craved it. She wanted nothing more than to stay in this room, with his touch and his passion and his perfection.

He tugged at the waistband of her pants, and she inwardly cheered.

"I've got a pair of cotton shorts and one of my T-shirts for you. They'll be more comfortable to sleep in."

Wait. What? He helped her undress, his calloused palms running over every inch of her legs. Optimism made her panties grow damp. She could sense the excitement in his touch, could hear it in his heavy breathing. Then he torched her arousal and tormented her by redressing her in shorts and a baggy T-shirt she refused to acknowledge were increasingly cozier.

"Rest." He nudged her shoulder, indicating for her to resume the spooning position.

"What if I don't want to rest?" she cooed. "What if I want exactly what you want?"

He groaned. "You're killing me. As if the guilt of taking advantage of you wasn't enough."

"You're not." She frowned. "There's no advantage to be taken."

He nodded his forehead against hers, but it felt like an appeasing gesture instead of agreement. "Just rest for now, OK? There's enough time for us to play later."

But there wasn't. Not really. The clock was ticking. Every second brought them closer to saying goodbye.

"Don't worry," he murmured against her lips. "I'm not letting you go any time soon."

She needed to believe him. She needed it bad enough that she rolled over and spooned into his chest, refusing to accept any other option. "Don't let me sleep long."

"I won't."

He wrapped his arm around her waist and hugged her close. Flashbacks of the blurred madness from the coffee shop entered her mind, then as quickly as they came, they left again, smothered by the memories of last night when Mitchell was on stage. She smiled at the recollection of his grin, the confident twist of his lips that made her melt.

Her brain grew heavy, her limbs too. His measured breathing lulled her into slumber, and she tumbled into weightlessness in his arms.

She groaned as noise registered on the far edges of her consciousness. The sound grew, the boisterous male voices becoming clear to her fuzzy mind.

"Mitchell?"

She sat up straight and opened her eyes to darkness. She blinked, blinked again, then woke up enough to realize she was alone. The heavy chatter seeped from outside her door, the deep sound of conversation becoming clearer the longer she listened. She heard Mitchell's laughter, followed by muffled words from Blake, and who she guessed was Mason.

This scenario was in complete contrast to what her mother had described to her throughout her life. Men were supposed to be deceitful, sleazy, hurtful, degrading—the list continued.

Mitchell was none of those. Yes, he was sexual and sensual, but she liked those parts of him. He'd shown her that intimacy could be fulfilling for a woman. He'd also taken the time to give her pleasure when he wasn't receiving any in return. And although she would never know for certain, she didn't think he had a dishonest bone in his body. The care he'd shown melted her heart. He went above and beyond to ensure her comfort.

Shifting her legs to the side of the bed, she stood on the soft carpet. Light no longer filtered around the edges of the curtains. Night had fallen. She must have slept longer than the power nap she had planned.

She worked her way to the bathroom, shuffling her feet in case her shins came in contact with something hard. After using the facilities, she took cautious steps to the bedroom door, led by the soft glow of light under the frame.

The rambunctious conversation died when she stepped into the dining room, and a chair scraped against the tile. She smiled at the familiar shadowed figure striding toward her, and her body tingled before they even touched.

"Hey, sweetheart." Mitchell's arm ran around her waist, and he placed a kiss in her hair. "Sleep well?"

"Mmm." She nodded and snuggled into the warmth of his neck. "Why didn't you wake me?"

"You needed the rest."

"Yeah, but I wanted to spend more time with you before Kate came to pick me up."

He pulled her into a hug, and she heard his deep inhale as he nuzzled into her hair. "I've already spoken to Kate. She's happy to do another sleepover, if you are."

She pushed back in his arms and squinted to focus on his face. His features were clearer than the fuzz of last night, even sharper than her vision this morning, but his eyes were still a cloudy dark patch amongst his lightly tanned skin. "You've spoken to Kate?"

"Yeah, she's out on the balcony, drinking wine with Leah and Ryan's wife."

"I should go see her. I need to talk to her."

"Later." He pressed a kiss to her lips and tightened his grip on her waist. The heat from his crotch sank through the cotton shorts he'd purchased for her, the sensation igniting a fire in her womb.

She reached on tiptoes, kissed him back with fervor, and melted into his arms. Just as her nipples began to burn and her stomach tensed with anticipation, he broke the kiss.

"Can I get you a drink? Something to eat?"

Nourishment of the food and beverage variety had been far from her mind. However, if Mitchell was strong enough to break their connection and move away, she supposed she should be able to do the same.

While she said her greetings to Ryan, Mason, Sean, and Blake seated at the dining table playing cards, Mitchell went to the kitchen, returning moments later. He led her to the darkened lounge room. The lights were off, making it harder for her to see. It also made their private picnic on the sofa more intimate. They sat side by side, their thighs touching while a plate of unrecognizable food rested on her lap.

He leaned into her and kissed her neck. "There's cheese, crackers, and some fruit. Just feel around until you find something you like." He cradled an acoustic guitar, the tan exterior the extent of what she could see. She wished she had the vision to appreciate the instrument he lazily strummed, to memorize the perfection of the moment. Instead, she listened with intent, letting the music seduce her.

In between bites of apple and sips of wine, he played softly. The notes were a beautiful weave of intensity and exquisite passion. The sound tickled her nerves, filled her heart, and made her shiver with sensory overload.

"Do you want a blanket?" The music stopped, and his hand traveled over her wrist and up her arm. "You've got goose bumps."

Her skin tingled at his touch. "Um, yes." She didn't want to tell him the sensitivity came from his close proximity. "Please."

He stood, resting his guitar against the side of the sofa, and walked away, returning moments later with a blanket he draped underneath the plate on her lap.

"Better?" He sat down beside her, resting his arm over the back of the sofa.

She nodded, trying to decipher his expression, and failed miserably due to all the shadows.

Light fingers trailed through her loose hair, behind her ear, and made her chest constrict. "What are we going to do?" he asked, his voice a soft murmur.

Alana remained quiet for a moment, unsure what he referred to, and not willing to look like a fool. "What do you mean?" She picked up the plate on her lap and lifted it forward until she found the table to rest it on. He continued to play with strands of her hair as she pulled her knees up to rest on the sofa between them.

"I mean about us."

Her eyebrows rose. On the inside, her blood rushed like lava through her veins. She tried to suppress her hope, not willing to become excited about the prospect of a future between them, only to have to hide her profound disappointment later.

"Once I leave tomorrow on this promo tour, are you going to mind me calling you?" His voice held no emotion for her to read. "Will you let me come see you?"

"Yes." She bit her lip and nodded. "I'd love for you to."

"Your mom won't mind? I was thinking I might be able to rent a car and come see you when we're in the Colorado area. Or if we get a day or two off. I'd need to check the schedule."

She cringed. At her age, she shouldn't have to worry about her mother. Yet there was no way he could show up at her home. "No, you definitely can't go to the retreat. My mom doesn't allow any men on the property unless necessary, but I'm actually thinking of staying in Richmond for a while."

His fingers stopped caressing her hair, so she continued. "I want to see the Bowens again and find out if they're my grandparents. My mom won't tell me anything. I know she won't, so it's something I need to do for myself. And if what they claim is true, then I don't have any immediate plans of going back to Colorado at all."

"You'll move to Richmond?"

She shrugged, still unsure of her plans, and not wanting to say them aloud until she confirmed things with Kate. "Maybe."

"Maybe," he repeated, swiping his fingers through her hair one last time. She jolted a little when both his hands gripped her thighs. He turned her body, pivoting her on the couch so her legs rested over his. The blanket came too. Her skin brushed against the stiff material of his jeans, and the heat of him made her insides burn.

She wanted him. Wanted nothing more than to cuddle into his body and be one with him. No other man had held this appeal. She may not have abundant experience, but she knew what she felt for him probably bordered on the unhealthy side.

Was it normal to fall for someone this quickly? Maybe the whole fame and fortune thing had affected her.

"Virginia is a hell of a lot closer to New York than Colorado," he whispered and leaned in to kiss her neck.

"Mmm," she groaned at the way her nipples tightened at his touch. "My mom never thought I was great at geography, but yes, I'd determined the same thing."

He chuckled and his tickling breath slid down her back, under her baggy shirt, and shot straight to her pussy.

"I'm going to miss you."

Take me with you, was poised on the tip of her tongue, but she bit back the stupidity, concentrating instead on the hand moving under the blanket to her ankle. He teased her flesh, making her want to moan at the exquisite way his fingers trailed over her calf, behind her knee, up to mid-thigh.

"Mitchell." She panted his name, trying to warn him to stop, yet the word came out more like a plea.

"Yeah, sweetheart?" His mouth was still on her neck, his tongue licking, his lips caressing. His hand went higher, the tingling of his fingers passing over the sensitive muscle of her inner thighs.

"Stop," she whispered and reached up to clench the material of his shirt in her fist. The voices of the other men came from only feet away. They were engrossed in conversation, only she couldn't see them to tell where their attention lay. What if they were watching?

"You really want me to stop?" He nudged the edge of her shorts, going under the material to swipe directly down the heat of her panties.

She clenched his shirt tighter and wavered with the unfamiliar burst of ecstasy.

"You're so wet." His voice came low beside her ear, so low she barely heard it. "I can feel your juices."

A moan escaped her lips, and she was thankful it wasn't loud enough to stop the banter from the dining table. "Someone will see." She moved into him, leaning on his shoulder while his teeth came up to graze her chin.

"No one's paying any attention." He kissed one side of her lips, then the other, while his fingers continued to torment her pussy through the moist material of her underwear. "And besides, the blanket is covering everything. They wouldn't be able to tell what I'm doing."

"Of course not." She panted and clenched her thighs together when the crotch of her panties was pushed to the side. "They would automatically think you were searching for your keys."

He licked the seam of her lips, and she opened her mouth to him, eager and waiting, even though she'd only just told him to stop. "Exactly." The heat of his breath entered her mouth, followed by the delicate slip of his tongue. "I love watching you. I love knowing I'm the only man to make you feel like this."

She ground into his fingers, letting the digits breach the entrance of her sex. Each movement forward was like a stroke of heaven, the sensation not only making her core clench, but her whole body shudder. "I want you, Mitchell."

"You've got me, sweetheart." His kiss was sweet against her lips, the gentleness in complete contrast to the erotic way he pleasured her body.

"No." She shook her head and broke the kiss. "I want you inside me. Now."

He pulled away and gripped the back of her neck with a firm palm. "God, I want that too." He squeezed her neck and rested his forehead against hers. "What is it with you, Allie? Why can't I take my mind off you? I can't take a single breath without wishing I was touching you."

Her heart grew wings and soared straight from her chest.

He felt it too.

Grasping the material in her fist tighter, she pulled him toward her. "Take me to your room and show me."

His fingers left her sex in an instant, and the blanket flew off her legs in a flourish. Before she moved her feet to the floor, he pushed from the couch and swept her into his arms. She squeaked and clasped her hands around his neck. The weight of heavy gazes from a now quiet dinner table settled on her, and she rested her head against Mitchell's shoulder, determined not to blush. They didn't say a word. She didn't have the luxury of reading their expressions, and right now she was thankful.

Mitchell was all that mattered.

Her limited sight faded as he carried her into the darkened bedroom, placing her feet on the floor before he closed the door with a hard push. The light flicked on, and she shut her eyes with a snap.

"Sorry." He moved in front of her, his dark hair and shaded face coming into view.

She reached out and smiled when her palm brushed the rough stubble of his cheek. Her vision was improving. She could make out the darker color of his lips and see the faint hint of a grin.

Her hand slid around to cup the back of his head and pull him closer. "What are you waiting for?"

He needed no further instruction. His hands gripped her hips, and she gasped when he lifted her from the ground. Her legs encircled his waist, clinging to him as her arms gripped his neck.

"In a few minutes, you'll be wishing I didn't rush." He backed her into the wall, her shoulders pressing into the smooth, cold plaster with a thump.

"Shh." She clung tighter in panic. His bandmates wouldn't need to be psychic to know what they were doing. She just didn't want to point it out with a big neon sign.

"A little late for that," Mason called from behind the door.

Alana cringed and rested her head against the wall.

"Forget about them." Mitchell's breath fanned her face. "It's only us in here." He kissed her lips, swept his tongue into her mouth. "Only me and you."

She moaned and ground her hips into him.

"Christ, I want you, Allie." He lowered her legs to the ground and proceeded to pull down her shorts, leaving her bare from the waist down. "You're so damn hot. So damn perfect."

She bit her lip, caught in a daze of compliments that she'd never experienced before, and let him undress himself. The crinkle of a condom wrapper broke her from the trance, and her heart increased from a gallop into a full-blown sprint. She could make out the frantic jerks as he placed the protection over his length, then he leaned back against her.

"As much as I love you wearing my shirts, I think you need to take it off." His voice was smooth as honey. Seductive. Delicious. Tempting.

She wanted him so badly her knees grew weak. He gripped the bottom of the material and pulled it over her head. He didn't spare it a second glance once it was off her body and thrown to the floor.

His hands found her hips, this time moving around to cup her ass and lifting her to rest back over his waist. The head of his cock nudged her entrance, but didn't penetrate. Her core convulsed in retaliation to the tease, commanding more. She sucked in a deep breath, wanting to voice her body's demand. "Please, please, please, please."

Her nipples were hard as stone and sensitive to every brush of his chest against hers.

"You really want me, Allie?" He nudged forward, and the hardness of his erection nudged her entrance.

She moaned and dug her nails into his shoulder, unable to form words. God, she wanted him. She didn't know how she would ever go without his passion.

His hands ran up her thighs, holding her steady while he leaned her into the wall, his face nuzzling her neck. "I'll take that as a yes," he murmured into her ear. He thrust hard, the full length of his erection sliding deep within her pussy. The invasion was smoother than silk. The desire already pooled between her thighs made it easy for him to sink home. "Goddamn."

She pressed her lips together, fighting back another moan, a scream, a plea for more. She felt him through every inch of her body, from her toes to the tips of her fingers. He devastated her senses, devoured her self-control, and she only hungered for more.

With agonizingly slow finesse, he retreated. Her core convulsed and her thighs clamped down tighter, her fingers dug in deeper. This time when he glided home, the pleasure burning in her throat burst free, and she cried out. His advances grew in demand, hitting harder, faster. His retreats became quicker, more frantic.

He pushed more of her body against the wall, and her shoulder blades rubbed with each thrust. She kissed his cheek, the side of his lips, his mouth, unable to get enough. The tension in her sex climbed to a height she'd never reached before, her walls pulsing around his hard shaft, sucking him deeper. "Oh, Jesus, Mitchell, please." She squeezed her eyes shut. She hoped taking away the visual would stave off her climax, but his image engrossed her mind, the memory of his smile and confidence on stage only bringing her closer to the edge.

Breath left her lungs with every plunge of his cock, and each time he pulled back she gasped for air. A strong arm wound around her waist and up her back. His hand gripped her hair and pulled, dragging her head back with it. He devoured the exposed skin of her neck, kissing, licking, and when he sucked, adding the sting of pain, she came undone.

Her core convulsed in tiny spasms of the most delicious pleasure. In and out, in and out. His penetrations became less frantic, more forceful, until her ears filled with a roar she felt all the way to the center of her chest. They jolted into each other, the stickiness of their sweat now fusing their skin. The world came back into view between panted breaths and shaking limbs.

"Wow." He puffed out the word.

She didn't know how he was still holding her weight. Her

feet hadn't even been touching the ground, and already her thighs throbbed from exertion.

Placing her arms around his neck, she leaned against the wall and lowered one foot at a time to stand on weak legs. Mitchell's softening length left her body and he grabbed for the condom.

"I'll be back in a sec." His heat disappeared, leaving her to slump against the wall.

She closed her eyes and stood rooted to the spot, her limbs too heavy to move. The noise from the dining room filtered into her recovery bubble and she cringed at the thought of going back out there. Mitchell hadn't been quiet. *She* hadn't been quiet.

When he returned moments later, she was still in the same spot, the slight breeze from the air conditioner drying the sweat on her skin.

"You still look good enough to eat."

Her eyes snapped opened, and she straightened. "Oh no. I'm definitely not edible at the moment." And as much as she wanted to spend the night doing sweaty, noisy things with Mitchell, she couldn't ignore the fact they were in a suite with many other people. People who weren't deaf and dumb.

She also wanted Mitchell to remember she wasn't a groupie who only wanted him for one thing. She was greedy. She wanted him all, the snuggling on the couch, the deep and meaningful conversations, and the comfortable moments spent together in silence.

"Regretting things already, sweetheart?" He walked into her and took her breath with the sweetest, most tender kiss of her life. There was no rush, no hunger, only a delicate mingling of lips and tongues.

When he broke away, she shook her head. "No. There are no regrets." She smiled and cupped his cheeks to bring him closer for one last peck. "I just don't want to be remembered as another one of your groupies."

He scoffed and rested his forehead against hers. "I know you're not a groupie, and my memories of you will always be respectful."

His words touched her heart, even though they had the faintest note of a goodbye.

He leaned down and picked up the shirt she'd been wearing and handed it to her. "Is this going to be your first walk of shame?"

She cringed and tried to swallow over the lump in her throat. "Unfortunately, yes." She pulled the material over her head and took the awaiting underwear and shorts he handed her next.

He chuckled. "Well, be prepared for humiliation of Titanic proportions. I'm pretty sure Blake likes you, and he never holds back on putting shit on the people he likes most."

Chapter Eleven

After Alana freshened up, Mitch held her hand and led her from the bedroom. The conversation at the dining table softened. Even Leah, Kate, and Ryan's wife, Julie, who had gathered in the kitchen, had turned from their gossip session to stare at them.

Alana squeezed his hand, and her nervousness made him smile. The atmosphere was different from any other time he'd had a woman behind the scenes with the band. Usually, they wouldn't pay her attention or acknowledge the sleazy X-rated noises that would've been the back track to their conversation. This time, the room churned with two parts uncomfortable silence and eight parts suppressed laughter.

"There's my dirty girl," Kate called from the kitchen, raising her half-empty wine glass in salute.

Julie gasped, Leah took a sip from her glass to hide her smile, and his closest friends chuckled.

"See, I wasn't the first person to highlight the latest prayer session." Blake shot him a smirk. "I didn't realize you were religious, bro."

Mitch grinned back, undeterred. "I've definitely found heaven."

Alana groaned. He glanced down to see her darkened cheeks and her gaze focused on the floor in front of them.

"I'm right beside you, if you hadn't noticed," she whispered, barely moving her lips.

"It's a rite of passage, sweetheart. Just go with it." He leaned down and placed a kiss below her ear. When he pulled back, she had one brow raised, and her shoulders were straight, ready to take the room head on.

"I don't blame you, girlfriend," Kate continued. "Now that you've finally experienced what the hype is about, I doubt you'll continue with your celibacy."

"Oh, Christ," Alana murmured, dropping his hand. "I need a drink." She stepped around him, her arms outstretched at her sides as she maneuvered and bumped around furniture.

Mitch stared at her retreating form, at the beautiful long hair cascading down her back, and the way her hips swayed in feminine beauty. A knot formed in his chest, and he fought the urge to rub his sternum. Kate was right. He didn't know why he hadn't thought of it earlier…probably because his cock had taken over his life. Alana hadn't experienced the pleasure sex provided before. He remembered what he'd been like as a teenager. Once he'd popped his cherry, he went around trying to pop everyone else's. It was a new and exciting experience.

Something she would want to experiment with.

Something she wouldn't want to wait around for.

Something Alana shouldn't *have* to wait around for.

He exhaled slowly, hoping to alleviate the pressure under his ribcage. He couldn't ask her to put her life on hold while he did the new album promo. Or the upcoming tour, for that matter.

Who was he kidding? His lifestyle didn't come with a happily ever after package. Ryan and Julie were proof of that.

Mitch continued to watch as Alana took a glass of white wine from Leah and proceeded to gulp the contents. He ignored the slide of a chair against the tile floor and didn't turn his gaze away from her until Blake nudged his shoulder.

"What's wrong?"

Mitch glowered and shook his head. He didn't want to talk about it. He didn't even want to contemplate what would happen when they left tomorrow.

"Alana seems like a top chick. Have you made plans for what will happen once we leave?"

Blake read him like a book.

"We're only having a bit of fun," Mitch lied. It was more than fun. More than passion. More than addiction. Alana was under his skin, and he didn't want to let her go.

Blake gave a derisive snort. "Oh, OK. So you won't mind me trying to have a bit of fun with her too?"

Mitch turned to the smug expression on his friend's face. Blake was trying to push him into admitting how he felt about Alana, but Mitch wasn't that gullible. Not when the likelihood of them having a future was slim to none. He enjoyed humiliation as much as the next guy.

He turned away, focusing his attention back on Alana and the way she spoke softly with the other females in the kitchen.

"Tell her how you feel," Blake murmured. "I've never seen you like this over a woman before. Don't let her go. She seems like a keeper."

Mitch smoothed his hands over his face, rubbing away the tension. Although his career didn't allow for it, he felt the…yearning sounded too sissy, but something similar told him it was time to settle down. The thought of coming home from months on tour to a wife and family seemed like a fantasy always out of reach.

He could see himself with Alana. He'd never contemplated a future with anyone else before, yet it came easily with her. With vivid clarity, he pictured how stunning she would look in white, the gleam in her eyes as he carried her over the threshold, and the way she would nurse a child.

Shaking his head, he ground his teeth together. She might be the perfect image for his future, but the timing couldn't be worse. Her life had just begun. She still wouldn't be able to fully grasp the opportunities the world had to offer—or the men who would eagerly fall at her feet.

"It isn't that simple." He wished it were. God, how he wished. If he had a normal life and a normal career, things might work out. But he didn't. His life was on the road, over numerous countries, and in and out of recording studios and rehearsal sessions.

"Love never is." Blake patted him on the shoulder and walked away, heading for the ladies in the kitchen. Mitch followed, ignoring the bite of jealousy when his friend spoke to Alana and brought a beaming smile to her face.

No. Things between them would be too complicated. Exactly the type of scenario both of them didn't need right now. The best he could hope for was a little more time spent with her in his arms and an amicable farewell.

Two hours later, Alana sat on the balcony of the hotel suite with another glass of wine in her hand. She couldn't remember how many she'd had, but her cheeks flushed with intoxication and her heart now beat in a slow waltz instead of the thunderous staccato she'd experienced for the last few days.

Since leaving the bedroom, she'd only spoken a few words to Mitchell, and her mind enjoyed the relief from the constant barrage of lust and love-filled thoughts. She'd also given up on trying to talk herself out of loving him. It took too much strength. They fit together too well. They meshed perfectly.

"Is everything all right between you and Mitch?"

Alana lifted her gaze from the glass in her hand to Leah's darkened face. The woman's voice held a hint of concern. "Yeah...I guess so. Why?"

Leah looked away. "No real reason, I suppose. He just seems down."

Alana watched the glint of a wine glass raise to Leah's lips before it descended again.

"Earlier, when you both…ah…came out of the bedroom, he was happy. More happy and carefree than normal. But over the last few hours, every time I go into the kitchen, he's sullen and detached."

Alana took a sip of her drink and squinted toward the side of Leah's face, trying to sharpen the darkened image. The inability to read people's expressions drove her crazy. She'd had to learn to concentrate more closely on the emotion in their voice.

"Do you want me to speak to him?" She felt stupid asking the question to someone who knew Mitchell better than she did.

"No." Leah shook her head. "It's probably nothing. I just get edgy when the guys aren't themselves, especially when we're about to go on the road."

Ryan's wife, Julie, let out a burst of laughter, and they both turned in her direction. Kate's soft chuckle came next from further along the balcony.

"Wow," Leah whispered. "I can't remember the last time she laughed. Hell, I can't remember the last time she smiled."

"Really?" Julie had been quiet since their two-second introduction. They hadn't even shared a conversation. Apart from the clouded outline of a tall, slim woman with blonde hair, Alana knew nothing about the rhythm guitarist's wife. "I assumed she must be upset about Ryan leaving to go on the promo tour."

Leah laughed without humor. "No. She prefers when he's away. Over the last year, they've done nothing but fight."

"Oh." Alana had nothing else to say. Ryan seemed like a nice guy. A damn attractive, wealthy, and talented nice guy.

"Come on." Leah rose from her chair and held out a hand in front of Alana's face. "Let's go inside and chat it up with my boys.

Maybe Mitch will cheer up when you're around."

The staccato flutter came back to life under her ribs. The mere thought of being near him sent her blood racing. "Sounds good." She gripped her now empty wine glass in one hand and allowed Leah to help her up with the other.

Half an hour later, she understood what Leah had meant about Mitchell. Alana didn't need her sight to notice the difference in him. He was distant even though they now sat side by side on the sofa. He still touched her, still kissed her cheek with affection, and spoke to her often, yet each time he did, he lacked his usual enthusiasm, as if his heart was no longer fully involved.

Maybe the mood change stemmed from the pressure of their upcoming album release and the nights he would spend away on the promo tour. She didn't know him well enough to judge. She wished she did, though, because every time he exhaled a heavy breath, it felt like she was one step closer to losing him forever.

"What are you doing before you leave tomorrow?" She nestled her head into his shoulder and snuggled close. They hadn't discussed anything beyond tonight, and her heart grew more demanding, needing to determine if they would spend more time together before he left.

"I've got promotional obligations for most of the day."

Her chest clenched, and she nodded to distract herself from the disappointment.

He slid his arm around her shoulder and pulled her a little closer. "Late morning, we're doing a pre-recording for an interview on the Daybreak Breakfast Show. Mason refuses to arrive at anything before eleven, so we have to tape it tomorrow for the following day's show."

She turned her head to look at him and raised a brow. "Nothing before eleven? Really?"

"When you've got as much money and pulling-power as the

all-famous Mason Lynch, you can kinda make whatever demands you want." He shrugged. "Then in the afternoon we'll visit the local drug and alcohol rehab center."

"Really?" Every day, almost every hour, he had her in awe at how different he was from her mother's portrayal of men. Pride melted her heart.

"It's something we try to do often. Especially since the near miss with the fan OD'ing. We like to show our support and reiterate that Reckless Beat doesn't condone the misuse of alcohol or the use of illegal drugs."

No, this man definitely wasn't what her mother described.

"Don't look at me like that." He chuckled.

She focused on the bright white of his smile and frowned. He read her so well already.

"It's mainly about exposure and to get the haters off our backs. The ones who think we encourage kids to take drugs." The smile faded, and the shadows from the light behind him made it hard for her to read his expression. "I enjoy it, though. It puts things into perspective. And if spending a few hours with people who are doing it tough is all it takes to ease the shit in their life, even for a little while, then I'm happy to do it."

"You're a wonderful man, Mitchell." She turned further into him and placed a kiss on his cheek.

He grasped the back of her head and held her close, their lips barely an inch apart. "I love how you say my name."

"And I love saying it." She kissed him again, this time on the lips. "You've opened my eyes and changed my life, in only a few days. I can't thank you enough for that. I can only imagine what you do for others."

He didn't respond with his usual passion. The burst of lust didn't hit. Instead, he stroked a hand through her hair and let out a heavy sigh. "You're special, Allie."

Her stomach dropped, not at his words, but at the resigned tone.

"Tell me what's wrong," she pleaded, framing his cheek with her palm.

"Nothing, sweetheart." He tilted his head into her hand. "Just tired, I suppose."

It was more than lack of sleep. He was shutting her out, and she didn't know why.

"Do you want me to go? Kate and I can call a cab."

"No."

She inhaled slowly. Deeply. At least his tone held a comforting fortitude. If it wasn't for his somber mood, she might actually believe him.

"What are your plans for tomorrow?"

She frowned at the change in subject, but let it slide. "I need to go back to the optometrist for a check-up."

"Shit. I completely forgot."

"It's OK. My sight is getting better, and Kate has the day off work, so I'll be fine to get there." She rubbed his chest to soothe the tension radiating from him. "I also want to determine if living in Richmond for a few months is feasible…and I plan on calling the Bowens and meeting up with them again. My mom has been the only family I've ever known, and I need to find out if I really am related to these people. I wouldn't forgive myself if I walked away not truly knowing if they were telling the truth."

His posture stiffened. "When do you plan on seeing them? You shouldn't go alone."

"I'll be fine. Truly. I'm not going to do anything stupid."

The tension in his body relaxed slightly, and she continued to soothe him with light strokes of her fingers down his chest.

"Plan it around lunchtime. I'll try and get out of the breakfast show gig as soon as possible and come with you."

Her hand paused, emotion freezing her movements. His sincerity and concern touched her more than she thought a man's interest ever would. "You don't need to do that."

"Please, Allie." He squeezed her tight. "Let me do this one last thing for you before I leave."

The reminder of his departure dried her throat to the point of pain. She cringed at the things he could learn about her from the meeting with the Bowens. Although she hadn't hidden anything from him, she didn't like announcing to the world that her life was forged from heinous adversity.

"Promise me you won't go without me." He lifted her chin and peered down at her.

She nodded, swallowed.

"OK." He brushed his lips against hers. "Let's go to bed. I want to make love to you this time." He ran his fingers through her hair and held her in place. "I want to take my time. I want to taste you, savor you, and have you fall asleep in my arms."

Alana blinked away the burn of forming tears. Although he hadn't said it, she still heard *for the last time* at the end of his declaration.

Chapter Twelve

MITCH GRABBED ALANA'S hand as she stood. "We're going to call it a night," he announced to his friends.

Leah left over an hour ago, heading to her hotel room a few floors down to get an early night. Kate did the same, choosing to sleep on Leah's sofa instead of in the crowded suite. And Julie still sat outside on the balcony, anti-social as always.

Blake and Mason raised their gazes from the dining table, both with knowing grins. Blake opened his mouth, then closed it again, the jovial expression fading from his face. Mason followed suit. These men were like his brothers—closer, in fact. They could see the pain he endured over needing to let Alana go. It clawed at his chest, made his palms sweat. Their time together hadn't been long, yet his body was preparing to sink into a drug-like withdrawal at the thought of leaving her.

Sean didn't raise his focus from the poker cards in his hand. "Have fun. Be safe. Just keep the vocals to a minimum. I've got sensitive ears."

Ryan sniggered, placing two of his cards on the pile in the middle of the table and grabbing two more. "What he said."

Blake frowned at him, his head tilting in an unspoken question. When Mitch didn't respond, Blake pushed from the table and made his way to them. "Night, Alana." He gave her a one-armed cuddle around the shoulders, while his gaze focused on Mitch. "Can I have a word with the priest before you two go and do your thing?" His toned lacked humor.

She replied with a soft nod. "Sure." She reached on tiptoes and placed a kiss on Mitch's cheek. "I'm going to go brush my teeth."

He let her fingers slide from his grasp and winced at the thought of doing it for good in the near future. He stared at Blake, both of them silent and unmoving until Alana left the room and the bedroom door shut with a soft click.

"You'd be stupid to let her go."

Mitch raised a brow. "You'd be stupid to give an opinion on matters you know nothing about." He didn't mean to be a jerk. Blake was only trying to look out for him. Mitch was just sick to death of the knot that had formed in his chest. A knot that grew and strengthened every time he thought about letting go of the woman he was falling for.

Blake's gaze bore into him, reading his thoughts, making him ache more with his blatant sympathy. "When was the last time you wanted to be with a woman for more than one night?"

Mitch scoffed and ran a hand through his hair.

"Getting her number and telling her you'll call isn't a lifetime commitment. It's an opportunity. If you cut yourself off before you even take a chance, you're a fucking idiot. And I may be stupid to give my opinion, because I don't know what her deal is, but you're a chicken shit if you let her walk away."

"You don't know shit." Mitch turned his back and stepped away. Blake didn't have a clue about her life or lack of it. He didn't know she was starting from scratch. That she didn't have time to wait around for a guy who would only be in her life for chunks at a time. She needed someone constant. Someone to give her the attention she deserved.

Blake grabbed his shoulder and tugged him back.

It may have been anger, the few beers he'd consumed, or the need to get back to Alana in a hurry, but something threw him off balance and he stumbled, slamming into the wall with a thud.

"Oh, shit," Mason swore, and three chairs scraped across the tile.

He righted himself and glared at Blake, not because of the shove, not because his friend was still trying to prove a point, but because there was now an unnecessary scene that was stopping him from being with Alana.

"What?" He raised his voice. "What the fuck do you want from me?"

Blake put his hands up in surrender and stepped back. "I'm sorry, bro. I didn't realize you'd had so much to drink. I'll speak to you in the morning."

"No. You won't," Mitch snapped. He'd gone through it over and over again. They weren't right for each other. Different lives. Different upbringings. Different futures. She needed a man who wouldn't jerk her around. A man who would be there to love her twenty-four-seven.

Sean stepped between them and turned to Mitch. "Back off."

"Are you fucking kidding me?" His blood boiled. "Blake's the one playing Dr. Phil or some shit, and you're telling *me* to back off? I don't have time for this. I'm going to bed."

When he turned around, Alana was there, half her body outside the doorframe, her eyes shining with emotion, her brow troubled.

He closed his eyes for a moment, took a deep breath, and walked toward her. Once they were both in the room, he slammed the door shut behind them, blocking out the rest of the world. He wanted to comfort her, to apologize for placing the worried frown on her face, but he was too emotional.

Instead, he strode to the bathroom, turned on the tap, and washed his face repeatedly, waiting for his heart rate to decrease.

When he calmed to the point of civility, he walked back into the bedroom and found her sitting at the foot of the mattress, her head bowed, her hands clasped in her lap.

He strode to the bedroom door, flicked off the light, and went to her. His sight took moments to adjust to the darkness, to the soft glow coming from beneath the door. When he reached the bed, he nudged between her legs, and her thighs parted without protest as he nestled between them. With gentle fingers he lifted her chin and peered down at her shadowed features.

"I'm sorry." He wished he had the perfect words for her. All he had was an uncomfortable yearning he couldn't relive.

"I'm not…comfortable with violence."

"I know, sweetheart. It was nothing." He caressed her cheek with his thumb, then her lips. "We're all stressed at the moment and… It doesn't excuse anything, but I swear you have nothing to worry about."

"You need to be honest with me." Her voice sent a white-hot blade through his chest, destroying everything in its path. "I'm not familiar with this, with us, and I have no clue what's going on. Have I done something wrong? Do you want me to leave? I…" She heaved a breath. "I really like you, Mitchell—"

"Hey." He knelt between her thighs and placed his hands on her hips. Her warmth surrounded him. The intoxicating mingled scent of her body and the hotel soap sank into his lungs like a hypnotic drug. "You have nothing to be sorry for." The urge to pour his heart out became overwhelming. He could tell her how he felt, and she would comfort him and persuade him into believing things between them would work. That she would always wait around for him, always be willing to put her life on hold so they could be together.

And that was what he feared the most. That he didn't have the strength to bite his tongue. To be a man and walk away for her sake. To give her the life she deserved.

"I'm sorry, Allie." He pulled her closer to the edge of the bed and circled his arms around her back. "I'm tired, and stressed, and overwhelmed. I usually get a little weird before promo or concert tours. It has nothing to do with you." The lie stung deep in his chest, like a back slap from God warning him of his inevitable trip to hell.

She didn't reply.

"The last thing I want is for you to leave."

Her hands slid to his neck. He held his breath, felt the pull of his cock as it hardened, and delighted in the buzz that ricochet through his body when her nails dug into the back of his head. A moan vibrated in his throat, and he leaned into her touch.

"You should go to bed," she murmured.

"Mmm, maybe I should." He moved to his feet and grasped her hands, pulling her up with him. "Want to join me?"

"Yes." The word was a breathless whisper.

Leaning in, he brushed her nose with his and hovered his lips over the warm satin of hers. He closed his eyes and let everything seep in. Her smell, her essence, her emotion. He inhaled it into his lungs and locked it away deep in his soul, never to be released.

His heart continued to taunt him, to flash images of a perfect future into his mind. One with passion and commitment and love. He wanted to reach out and grab them, to open his mouth and kiss his love into her, but he straightened his shoulders and remained firm.

Alana would find a man. A better man.

And the realization hurt more than the thought of letting her go.

He ignored the turmoil threatening to tear him apart and bent over, lifted her, one arm under her knees while the other supported her back.

She didn't protest, didn't say a word as her arms came around to encircle his neck. He carried her around the bed and laid her down. When she scooted away, he pulled at the cover, working it to the foot of the bed as she maneuvered under the sheet.

He took his clothes off. One by one. His jeans. His underwear.

His shirt. Until he stood completely bare in front of her—physically and emotionally. He didn't know if she could see him, but her gaze burned his body, over every inch of his skin.

He grabbed a condom from the bedside table and placed it under his pillow. His cock tightened in anticipation as he pulled back the sheet, climbed onto the bed, and positioned himself beside her. She lay on her side with her face turned toward him. He could barely see her, not through his eyes, yet the picture in his mind was clear as day. He'd never let go of that image. Not tomorrow, or next month, or twenty years from now. She'd burrowed herself into his heart and would remain there forever.

"You should get some sleep." Her voice held no humor, only resignation.

Fuck sleep. His tiredness had been an excuse to cover for his crabby mood. He wanted to spend the whole night loving her, touching her, devouring her. For once, his band commitments could come second. The last hours with Allie were all that mattered to him.

"Right now, I should be doing a lot of things, but the only thing I want is you." He moved into her, placing an arm over her waist, letting the hardness of his erection push into the soft cotton of her shorts.

He heard her deep inhale and leaned in before she let it out, taking her mouth in a passionate kiss. Their lips meshed, their tongues danced, and slowly the rigidity of her body flittered away, leaving her malleable in his arms.

Her hands found his hair, always his hair, always his undoing, and glided the strands covering his face behind his ear. He didn't usually allow anyone to play with it. He'd never enjoyed the sensation, but with Allie, it was different. Every stroke made his scalp shiver, every tug and scratch shot desire straight through his body to harden his aching cock.

He ground into her, groaned over the delicious friction, and kissed her harder. He was crazy for her, his thoughts and desires making him insane.

Damn it. He wanted to go slow, to savor and sample every inch of her. Pulling back, he gasped for air and tried to calm himself. "Take your clothes off. I want to feel you…every part of you, against me."

She complied, removing her shirt, then shuffling under the sheet before she dragged out her shorts and panties and threw them away.

They lay in silence, his erection pressing into her curls, his arm over her waist, her breasts resting against his chest. He played with the skin at the low of her back, ran his fingers around in intricate patterns while they enjoyed each other's warmth.

One of her hands roamed his body. She trailed her fingers over his arm, down his ribs, along his thigh. His skin burned wherever she touched, turning his blood to lava, and his cock to stone. He wanted to change positions, to make her writhe in pleasure, to distract her with her own need instead of his own. Leaning down, he sucked her nipple into his mouth, rolling his tongue around the stiffened peak. She mewled, rubbed her crotch against him, and dug her nails into his ass.

Her reaction only made him hotter. He moved to her other breast, paying it the same attention while his hand slid up her waist to cup the one he'd just been savoring.

She arched her back, moaned her pleasure, yet it still wasn't enough. He needed her as hot as he was, as needy, as crazy with lust and adoration. He tweaked her nipple with his fingers, relished her gasp, and then released her. Slowly, he ran his hand down her belly, over her abdomen, and through the patch of curls at the apex of her thighs.

Her breathing increased, the pants of her breath brushing over his face as he moved his mouth from one breast to the other. He teased her pussy, gliding his fingers around her swollen lips, back and forth, until she was undulating against him.

"Mitchell…Mitchell."

He glanced up to see the darkened beauty of her face.

She nuzzled into his neck and tasted his skin with her tongue. "Please. Oh, god, please."

"What, sweetheart?" He applied more pressure to the fingers circling her clit. "Tell me what you want." He craved the words, hungered to hear the disorder in her voice. "Tell me what you need."

She ground into him, scouring her nails up his back. "You," she whispered into his ear, sending a shiver down his spine that pooled in his balls. "I want you, Mitchell." She sucked on the skin of his neck. "Only you… Please."

He stroked his fingers down the center of her pussy, straight through the juices of her arousal.

"I want you inside me now."

He couldn't wait either. Leaning back, he grabbed the condom from under the pillow and sheathed himself. Gently positioning his body on top of hers, he rested on his forearms so she didn't take his entire weight. He settled his erection against her wet folds, his stomach pressing into hers. The room fell quiet as her hands lay at his shoulders, and for long moments they just stared.

Her eyes were too dark to make out, too shadowed to see the light green irises he loved so much. Her heart beat hard against his chest, the rapid succession matching the pounding that echoed in his ears.

Damn. He had it bad. Even in shades of gray, she was beautiful. And never before had he wanted to make love. He couldn't remember ever having slow, emotional sex. As a teenager, he'd concentrated on his mantra of "This is a marathon, not a sprint. This is a marathon, not a sprint," and spent his time concentrating on getting his partners across the line, one way or another. Then Reckless Beat became famous, and women flocked to him. They didn't care if he pleasured them or how the situation ended as long as they had the opportunity to tell their friends they'd screwed a rock star.

He'd never sought the intimacy of the missionary position, yet right now, he wanted nothing else. To feel her breath, the touch of her breasts against his chest, to see the dark outline of her face.

With a slight tilt of his hips, he rocked into her, the head of his cock finding her slick entrance. Her hands gripped his shoulders tighter, and he closed his eyes to press his lips against her. He pushed into her sex and groaned over the tight ecstasy.

Their kiss was lazy and deliberate, soft strokes of tongues, tender pressure of lips, and he mimicked the rhythm with each gentle thrust of his hips. With each slide, he gave his heart and soul to her, and his insides crumpled under the weight of love.

I love you...I love you...I love you.

He couldn't say the words aloud, but he showed them with every touch.

Her thighs parted further, and her legs rose to encircle his waist. With the next pulse of his hips, they groaned in unison, the deeper penetration driving him so close to the edge he thought he would go over. He broke the kiss, paused, and leaned over on one elbow to break the connection his soul seemed to have made with this woman.

The pleasure didn't just pool in his usual zone of awesome, it rushed along his stomach, through his chest, clenching his heart. She consumed him from head to toe, mind and soul.

"Don't stop." She pulled him back down to her chest.

"Just give me a minute." He rested his forehead against hers.

"No," she whispered and lifted her hips, making his cock sink deep inside her core. "I'm so close."

"Christ," he moaned, biting his lip to control the orgasm threatening to explode. He kept his movements slow, deliberate, but hit harder, sinking to the hilt. Each time he retreated, he paused to take a breath and rebuild his restraint.

"Mitchell." Her plea was his undoing.

He reached around to cup the back of her neck and smashed his lips against hers. This kiss wasn't soft, it wasn't sweet. It freed his passion, his weakness, and left him raw and vulnerable. Her thighs gripped him to the point of pain, her back arched, and with each hard thrust of his hips, she panted.

"Mitchell, I'm coming."

His release hit in an instant, her pussy milking him harder with every slide between her tight walls. He shot his seed and moaned with each rhythmic pulse, until his legs burned with tension. Burying his head in her neck, he let the feminine sounds of release wash over him with the last bursts of paradise.

Her thighs began to relax, their grip loosening from his waist, to fall back down on the bed. His mind was a frenzied blur, caught between his desire to make Alana his, and his conscience battling to let her go. The struggle tore him apart as he panted into her neck.

He wished he had all the answers and knew which path to choose, the one that was right for both of them. But as exhaustion settled in, pulling him into slumber, he realized no matter what happened between them, even if he did leave her, he would never truly be able to let her go.

Chapter Thirteen

Alana came to consciousness, warm, sated, and still wearing the smile she fell asleep with the night before. Mitchell lay behind her, the hardness of his hip resting against her bottom. The heat of his hand sat against the top of her thigh.

She began to rise from the bliss of sleep into reality, and the happiness slid from her face. She didn't want to open her eyes and begin the day. Beginning the day meant she came closer to the end where she would have to say goodbye to the man she adored. The thought of their upcoming last kiss made her stomach turn.

Sliding her hand from her pillow, she ran it under the sheet, over her naked waist, to rest on top of Mitchell's. She touched him for strength. Above everything, she wanted to be able to say her farewell without drama. There wouldn't be a fangirl moment. She wouldn't cry. As much as her eyes burned and her hands trembled, she wouldn't shed a tear in front of him.

She gripped his fingers and startled at the groan that followed. A groan that vibrated from in front of her, not behind. Her eyes snapped open. She followed the lump under the sheet beside her, all the way up to the tattooed arm coming out from the covering, to the spiky dark hair of a man resting face down on the pillow.

A squeak escaped her throat.

"Blake," she whispered and swallowed to alleviate her dry mouth.

He groaned again. "What?" His voice came out garbled from the pillow.

"Your hand is on my thigh." She didn't move, not an inch, and kept her voice low in an attempt not to wake Mitchell.

"Mmm."

"Blake!" she pleaded. Her skin buzzed at his touch, making her hyperventilate. "I'm naked, and your hand is on my thigh."

He tilted his head, gave her a flash of his crooked grin, and slid his hand away. "Sorry, I hadn't noticed." His tone and gleaming eyes told her the exact opposite. He stretched and turned onto his back, placing his heavily inked arms behind his head.

She raised a brow at his arrogance, but couldn't muster any annoyance. Blake had been kind to her. A little cheeky at times, and yet, along with the man lying behind her, they both reiterated the message that the opposite sex wasn't the enemy. He had been the echo to Mitchell's perfection, the person who backed up the kindness and trust.

"Why are you here?" Her voice was breathy. She wanted to believe it came from the shock of waking up with an unwelcomed guest in the bed. The way her nipples tightened told her otherwise. Not that she was attracted to Blake. He did have the most gorgeous, dark brown eyes she'd ever seen, but he didn't match her like a jigsaw puzzle the way Mitchell did.

He kept his eyes closed. "Ryan and Julie took my bed…even though they weren't going to make good use of it. And Mason and Sean drank too much and passed out on the couch and floor. I had nowhere to sleep."

"And your hand on my thigh?"

His grin widened and he opened one eye to glance at her. "I snuggle in my sleep."

She shook her head at him and diverted her gaze to his arms. She followed the intricate designs marking his skin from his wrists to his shoulders, and her heart fluttered with slow dawning realization.

She could see.

There were still fuzzy patches, parts of her vision melted into others, but overnight her sight had improved enough for her to make out the finer details. If Mitchell weren't asleep, she would place her face an inch away from his and stare into his eyes forever.

As if reading her thoughts, he moaned from behind her and wobbled the mattress as he shifted on the bed. He changed his position so they were spooning, his erection nudging against her ass, his arm moving to cuddle her waist and lay against her belly. He ground into her, once, twice, then went languid against her.

She remained silent until his breathing grew heavy against her neck. When she was convinced he'd fallen back asleep, she turned her gaze to Blake, who now stared at her.

"You like him."

She took a deep breath and pulled the sheet up to her collarbone, taking the extra moments to compose herself. "Yes." There was no need to elaborate. She wasn't sure what her feelings for Mitchell meant. She only knew her heart was full, all because of him.

"Have you two spoken about what's going to happen once we leave?"

His voice was flat, and she hated the unfamiliar seriousness in his tone. He no longer smiled, the humor having left his face entirely. The change in him unsettled her. She prepared for the best friend speech, where he would ask her to walk away quietly. Or explain to her the time with Mitchell was nothing more than a fling.

She focused on the white hotel sheet and made swirling patterns with her fingers against the cotton. "No." She gave a slight shrug. "He mentioned maybe calling me. But apart from that, we haven't discussed anything."

Her heart beat stronger waiting for his reply. When it came, his words were barely audible. "He likes you."

Her gaze snapped to him, needing to read his expression. What she saw made her chest constrict. His eyes held an anguish she knew would be echoed in her own. She hadn't expected him to voice the hopes she bottled inside. She'd figured he'd let her down gently.

"Don't let him go, Alana," he implored her. "He wants you just as much as you want him. Don't let the hurdles surrounding his career stand in your way."

Relief and hope burst to life, flooding her with happiness. His career had never scared her away as much as it made her feel out of his league. She lay in silence, picturing what their future would be like if they did commit to one another.

He would be away a lot, which would be tough to handle when she wanted nothing more than to spend every second of the day with him. But her life seemed to be evolving. She had so many things she wanted to do and was positive the excitement of finally living would dull the loneliness of being apart. She'd never been a dependent person. Although she grew up in isolation, she'd forged her own career and made her own income.

Being separated might give them time to get to know each other without the lust which currently had them falling between the sheets at every opportunity.

"I won't." She smiled, and Blake returned the gesture with a slight tilt of his lips. "I like him, too."

Mitchell inhaled deeply and moved against her again, his erection sliding between the crack of her bottom. He groaned, and she blushed, her gaze still focused on Blake. She gripped the sheet tight and made sure the material covered her breasts, which now prickled with desire.

"Christ," Blake murmured and turned his gaze to the ceiling.

Mitchell jolted and his hand pressed hard against her belly. Then he was up on one elbow, hovering over her to glare at Blake. "What the hell are you doing in here?"

Blake scrubbed his hands down his face and groaned. "Torturing myself."

She turned into Mitchell's warmth and placed her hands around his neck, pulling him back down to the pillow. "He had nowhere else to sleep." She kissed him softly on the lips.

She leaned back and took her time taking in his features, memorizing the things she hadn't been able to see properly before. The dark stubble, the loose, sexy hair that shadowed his face, the sensuous mouth that held her attention and made her want to stay in bed all day to taste it.

Oh, boy. She'd been missing out with her lack of sight. Her memories hadn't done him justice. Not a damn bit.

Mitchell quirked a brow and a grin tilted his lips. "You seriously fell for that?"

She frowned and peered over her shoulder at Blake, who was now chuckling to himself.

"Sweetheart, this isn't the first time he's used that line." Mitchell placed a kiss on her extended neck, the sensation quickly fading as she turned fully to Blake.

"That was a line?" She slapped him on the chest and appreciated the loud crack of flesh on flesh.

His laughter increased until he was holding his ribs.

"Did he use the excuse about cuddling in his sleep?"

"Snuggling," she growled, trying to keep the smile from her face. She slid her feet up the bed and maneuvered around to aim them at him.

Mitchell began to chuckle while Blake laughed so hard she could barely think. Making sure she didn't hurt him, she gently rested her feet against the silk boxers at Blake's hip, and with all her might, she pushed.

His arms flew in the air and he toppled from the bed, landing on the floor with a thud. The impact didn't interrupt his laughter. Only made it grow.

Mitchell rubbed against her back, and the reminder of his thick erection made her squirm with pleasure. "You can pay him back," he whispered into her ear.

The brush of his breath sent a shiver down her spine, and she swallowed before answering. "Yeah? How could I do that?"

His hand slid around her hip, over her waist, and his fingers found her clit. She sucked in a breath and closed her eyes as he ground into her.

"Tease him with something he can't have."

The air in her lungs congealed and she let it out in a long rush. There was no mistaking the implication. She opened her eyes and found Blake kneeling on the floor, his hungry gaze making her body burst alive with a turbulent mix of apprehension and excitement.

"Alana's too nice to tease, aren't you, Alana?" Blake's voice held a hint of arousal, something she hadn't heard from him before. Yes, he'd flirted with her on occasion, but this was different. This was raw and primal and thrilling.

She swallowed her nervousness and fought to sort her scattered thoughts.

"Alana may be too nice to tease, but I definitely won't be sharing her."

Blake turned his focus to Mitchell and raised an eyebrow. "So you're just going to fuck her in front of me?"

Alana held back a whimper. The image of Mitchell deep inside her while Blake witnessed the intimate act made the moisture between her thighs increase. She didn't want anyone else except Mitchell, yet having an audience made her body break out in goose bumps.

"The choice is up to Allie."

This time she did whimper.

Blake stared at her while Mitchell ran his fingers between her pussy lips, taunting her entrance with slow swipes. He ground his cock harder into her ass and she arched her back, still clutching the sheet to her chest.

"What's it going to be, sugar?" Blake moved to his feet and knelt on the bed, his erection tenting the front of his boxers. "Are you going to be my pretty little exhibitionist?"

Could she? His hand moved close to brush the wisps of hair away from her face. She shuddered, her entire body igniting at the swipe of his fingers. Mitchell gently bit into the sensitive hollow at the base of her neck, and she mewled her affirmation.

She trusted him, and in return trusted Blake, but most of all, her trust lay within her own judgment. They wouldn't pressure her. This was what life was about–experiencing new things to determine what you enjoyed and what you didn't. With the way Mitchell made her soul sing to the heavens, she doubted she would even notice Blake's presence.

She nodded to reiterate. Mitchell rewarded her with a hard suck on her neck and two fingers plunging deep into her pussy. She clutched the sheet, bit her lip, and let her eyelids flutter closed.

"Are you sure, sweetheart?" he whispered in her ear. "You don't have to. I won't let him touch you either way, but it's up to you whether he stays or goes."

She opened her eyes and focused on Blake. He peered down at her with an expression akin to adoration. There was no cockiness, no superiority or arrogance. Only raw heat and passion and lust. The image would've made her smile if her body weren't overwrought with pleasure.

"Yes," she breathed.

Blake shuffled closer on his knees.

"I want to," she moaned.

Mitchell growled into her hair. The animalistic sounds sent electricity through her veins. His body moved away, and she heard the slide of the bedside drawer, a crinkle of a wrapper, and then felt the jerks as he sheathed himself with a condom. Moments later he was against her again, his hard chest molding against her back.

Blake lay down beside her, his gaze intent on her face while

Mitchell slid his hand over her bottom, between her legs, and stroked her pussy from behind. He worked her sex with deliberately slow penetrations, his fingers moving in and out, while the head of his shaft rested at her opening, nudging where his digits already filled her. She stretched to accommodate him, and the pinch of pain felt better than she expected, sharp and sweet. It made her core clamp down on his fingers and her butt grind hard into him. Her back arched while Blake's fingers slid toward her and came to rest against her hand clasping the sheet.

"Let me see you."

She shook her head in panic, the arousal slipping from her grasp. She wasn't ready to be on display. A part of her mind still lingered in the present, instead of the passionate plane where the rest of her consciousness hovered. Until she was lost to sensation, she didn't know if she could allow it.

"All right." He nodded and pulled his hand back, moving it to the waistband of his boxers. He turned onto his back, lifted his ass off the bed and removed the only piece of material left covering his toned body. She didn't take note of where the clothing landed. Her eyes were fixated on his erection. His girth and length made her blink. Again and again. And she clamped down on Mitchell's fingers.

Impressive.

"Don't get too excited, sweetheart." Mitchell nuzzled her neck. "You're mine."

She nodded and whimpered when he stroked her clit.

It wasn't until she went to mentally compare Blake's size to Mitchell's that she realized she hadn't actually seen her lover naked. Her only experience had been through touch, and that alone had been profound.

Needing to see him, she turned her back to Blake and encircled Mitchell's waist in a hug. She regretted his touch leaving her most sensitive flesh, but she craved the image of his lips, the sexy swoop of his hair. "I've hated not being able to see you." She gazed at his face and savored the way he peered at her with intensity.

"Your sight's better?"

She nodded. "Almost back to normal."

He kissed her jaw and pulled her close so their bodies touched from toe to chest. She snuggled into him, her nipples beading at the friction of his skin.

"You're not disappointed?"

She leaned back and scrutinized his expression. The slight tilt of his lips tried to convince her he was making a joke, yet his eyes spoke of insecurities she hadn't noticed before. "What do you mean, am I disappointed?"

His gaze flickered to Blake, then returned to her as he leaned closer to her ear. "In me."

Her heart contracted at his vulnerability. "No." She stroked his cheek with her palm and smiled. "You're perfect. The most gorgeous man I've ever seen."

It was true. She'd never been more infatuated. Not even during her teen years when she experienced her first boy band crush. Mitchell Davies had stolen her heart, and she didn't think she would ever want it back.

Blake cleared his throat. "Except for me, she means."

Her smile widened, and so did Mitchell's. Ignoring Blake, she placed a kiss on the smooth flesh of Mitchell's chest and stroked her fingers down his arm, over his waist, and grasped his arousal. He hissed in a breath and thrust into her hold. He continued to pulse in her hand, back and forth, each movement bringing him closer to where she wanted him to be.

"I want you." He cupped the back of her head with his hand.

"I'm right here. Take me."

He was on top of her before she finished the words, the heavy weight of his body sinking into her. He thrust between her thighs and his thick cock slid to the entrance of her sex. He did it again and again, his arousal teasing her with gliding strokes through her juices until finally he angled his hips and sank home.

She gasped and arched her back, the sensation rocking her entire body, his adoration consuming her. Blake groaned from beside them, and she glanced his way, her attention immediately straying to the erection he worked in his hand. He stroked himself with lazy deliberation. Her gaze crept up his tattooed chest, to his face straining with determination, while Mitchell retreated and thrust into her over and over.

Blake's eyes didn't focus on her face. They were lower, hovering around her breasts that were now squashed against Mitchell's chest. She didn't cower, didn't suffer an ounce of shame or embarrassment. Instead, she turned back to Mitchell and hitched her legs around his waist, giving him deeper penetration and making the sheet glide further down over their bodies.

He leaned in, kissed her shoulder as he thrust, and moved his lips to her ear. "Have you been taken from behind?" His words were low, the volume too quiet for Blake to hear.

She closed her eyes with the mental image of her lying on her stomach while he sank deep within her core, and shook her head. No. Missionary was all she'd experienced with her former lovers, and those experiences had been sterile compared to the way he'd pleasured her in the same position.

"Let me be the first." He left a trail of kisses along her shoulder, each press of his lips followed by a thrust of his hips. "I want to show you things no one else has."

She encircled his neck with her hands and held him close. "Yes."

He continued to make love to her, his penetrations never faltering. The hard pulse of impending climax started to soak into her core and she released her hold on him, wondering when he was going to turn her over and take her the way he desired.

"Mitchell." She gripped the headboard trying to ground herself. "I'm close."

"Ohh, Jesus," Blake murmured, and she turned her head to find him gripping the base of his cock. His eyes closed. His breathing deep and measured.

Mitchell slid out of her and rose to his knees, taking the sheet with him. For a moment she was exposed, entirely on display. Instead of shrinking under the gaze of two fierce men, she used the few seconds to relish the perfection of Mitchell's body, the daunting size of his arousal, before he grabbed her hip and turned her onto her belly.

She waited for instruction, for him to tell her if she should be on all fours. He didn't say a word. He moved to lie on top of her, his weight barely registering as he rested on his forearm and guided himself back inside her heat.

"Damn, Allie. You feel good."

Words escaped her. Her focus firmly concentrated on suppressing her climax. The new position brought a deeper penetration, a more fulfilling pleasure. When his arm grazed her hip, his fingers finding her clit, she had to bite her lip to fight for control.

The sensations were too much. Her nipples against the sheet, his mouth on her neck, his fingers on her clit, his cock in her pussy. She panted, sucking in breath after breath and raised onto her elbows.

Blake groaned. "Oh, Jesus, Mary, and Joseph, those are the best breasts I've seen in my entire life."

Alana flipped her head back, her loose hair cascading over her shoulders, and no doubt in Mitchell's face. He growled in her ear, slammed into her hard, and brought her straight back to the edge of climax.

Blake's gaze bore into her, his focus on her eyes, not the feminine part of her anatomy he evidently enjoyed. Sweat beaded on his forehead, and his eyebrows were creased with restraint. "You gotta let me touch."

"No," Mitchell growled, reiterating his refusal with a hard slam into her heat.

Blake threw his head back on the pillow and raked a rough hand through the short spiky lengths of his hair. "Come on. Just a touch. Or a taste. You've gotta give me something."

Alana continued to pant, her lungs struggling under the pressure of unyielding stimulation. Mitchell's fingers lowered from her clit, down to her entrance, and squeezed inside her core. She was so deliciously full she had to push her face into the pillows and hold her breath to stop from crying out.

The pressure vanished and Mitchell leaned into her shoulder, stretching toward Blake.

"This is all you get."

She tilted her head on the pillow and peered over at Blake. The vision sent her over the edge. He lay there, his eyes closed, his hand jerking his cock as he licked her juices from two of Mitchell's fingers and moaned. Her walls clamped down and began to spasm and still she couldn't drag her gaze away. She'd never seen anything like it.

Ecstasy personified.

"I'm coming," she groaned and turned her face back into the softness.

Both men swore.

Mitchell positioned himself back over her, his thrusts matching the convulsions of her sex. Moments later he growled, low and brutal, and followed her into the black abyss of orgasm.

When her release faded and his motions slowed, she slumped into the bed. Mitchell rolled off her, his softening erection sliding from her body. She felt the bed dip where Blake lay beside her, then it straightened out again, but she didn't have the energy to see what he was doing.

"You're amazing." Mitchell kissed her shoulder.

"Oh, shit," Blake swore from the other side of the room, and both Mitchell and Alana turned to look at him. "We've got thirty minutes before we need to be at the studio." He strode back toward the bed, completely unabashed by his nudity.

"Fuck!" Mitchell placed a hard kiss on her shoulder and slid from the bed. "We need to wake the others." He threw the sheet up from the bottom of the bed and smiled. "You might want to cover up before I open the door."

She reached for the material and pulled it over her breasts as she sat.

Mitchell's sexy ass flexed with each step as he padded to the door and yanked it open. Alana didn't know what he found on the other side, but it made him curse and slam the door shut again.

"They're awake?" Blake asked.

"Yeah." Mitchell gave a nod with wide eyes. "And I'm pretty sure Julie just got an eyeful of my package."

Chapter Fourteen

There hadn't been time to say the proper goodbye Mitch had been hoping for this morning. After they rushed to shower and eat breakfast, Leah had dragged him and Blake out the door. He'd only had the chance to give Alana a quick peck on the lips and type her cell number into his phone before he had to hightail it.

They still planned to meet up in between his promotional commitments. He didn't want her going to the Bowens on her own. But not having her beside him, after the time they'd spent together, left him hollow.

"I assume you're giving the long distance thing a try." Blake raised his brows from the couch across from him. The five of them were seated around a small coffee table. Mason, Ryan, and Blake on a three-seater, Mitch and Sean on the other while they waited for the television host to sort her shit out on the side of the set.

Mitch worked his jaw and shook his head. "You assume wrong." His opinion hadn't changed from his last confrontation with Blake. Not even fantastic sex…truly fantastic sex would change his mind. Alana was starting a new life. She would need stability—something he couldn't provide with his schedule. Not to mention how fucked up a committed relationship could get in his line of work. He didn't want to ruin what they'd shared. Better to end it now before they turned into Ryan and Julie.

"What the hell, Mitch? It's obvious you love the girl. Why can't you pull your head out of your ass and give it a try?"

Mitch glared. "Mind your own business."

His friend gave a sardonic smile. "I'm making it my business."

"Just because you're a nosy-ass bastard doesn't mean you can make it your business," he growled, struggling to keep his tone down as members of the studio crew turned to see what the fuss was about.

Blake returned the glare, his dark brown eyes turning black. "And you think your fucktard, moping, bitch attitude won't piss all of us off once we leave Richmond?" He scowled. "I can tell you now that if you break things off with Alana, I'm gonna want to high five you in the face with a hammer before we reach New York."

"Guys, settle down," Mason murmured from his position beside Ryan.

Mitch gave Blake the bird and backed it up with a *bing* sound effect.

"Real mature." Blake rolled his eyes.

"You think I want to leave her?" He pushed to his feet, and Blake followed suit.

"Guys," Mason warned.

"I think you're being a pussy and need to man up. Try taking the hard road for once. Life wasn't meant to be easy."

Mitch scoffed. "Like you know anything about taking the hard road."

Blake's shoulders straightened, and his eyes flashed, this time not with anger but with anguish. "I know enough." His nostrils flared. "What about Alana and what she wants? Are you just going to break her heart and forget about her?"

A lead balloon settled in Mitch's chest and expanded with every breath. "She doesn't know what she wants." He stepped around the coffee table, getting in Blake's face. "This is her first time in the real world. What she feels is infatuation, nothing more." He'd convinced himself of the truth overnight…when he'd spent every minute lying awake, smelling the floral scent of her hair.

"She loves you, jackass," Blake spat.

He swallowed the bile rising in his throat. No. Alana had never been in a relationship before; she wouldn't have a clue what love was. He wasn't sure of it himself. All he knew was what he felt for her was the closest he'd ever come to the emotion. Evidently not close enough to want to settle down.

"Yeah, well, I'm sure she'll feel the same about the next guy who pays her attention too." The harsh words burned his throat, and his self-loathing tore at his insides. There were too many reasons to make a clean break and move on with his life. He didn't want to end up like Ryan—bitter and resentful of his marital status.

"Quit it!" Leah hissed from the far side of the studio stage.

He glanced at her from the corner of his eye and ignored the anger radiating from her direction. She jerked her head toward one of the cameras and shook her head at them in disgust.

Great. Another fucking PR nightmare.

He sat back down and glared into the camera lens in the hopes the man behind the machine would stop taping. No such luck.

"Good job, bro."

Red flashed through his vision, and with all his might, he held back from decking his best friend. He clenched his hand, bit his tongue, and ground his teeth. He'd never hit anyone in his life, probably never would, but Blake was getting pretty damn close to being on the receiving end of his fist.

Mitch had no choice but to make the hard decisions so Alana didn't have to. He made the choices to better her future. To save her heartache.

And the choices were shredding his soul. Couldn't Blake see that?

Kate had said it herself—Alana was only starting to live. She would yearn to experience other men, other heated situations. The pressure of not being enough for her would be too much. His job provided enough anxiety. He didn't need more.

No, it was best for both of them to make a clean break. His lifestyle didn't allow for relationships. The separation, easy women, and paparazzi always tore them apart.

They both sat in silence, the other guys speaking amongst themselves until the female interviewer stepped onto the stage platform. Middle-aged, dressed in a pantsuit, and smothered in make-up, she glanced at Blake, then toward Mitch, as if calculating a plan in her mind.

He wished he didn't have to do this shit. He lived for music. Not for never ending questions which had nothing to do with their songs. Who they screwed and where they chose to spend their spare time shouldn't be up for discussion.

The woman introduced herself, Sarah or Sally or something. He didn't care. He zoned out of the speech on how things were going to run and turned his thoughts to Alana and how he would say goodbye without breaking her heart. Chatter echoed around him. Mason did most of the talking, as usual. Then everything became uncomfortably quiet.

"Mitchell?"

He raised his gaze from the coffee table to the woman requesting his attention. "Yeah?"

"I was just saying I overheard a conversation between you and Blake earlier. I wanted to know—and I'm sure your female fans are dying to find out too—who is the mystery woman you've been seen with lately? First there was the newspaper article, then the mention on the radio. Are you officially off the market?"

Mitch sank into the role of a deer in headlights. His brain was still there, inside what felt like a puny little skull, but no helpful thoughts were bursting to break free. "Ahh..."

He glanced at Blake, who had a superior smirk on his face, then to Mason, whose frown deepened, then back to the interviewer. "No, not at all. My fans know I'll never settle down. It's not in my blood, and relationships in the music industry rarely last these days. I'm just having a good time."

She nodded her head solemnly. "Yes, there always seem to be celebrity breakups in the news. However, Ryan's happily married. Doesn't his relationship give you hope that you can settle down someday?"

He held back a snort, and Sean cleared his throat beside him. First of all, he wanted to tell her "happily married" was an oxymoron, and Ryan's "relationship" was far from wedded bliss. Instead he gave a lazy smile. "Ryan's marriage has affected us in different ways. But his *relationship* with Julie is *always* in the back of my mind when I'm with a woman I find myself caring for. Our lifestyle is hard to put up with, and temptation isn't only around the corner, it's in our dressing rooms, on the tour bus, and even in our hotel suites." He shrugged. "I've given up a lot for the band. We all have. And being in a relationship isn't a distraction I need." He noted Blake shaking his head in annoyance from the corner of his eye. "At the moment, anyway," he added as an afterthought.

"Distraction, my ass," Blake threw in.

Mitch breathed through his nose, his jaw now pounding in anger as he turned to Blake. He gave him a death stare. One that said oh-no-you-fucking-didn't and you-better-shut-your-mouth all in one hard squint of his eyes.

The studio fell silent, until Sean started to whisper in a barely audible tone, "Dah, dah, dah, dahhhh."

Sarah or Sally, whoever she was, cleared her throat. "What do you mean, Blake?"

Mitch's nostrils flared, and he gave an indiscernible shake of his head. If the bastard said anything about Alana, he would find himself in a world of hurt as soon as they were alone.

Blake rubbed his chin in a lazy fashion. His chest rose with a deep breath, and he turned his focus to the woman. "I was commenting on Mitch's choice of words." He flashed one of his trademark bad boy grins. "Being on the road is tough. The food's crap. Sleeping on the tour bus, and in and out of hotels is a pain in the…it's a pain. I couldn't think of anything better than knowing you had someone you—" Blake turned his gaze back to Mitch, "—*loved* waiting for you at home. I'd take the distraction over the loneliness any day."

"Ohh." The supposedly professional breakfast show interviewer melted in her seat, practically sliding to the floor in a big puddle of sympathy.

"It ain't all bad." Blake turned back to smirk at her. "There are a lot of lovely ladies out there." He winked at her, and Mitch rolled his eyes. "I just think it's time for my boy Mitch to suck it up and give it a try."

"So, you're looking for a relationship?" She raised a brow, now on the edge of her seat.

Mitch held his breath, his heart beating overtime as he waited to be sent back into deer-headlight mode. This shit made him nauseated.

"Not exactly looking, but if I found someone who made me happy, I wouldn't throw it away."

Mitch leaned into the couch and sighed in relief when she directed her attention to Mason and some of the erotic lyrics in their upcoming album. The voices began to fade again, and he settled into his own thoughts, concentrating on leveling out his breathing. He fucking hated interviews. He hated the horror that filled his gut when he was asked a question. Blake knew that, and still his friend couldn't keep his mouth shut.

When performing live, confidence consumed him. The stage was his home. His guitar an extension of his body. The songs a part of his soul. Nothing dragged him down.

Places like this were different. The atmosphere was sterile. The questions intrusive.

Quiet descended again, and the bright lights burning his retinas snapped off, leaving them with the dimmer house lights.

"Thanks for everything, guys." The woman rose to her feet, and the five of them followed.

He grabbed his cell out of the back pocket of his jeans and turned it on. He'd promised to call Alana when the interview finished, and damn it, he needed to see her. He stepped off the stage and began searching his contacts for her number. Not only did he want to speak to her, but he had to get away from Blake. His restraint was non-existent, and if his friend tried to push him again, he'd push straight back, and maybe break the fucker's nose at the same time.

"I thought you liked her," Sean commented from behind him.

Mitch heaved an impatient sigh and continued to move around the cameras to the back exit where their bodyguards waited. "I do like her, but as I said, I don't need the distraction right now. None of us do. It's hard enough for me to remain focused on promotional shit without obsessing over a woman twenty-four-seven."

Sean clapped him on the shoulder. "Seriously, you need to pick up some tampons next time we go shopping. You're starting to sound like a chick."

"And yet I've still got a bigger cock than you." He shrugged off Sean's touch and pressed Alana's name in his phone index.

Sean chuckled. "Are you heading off to see her?"

He placed the phone to his ear, listening to the ring of the connecting call as he turned to Sean. It was already after lunch, and he'd expected they would've been finished earlier. He hoped she had the patience to wait around and not go without him.

"What's it to you?"

"No need to get aggressive, sugar plum. I thought you might want some backup. I can come with you and help out if she goes all psychotic-fan-girl."

"She won't." He was sure of it. She didn't have an irrational bone in her body. He pushed open the exit door, squinted at the bright midday sun, and made his way down the back entrance stairs toward the waiting car. Fans screamed from behind the mesh fence and called out his name. Their excitement grew when Sean followed him outside.

The call connected and he paused, his chest clenching the slightest bit at the sound of her voice.

"Hey, Allie. The interview's finished. Did you get in contact with the Bowens?"

"Yeah, I did. I'm actually standing out in front of their house right now."

He hated that his heart began to pound. He was too damn protective of her. "You said you'd wait for me. Where are you?"

"It's all right. Kate and I did our research this morning. Mr. Bowen is a retired lawyer from one of the biggest firms in Richmond. I'm no longer concerned about his sincerity. I wouldn't have come if I didn't feel safe."

"Give me the address and I'll head straight there."

With a sigh, she relayed the details, which he spoke aloud in the hopes Sean would remember. "All right, I'm on my way."

They said their goodbyes and he disconnected the call.

"Can you give me directions?"

"Do I look like the type of guy who memorizes the street directory?"

Mitch let out a huff and turned his back to Sean. The car would have a GPS. He stalked forward and opened the driver's door to the hired car.

"Doesn't mean I can't help," Sean added over the roof of the car. "It's the same suburb where Mason's parents live. I might not know the roads, but I know how to get there."

Mitch eyed the computer screen in the middle of the dash, then glanced up at Sean. He didn't need anyone holding his hand, yet if Sean came with him, he'd be sure to stick to his mantra of making a clean break. Nothing made a guy man up more than having a friend watch.

"Fine. Tag along. But you're staying in the car."

Chapter Fifteen

ALANA SAT ON the Bowens' sofa, sipping coffee from fine china. Whiplash from her rubbernecking left her reeling. Originally, she'd expected a dilapidated house from a couple who planned to con her out of a non-existent fortune. Reality didn't come close to her assumptions. Theirs was an immaculately clean, two-story mansion with extravagant furniture.

She came prepared, though. Once she left Mitchell this morning, Kate had driven them back to her house with research being one of the top items on their agenda.

First, Alana made an optometrist appointment, which the receptionist kindly scheduled within the hour. Then she'd called the Bowens, who encouraged her to come over after the appointment to save Kate driving back and forth.

That left little time to snoop into the Bowens' lives. Kate had searched the internet, finally coming up with an image of Mr. Bowen on the Channing, Slater & Bowen law firm website. Alana hadn't expected a wealthy, highly educated man. When they first met, she hadn't even been able to determine if he dressed in cheap clothing. Thanks to the World Wide Web, she found out he was a retired criminal defense attorney who lived in a wealthy neighborhood with his wife and two Maltese.

"Is there anything you would like to discuss, Alana?"

Mrs. Bowen treated her with fragility, keeping her distance, not asking too many questions or holding eye contact for too long. Her soft smile and gentle gaze added to the wholesome appeal of her friendly nature.

Alana gave a derisive laugh. "I want to know everything… How did you know my mother? Had she met your son before the…incident? And how did he die?"

Mrs. Bowen's mouth gaped and she turned her wide-eyed expression to her husband, whose face was set in a deep frown.

Had she said something wrong? Husband and wife stared at one another for endless seconds, communicating on a level Alana couldn't decipher. She could only assume the death of their son—her father—still affected them. Maybe the reminder of their son's actions wasn't a topic for discussion.

"There are many things we need to discuss." Mr. Bowen turned his attention back to her with a grave smile. He scooted forward on his recliner, leaning toward her, and clasped his hands in his lap. "Most of which will be hard for us all…but, child, your father isn't dead. Chris is alive and still living in Richmond."

Her lungs constricted, cutting off her oxygen. She dug her nails into the soft leather sofa and swallowed, again and again, trying to alleviate the pain. "No." The word rasped from her throat. She shook her head. "No." She refused to believe her mother would betray her to this extent. It was too much. Past the point of forgiveness.

There had to be a mistake.

The bright blue of Mr. Bowen's eyes turned gray. "I'm sorry you've been misled, Alana. Your mother went through a lot of mental trauma because of our son's actions, which resulted in her leaving town. But he *is* still alive. If what he tells me is true, he purchased a large expanse of land for your mother a long time ago and was sending her money for your upbringing."

Her eyes burned, and she blinked away moisture. Her whole life was a lie. She'd been led to believe she had no family, no grandparents, no father. Yet what the Bowens said contradicted everything she'd been told as a child.

"Did he rape her?" Her voice cracked. Emotion engulfed her. The panic, despair, and hopelessness that came with realizing her mother was not only protective, but suffering from mental problems beyond Alana's grasp was overwhelming.

Everything was fake.

False.

Her entire existence was one convoluted lie.

Mrs. Bowen sniffed and dabbed her nose with a white lace handkerchief.

"That much is true." Mr. Bowen stared at a spot on the cream carpet. "Chris and Susan used to date in high school. She spent a lot of her youth here, studying and playing in the pool. They were inseparable." He gave her a quick glance; his eyes filled with tears, then turned his gaze back to the floor. "We weren't aware he'd been experimenting with drugs until the night the police turned up on our doorstep. They'd been at a friend's party. Chris had been drinking and also stole some Valium from my medicine cabinet. The combination of alcohol and drugs altered his perception and emotions."

Alana's head nodded of its own accord. She was empty, completely devoid of sensation, except for the big, gaping hole where her heart used to be. Her mind, her soul, her emotions, all numb.

"Your mother noticed his change in mood and wanted to go home. On the drive back to her parents' house—"

She held up her hands, unable to hear any more. She wanted to crawl into a hole, to disappear and hibernate until this nightmare dissipated. Yet she couldn't move, couldn't even lower her hand.

"If you have any questions—"

Alana shook her head with vehemence. She had nothing. Not a

damn thing to cling to anymore. Her arms shook, her vision blurred, then the doorbell rang and startled her to the point of retching.

They remained silent, all of them unmoving for long, loud heartbeats until Mrs. Bowen rose from her seat and strode from the room. When she returned, Mitchell was by her side, his frantic gaze searching Alana's face as he approached.

She stood on shaky legs and sank into the warmth of his arms, needing his strength and protection.

"What's wrong?" he whispered into her hair, clutching her body to his chest. "You're trembling."

She shook her head, unable to speak. She rested her palms against the muscles of his chest and closed her eyes.

"I'm sorry to have upset you, Alana."

She pulled back from Mitchell's embrace, glanced at Mr. Bowen, and nodded in response. "I-I know."

Mitchell lifted her chin with a delicate finger, gaining her focus. His gaze scrutinized her features, his eyes pleading for answers while he held her upper arm with a gentle grip. "Tell me, Allie. What's happened?"

She swallowed the lump in her throat and winced at the pain that followed. "M-my dad." She shook her head, breathed deep. 'Dad' was the wrong word. 'Dad' implied a familiar bond, a connection, something she had never, and would never feel for the man. "My father. The man who raped my mother, is alive."

His eyes widened, and he recoiled as if he'd been struck. "You were…"

She hadn't mentioned the attack before. Shame kept her from admitting how she'd been conceived. Every day of her life had been a constant reminder of the traumatic event. Every time she stared into her mother's eyes, she glimpsed the pain of remembrance.

"I'm the result of a man raping my mother." She peered into his eyes and waited for the disgust to cross his features, for him to realize half her DNA came from someone capable of such a horrendous act.

He frowned, his grip on her arm tightening, and he blinked, once, twice, three times, batting away the shock from his eyes. He pulled her into his arms, hugged her close, and pressed a firm kiss on the top of her head.

"I'm sorry." His hold tightened. "Allie, I'm so sorry."

A burning tear broke free, leaving a scorching trail down her cheek. She leaned into him and grasped what he offered, the warmth, the support, the protection. He gave her what she needed without a single word.

The doorbell rang again, the dull ring like a gunshot blast through the silence. Mrs. Bowen gave an apologetic glance and moved from the room.

Alana stepped back from Mitchell's grip. "I need to get out of here."

He nodded and dropped his arms to his sides. She turned to Mr. Bowen, who now stood at the far end of the sofa.

"I'm sorry, but I need to leave."

He tilted his head in acknowledgement. "I understand. I'm sorry to have been the bearer of…unwelcomed news."

The regret was evident in his sad smile and troubled gaze. He was a caring man, with a successful career. She could only imagine how her father's actions would've affected their perfect existence.

"It isn't your fault. It seems I've been misled my entire life."

Mitchell clutched her hand, entwining their fingers, and led her from the room into the entrance hall. Mrs. Bowen spoke in a hushed whisper to a middle-aged man. Her tone was alarmed, her gaze panicked as it drifted back to Alana.

Words weren't necessary. Instinct told her the stranger in the expensive tailored suit with his back to her meant something. Was he an uncle, a cousin, a high school friend of her mother's? She diverted her gaze to the marble floor as time slowed. Each step toward the door made her pulse thud, her nerves skitter, and her stomach roll.

Mitchell's hand came to rest on the low of her back, and she realized she'd stopped. Even though her knees threatened to fall out from under her, she glanced over her shoulder and focused on the man who now stared on her.

He had a slim face, his dark brown hair a similar color to her own. But there was no mistaking the eyes. The light green irises matched the ones that reflected back at her every time she looked in the mirror.

Mitchell stepped in front of her, blocking her view. She wasn't sure if he could sense the approach of her breakdown, didn't know if he was aware she was losing hold of her sanity. Reality was slipping from her grasp with every dazed blink of her eyes. She felt drugged, as if she were living an out of body experience.

"We need to go, sweetheart." He raised his hand to indicate the door.

"Alana." The stranger spoke her name with reverence. It was only one word. One emotionally devastating word. That's all it took for her to realize. Without doubt.

This man was her father.

Mitch kept his gaze trained on the man causing the palpable hostility to churn in the entryway. Mrs. Bowen seemed paused on the brink of a meltdown, her skin clammy, her hand shaking as it rose to her mouth in horror. He sensed her husband behind him and his apprehension over the unexpected visitor.

But it was Alana he worried about. She was close to catatonic, her eyes blinking without sight, her lips parted without words.

He stepped toward the door, his palm still on her back, and grasped the handle tight.

"Wait." The man's voice broke, and Mitch glanced over his shoulder to catch the asshole approaching.

"Back off," he growled and felt Alana's spine stiffen as she staggered forward.

"She's my daughter."

Mitch let the anger in his veins take hold. He turned, squared his shoulders, and got in the man's face. "She'll be your ticket to unconsciousness if you dare to touch her."

"Mitchell." Alana's plea acted like a leash, pulling him back.

He glared, and his nostrils flared. Her father may seem innocent with his remorseful eyes and professional suit, but Mitch didn't give a fuck. A man capable of rape was a man undeserving of life.

"Let's go," he said to Alana, his gaze still boring into the man before him.

Her heels clicked on the tile, and when the door creaked with her exit, he followed, striding from the house and down the front steps.

Fresh air hit him like a burst of clarity, the bright sunlight giving him perspective. This was far from his normal reality. Family drama gave him hives. It reminded him of Ryan and his miserable marriage.

"No." Her father barreled past, knocking Mitch's shoulder in his effort to get to her. He grabbed for Alana's elbow, and she turned with a gasp.

Mitch snapped—a faint mental pop signaling his break with restraint. He didn't think, didn't contemplate. He took action, slamming his fist into the man's cheek. The pain was immediate, the searing agony coursing through his knuckles, down to his fingers, and all the way up his arm.

Alana screamed. A car door slammed, then another. Mr. and Mrs. Bowen rushed forward, helping their son to his feet. And Mitch stood there, frozen in place. Unable to understand what had just happened.

Sean's face moved in front of his, asking questions he couldn't hear, speaking words he couldn't understand. His gaze sought Alana through the confusion. She was walking away from him, glancing over her shoulder in shock, or maybe disgust, while Kate ushered her down the path.

The noise from the Bowens didn't register over the static in his head. The elderly couple helped their son to his feet, avoiding eye contact as they rushed inside.

"*Mitch.*" Sean grasped his shoulders and shook. "Mitch! They're probably calling the cops, bro. We need to get out of here."

He tried to blink away the haze. Where had everyone gone? What had he done? A car door slammed, jolting him back to life. "Shit. Alana." He shrugged off Sean's hold and strode down the path, his pace quickening with every step. "Hurry up."

"I've been trying to get you to move for five minutes, dickwad." Sean's footsteps thumped behind him. "Why the sudden need for speed?"

He concentrated on Alana and the tortured expression that skewered him from the passenger side window of Kate's red compact car. He mouthed for her to stop and held up his hands. Instead of acknowledging his plea, she looked away, embedding a knife straight through his heart.

"Fucking hell." He didn't mean to yell. He couldn't help it. His entire body ached, his chest, his lungs, his arms, all the way to his fingers. And that didn't include the pain pulsating in the knuckles of his right hand. "Hurry up, Sean."

He began to run, making it to his rental car and opening the driver's door as soon as Sean released the lock.

"What's the fucking hurry?" Sean asked, sliding into the passenger seat and slamming the door.

"I have no idea where Kate lives. If Alana's too pissed to stop and let me apologize, she'll probably be too pissed to answer her phone before we have to jet outta here."

Kate's car passed as Mitch fastened his seat belt and turned the key in the ignition. Before he pulled from the curb, he yanked his cell phone out of his pocket and threw it at Sean. "Call her. If she answers, find out where they're going."

"Awesome. I always wanted to be your secretary."

He steered onto the road to follow Kate, his tires screeching. By the time she turned the corner, he was right behind, but had to stop and wait for traffic. Blue car, green car, white truck. He accelerated with a burst of speed, the little red car barely visible up ahead.

"She's not answering." Sean handed the phone back.

"Try again."

"I don't think she's going to answer. She seemed pretty pissed when you snap-crackled that old-timer."

Mitch pushed the phone back. "Try. Again."

"Fine…Who was the guy, anyway?" Sean dialed again.

A sigh of regret escaped Mitch's lips. "Her father." He placed his foot down harder on the gas.

Laughter filled the car. "That's badass."

"Yeah, pretty fucking badass, seeing as I've completely totaled my hand." He wiggled his fingers and winced at the thousand shots of pain that followed. "How come you never told me how much it hurt to punch a guy?"

"'Cause you've always been too prissy to wanna break a nail. If I even contemplated the thought of you cracking someone, I would've told you to aim for the stomach to avoid damaging your hand. Good luck playing during the promo tour with swollen knuckles, loser."

Sean gripped the door's armrest as Mitch took a sharp turn without slowing.

"How's it feeling?"

"Like I've got Wolverine's blades embedded under my skin."

"Yeah," Sean sniggered. "That sounds about right…and you might want to slow down."

Damn it. Where the hell had the red car gone? He was stuck in suburbia with only two lanes of traffic. Why couldn't he be playing Speed Racer on the freeway?

He swerved into the opposite lane and veered straight back when he sighted an oncoming van.

"Holyfuckingshit. You're gonna kill me," Sean wailed, gripping the dash with his free hand. "I'm too pretty to die. I'm too damn pretty."

"Are you still trying to call her?" Mitch shot him an incredulous look.

"I no longer have the use of my fingers. They're frozen in fear."

Mitch shook his head and gripped the wheel with his swollen hand, snatching the phone from him with the other.

"Oh, hell no." Sean raised his voice, grabbing it back. "Your driving is bad enough without another distraction."

"Well keep dialing—oh shit." He noticed too late that Kate's car had turned down the street he began to pass. He didn't think, didn't falter. He jerked the steering wheel to the left, almost clipping a parked car as he straightened onto the new road.

"I'm gonna kick your ass as soon as we get out of the car," Sean mumbled, his attention now on the cars streaking past in a blur of color.

Mitch closed the gap between them and Kate. He breathed a sigh of relief when, a few minutes later, she pulled into the driveway of a small brick house. He followed her up the drive and came to an abrupt stop mere inches from Kate's car.

Oh, shit. Now what should he do?

Trepidation clogged his throat. He loved the irony of having to race here to do something he loathed doing in the first place. He'd only come to say goodbye, and now he wasn't sure she'd let him get the words out after he'd slammed his fist into her father's face.

"Fuck it."

He yanked the keys from the ignition and unfastened his seat belt. This was it. The last time he would see Allie. Pain exploded in the back of his head and he fell forward, gripping the steering wheel. "Mother fu–"

"If I didn't feel so sorry for you, you would've got more than a slap."

Mitch glared at Sean, then lightened the harshness of his gaze when he notice the beads of sweat on his friend's forehead. He inhaled deep and let it out in a sigh. "Wish me luck."

"Good luck, buddy." Sean's gaze held sympathy. "Alana seems like a mighty fine woman. You sure you still want to break things off?"

Alana climbed out of the car, her long, brown hair flowing over her shoulders while she slowly turned to face him.

No, he didn't want to sever his ties with her. He wanted to stay here and do whatever it took to gain her forgiveness. "Oh, shit, what am I doing?" he whispered to himself. She was so beautiful. Her full lips, her dimples, her bright eyes, and flawless skin. She was brave and loving and trusting and caring, and… Oh, Christ, he needed to get a grip.

They lived in different worlds. Hers was just beginning. His was a washing machine of drama, lies, and sleazy sex.

"No. I've gotta do this." He opened his car door and his heart dropped to his feet when he stood.

Alana lifted her chin and wandered around the front of the car, her fingers trailing along the hood. She needed a few moments to compose herself, to stop the tears from falling. Life had been such a rush the past few days. She'd changed from being a caterpillar into a butterfly, yet she hadn't learned how to use her wings.

The real world was harsh. First the violence of Mitchell's dismissed bodyguard, then the betrayal upon betrayal from her mother, followed by more violence from the man she had begun to trust. The lows had rocked her emotional foundations, yet the highs were more than she ever dreamed. If only she could overcome the vertigo which stemmed from the back and forth between ecstasy and trepidation.

"I'm sorry."

She raised her gaze from the cement driveway to his gorgeous hazel eyes. Mitchell stood before her, hands in pockets, his face gloomy with regret. She tried to smile, to show him everything was all right, but it only made her eyes burn.

"I don't understand what happened to me, Allie. I just snapped."

That's what scared her the most. She hadn't contemplated Mitchell being a violent man. Two days together, and she thought she knew him. Two days where she hadn't even been able to see him or read his expression.

Oh, how naive and delusional she was.

She understood his protective anger, but couldn't excuse the violent reaction. He glanced down at his hand and tilted it back and forth. His knuckles were red and swollen, and she felt the urge to comfort him.

The whole situation was a mess.

"I've never hit anyone before." He spoke softly. "I…I…" He shook his head and slumped against the car.

Her heart ached for him, yet it comforted her to find out the violent outburst wasn't a common occurrence. She walked the remaining steps around the hood and stopped in front of him.

"The past few days have been emotional." She sighed. "I've been a strain on you. We haven't had much sleep. You're dealing with the start of your promotional tour and album release…and you were protecting me."

He glanced up at her from underneath his dark lashes.

"I'm not making excuses for you. Please don't think I am." She shook her head. "I don't condone violence. It's the way I've been raised, and that part of me will never change. But I do understand why you did it." She stepped into him, needing a connection, and gently raised his damaged hand in her palm. "Thank you for looking out for me." She rubbed a delicate finger over the swollen skin. "Does it hurt?"

"Like a mother… Yeah, it hurts." He gave her a sad, lopsided grin. "I'm not sure worker's compensation covers me for acts of stupidity."

Her eyes widened. "You won't be able to play?" She hadn't realized what he'd risked in an effort to protect her. His career could hang in the balance. All because of her.

"I don't know." He shrugged. "I'm hoping some ice will help."

He pushed from the car hood and moved into her, encircling her waist in a hug. She rested her head against his chest and wrapped her arms around him.

He sighed, long and loud. "I've gotta go."

She tightened her grip. Blake had prepared her for a fight to keep Mitchell, but at the moment she was too despondent, too broken to show enthusiasm for anything.

"I think it's best if I don't call you."

There it went, the line she'd been waiting for, and although she'd prepared herself, it didn't stop her heart from cracking under the rejection.

"I like you, Allie, but you've got too much going on in your life, and I'm constantly flying from one place to the next. It's not worth dragging out the inevitable."

She placed her palms on his chest and leaned back to look him in the eye. "I like you, too, but no matter how much I have going on in my life, I will always find time for you."

That was what it came down to.

Effort.

Enthusiasm.

"If you truly care for me, we can make it work."

He frowned and broke eye contact, focusing his gaze on the green grass behind her.

"I'm an independent person," she continued when he didn't reply. "I can deal with time apart. I just want the chance to see if things between us can be something more."

His Adam's apple bobbed and his arms dropped from her waist.

"I'm not what you need right now."

She winced and tried not to take his assumption of what he thought she needed too personally. "What are you scared of?" she whispered, tilting her head into his line of sight.

"I'm not scared," he huffed and stepped back.

"Then why are you pushing me away?"

"Because I'm not what you need!"

She jerked back. "The assumption that you know me better than I know myself is insulting."

"You're starting a new life, Allie. You need constant support, which I can't give you."

"Stop telling me what I need!" Her hands were in the air; her heart was in her throat. This was ridiculous. They barely knew each other.

"OK, fine." She retreated and shook her head to dislodge the frustration. "I'm not so virginal that I can't see the brush-off right before my eyes."

"No, it's not—"

"Mitchell, I've had fun these past few days, and I thank you wholeheartedly. I enjoyed spending time with you and admit my feelings for you are a lot more than friendship." She blinked faster and faster, hoping to stem the flow of tears, at least until he left. "But I've had enough of people telling me what to do and trying to shape my life. I *know* what I need, and more importantly, I *know* what I want. I'm not a child, and I can make decisions for myself."

She raised her chin and took a deep breath. "I wish you all the best." Her voice cracked, and before the first tears fell, she turned and strode toward the house.

Her chest was cracking open with the pain of loving him, but it wasn't enough to accept that he thought he knew what was right for her. His opinion was wrong, and if he couldn't see that, there was no point fighting for a future that was destined to fail.

She wouldn't allow someone to have a controlling hold on her again.

Never again.

With each step, she prayed he would understand why she was walking away. Why she had to remain adamant. She wanted him to see the light, to wake up and call out her name.

Not a single word whispered past her ears. Not even a goodbye.

Silence reigned as she opened the front door and locked herself inside. She rested her back against the thick wood, her heart pounding, still holding onto the hope he would change his mind.

They were good together. Even with her limited experience, she knew it to be the truth. So why wasn't he just as eager to make this work? Why wasn't he fighting?

She released a sob and clasped a hand over her mouth to stop another breaking free. Maybe this was another case of warped reality. Maybe what they had wasn't as perfect as she made it out to be.

Her mother had built a fantasy universe, spinning the web of lies with such finesse that she had grown to believe them. What if Alana had done the same? Had she constructed a false sense of what they shared?

A car door slammed, followed by the rev of an engine. She squeezed the hand over her mouth tighter and allowed the destruction of the past days to take hold as she crumpled to the floor.

"Goodbye, Mitchell."

Chapter Sixteen

"Can I borrow your laptop?" Mitch stood in front of Blake, eyebrows raised, heart on his sleeve. They'd barely spoken since leaving Richmond over a week ago. Mitch's social skills had lacked civility, apparently, so he spent most of his free time alone.

"Ahh, yeah. Sure." Blake frowned. "Give me two minutes to end my chat session and it's yours."

Mitch sat down beside him on the penthouse suite sofa. "Who are you chatting with?"

Blake shot him a glance before turning back to the computer, his fingers madly tapping the keys. "A friend."

Riiighhhht.

If Mitch weren't shoulder deep in his own dramatic-self-loathing-depression-bubble he would've asked more questions.

"Here ya go."

He grasped the outstretched laptop, placed it on his thighs, and stared at the screen while his heart did a drum roll.

"What do you need it for?" Blake reclined into the corner of the sofa, outstretching his legs and crossing them at the ankles.

Mitch cleared his throat and continued to blink at the computer.

"I just…thought I'd play around on the internet."

"By Googling Alana, you mean," Mason added from the kitchen.

He didn't reply. His friends knew him too well.

"Why don't you call her?" Mason strode over and sat in front of him on the coffee table.

"I already have."

"What?" Blake straightened. "When did you do that?"

"What did she say?" Mason asked.

He shrugged, brought up a Google internet page, and typed in Alana's name. "I hung up."

They laughed. Assholes.

"You're a pussy." Mason pushed from the table and walked back to the kitchen to grab a beer from the fridge. "A grumpy-ass pussy."

"I'm not fucking grumpy," Mitch snapped.

"Umm, you remember the chick who wanted you to sign her tits? You told her to 'get her skanky ass away from you.'" Blake raised his brows. "I think that constitutes grumpy."

"And she had a great rack, too." Mason added.

"So what? I don't have time for that shit anymore." He didn't. Easy women were off his menu. For good. He wouldn't slum it again, not after Allie.

"Just admit you fucked up, and I'm sure we'll leave you in peace," Mason taunted.

"I didn't fuck up," he spat. "You did." He pointed a finger at Mason. "And you did." He pointed at Blake. "And Ryan and Sean, too. It's not like you assholes are great role models. Maybe if your love life was peachy and I had even the tiniest insight into what it takes to make a relationship work, while also dealing with a crowd of groupies stuck up my ass, I would've had some sort of hope."

He waited for a smartass reply. Waited and waited. "I'm glad that's finally settled. Now leave me the hell alone."

His Google search brought up a page full of links containing the words Alana Shelton. He clicked on the top one – *My Life in Focus, a photographic journey through my eyes*. A pink screen loaded, the title of the blog standing out in bold script. He scrolled down and sucked in a breath at her image on the side bar. The photo was black and white, in a meadow or a playground. She smiled at the camera, her dimples showing, wisps of dark hair framing her beautiful eyes.

Why hadn't his desire for her faded? He'd depended on it, had gone to sleep every night hoping to wake up anew. But, nope. The hard stone of regret which lodged in his chest the day he said goodbye had grown.

To the size of a fucking melon.

"Damn, she's hot."

Mitch pushed Blake away, ignoring the comment. He scrolled further, to the first post that read 'Moving On.' There were no words, only images. One of Kate in a nightclub, dressed in a sparkly red dress with men on either side of her. Colored lights flashed in the background, people danced.

The next was of Alana, the same guys in the image. Her delicious curves were hugged by a tight pink camisole, her hand clutched a cocktail. He focused on her lips. Her beautiful, full, kissable lips, and tried to ignore the man beside her who had his arm around her waist, his mouth on her cheek.

"If you throw my laptop, I *will* hurt you."

Shut it, Blake.

"Call her." Mason sat back on the coffee table and chugged his beer. "Once we finish the promo tour, you'll have a couple of weeks to catch up with her again."

A couple of weeks. Mitch scoffed. Weeks would never be enough. He needed more. He needed forever. Unfortunately, it wasn't an option on the table when his career had him flying around the globe.

He scrolled further down the page to an earlier post—*Fractured, Not Broken*. Underneath the heading was another photo of Alana. Her eyes glistened, a single tear streaked down her cheek as she focused to the side of the camera. The background blurred behind her and even with anguish distorting her features, she still took his breath away.

"Wow, kinda grips you by the balls, doesn't it?" Blake murmured.

Mitch frowned and wriggled his nose, trying to dislodge the unwelcomed tingle. His sight blurred and he had to blink to regain focus. The weight of regret increased, squashing his lungs. How would he get through this? He hadn't even boarded the jet from Richmond before doubt started to gnaw at his insides. He hadn't realized how much their time together had affected him. Well, not until it was too late, anyway.

Before he chickened out, he clicked on the link to the last post and placed the curser in the comment section. *I miss you, Allie.* He typed his name with shaky hands then pressed submit, not allowing himself time to contemplate his actions.

"What are you doing?" Blake leaned closer, rubbing his shoulder. "Oh, no you didn't."

Mitch shot him a glare. "What? I wanted to send her a message to let her know I'm thinking about her."

"Stalker." Mason chuckled. "Hang up calls, tracking her down online… You sure you don't have a pair of her panties hidden under your pillow?"

Mitch wished.

"I just want to know if she's all right."

He needed to reach out. Maybe his conscience wouldn't allow him to move on because their farewell had been hostile. He never wanted to hurt her. Her future happiness had always been the reason for the decisions he made. Ending things on bad terms had almost killed him. Nothing felt right anymore.

For those few days with Alana, his life had been full. Content. The entirety of his existence had some semblance of meaning.

Now…now nothing mattered.

He didn't want to smile, he didn't want to perform, he didn't even have the motivation or desire to get drunk and screw around with groupies.

He was broken.

Lost.

And unlucky for him, he'd thrown away the only thing able to turn his life around.

Alana had done a great job occupying herself for the last ten days, yet every so often she needed to stop and breathe and think.

Those were the times when Mitchell invaded her thoughts and wouldn't let go.

The day after his rejection had been the worst. She'd woken to the sound of Kate's shrill voice echoing up the hall. Reckless Beat's interview with the breakfast talk show blared on the television, and apparently waking Alana required the call of a banshee.

She'd shuffled into the lounge room, her mind still half asleep as she listened to him announce to the world that she was a 'distraction.' His words not only fractured the cracks in her heart, they smashed her wide open, exposing her heartbreak to anyone who cared to notice. She'd foolishly thought he'd been too scared to fall in love, or commitment might've been the issue. Now she knew better.

A distraction. Christ.

He cemented the notion that she had no concept of reality. She was her mother's daughter, after all. At least it turned her mood from weighty despair to energized fury. She wanted to remind him that she never asked for his help. He'd pushed to be her knight in shining armor, not the other way around. Only she didn't have his phone number to give him a piece of her mind. He'd conveniently taken hers and not shared his in return.

"Are you still staring at his message?" Kate walked into Alana's bedroom and peered down at her computer screen.

Alana sighed and read the line again. *I miss you, Allie.* "I can't help it." Anger had been her constant companion. Finding the comment only made things worse, ripping her to pieces all over again.

Talk about a damn distraction.

She started the blog the night he left Richmond. She couldn't sleep, couldn't eat, so she threw herself into work. A new blog, a new life, a new outlook. Only Mitchell ruined that too.

"Delete it."

Alana nodded. She should, yet what she really wanted to do was re-wallpaper her room with those few simple words. "I'm going to remove it all. The whole blog. Every post."

"What? No way! I'm not letting you do that."

"No." She inhaled deep, filling her lungs for strength. "I need to. I started the blog to get over him, and it worked for a while, but now every time I check my email I wonder if he's left another message. And every time I start another post, I wonder if he'll read it." She turned to Kate and gave a sad smile. "I need to delete the whole damn thing."

Kate winced. "That sucks!" She moved closer, and scooted her ass onto Alana's desk to face her. "Why don't you do a post on why sex toys are greater than a man? Or a certain guy in particular. I can buy you the rabbit vibrator I promised you for your break-up gift, and you can review it. Tell the world how only the finest medical grade silicone is better than the famous Mitchell Da—"

The house phone rang, and Kate scooted off the table. "We'll finish this in a sec."

Alana sighed and stared back at the words. *I miss you, Allie.* Her heart clenched. She missed him, too.

With a deep breath, she clicked onto the control panel of her blog and went to the settings tab. Kate had been kind enough to stop playing Reckless Beat's music and removed memorabilia from view. The least Alana could do was take away the distractions on her end. There were only a few posts anyway. Nothing she couldn't replicate when her memories of Mitchell faded.

She moved the mouse curser, hovered it over the Delete Blog button, and paused.

"Alana?"

She glanced over her shoulder at Kate who stood in the doorway. Her face was troubled with a frown, her skin pale.

"What is it?" Her mouth dried. She stood, her legs shaking as she stumbled forward and grasped the outstretched phone.

"It's Patty from your mom's retreat. There's been an accident."

Chapter Seventeen

ALANA RAN INTO the hospital, her hair a mess, her clothes wrinkled from travel as she pulled her suitcase behind her. She'd caught the first flight out of Richmond the morning after the phone call, and spent an hour and a half at the Chicago airport before flying into Colorado Springs.

She hadn't spoken to her mother yet. The only information came from Patty, and that news wasn't entirely forthcoming. There had been a problem on the tractor. A fall. Alana wasn't clear on details, and she wasn't sure if it was because of her mother's need to build guilt and drama, or Patty's annoyance that Alana hadn't returned home.

All she knew for sure was the injuries weren't life threatening. The main concern was her mother's anxiety over being confined to a bed and vulnerable to the male hospital staff.

"I'm here to see my mother." She leaned over the chest-high reception desk and gave a half-hearted smile to the lady on the other side. "Susan Shelton."

A lifetime passed before she was given a room number and directions to the elevators. That's when the need to hurry became less cloying. She began to drag her feet as she walked down the hall. She was preparing to mourn, to look over the slain body that was their relationship and fight to find any salvageable memories in the carnage.

The last time she spoke to her mother was the day the Bowens entered her life. Dialing the number had been impossible ever since. She hadn't been ready to face the truth. And she refused to answer any calls that came from Richmond—from Patty, her mother, or any one of the numerous women who called the retreat their home.

Now she had no choice.

The open door to her mother's room loomed in front of her. Devastation was inevitable once she passed the threshold. Tears and harsh truths too. They were different people now. At least Alana was. And it was funny, but the few days spent with Mitchell had strengthened her. She truly felt like a woman now. Not only sexually. She had a sense of ownership on the adult world. She was strong. Stronger than ever before. But maybe not strong enough to say goodbye to her mother forever.

She inched closer, seeing the bed, the feet covered in blankets, the legs, the chest. Then finally the familiar face. Her feet rooted in place as she stared at the woman who had given her life, given her love, yet given her enough heartache to carry into the afterlife.

"Alana."

Her heart stopped as their gazes collided.

She loved this woman, loved her so much that the betrayal hurt ten times more. "Hi, Mom." She stepped past the threshold and placed her suitcase inside the door. "How are you?"

"Much better now that you're here."

Alana released a sardonic laugh. She wanted to voice an assurance that the comforting sensation was only temporary. They had a lot to discuss, and none of it would be pretty.

"What happened?"

"I fell off the tractor." Her mom looked down at the sling that partially hid her arm in plaster. "It was stupid, really. I wasn't concentrating and received a broken ulna and three fractured ribs for my trouble."

"I guess you're lucky, then." Alana pulled a plastic chair from the side of the room and placed it beside the bed. "I didn't know what to expect. Patty didn't give me a lot of information over the phone."

"We were all a bit frazzled at the time. She did well to get me in the car and drive me here when I would've much preferred to call my normal doctor and have her look over me." Her mother shuffled uncomfortably. "I don't like the doctors here, Alana. They're men."

"A lot of doctors are male, Mom."

"They sedate me for no reason."

"No reason?" Alana raised a brow. "Patty told me you've been hostile to the male staff."

"It's anxiety. *Mild* anxiety. It certainly wasn't enough to warrant them knocking me out. Who knows what they're doing to me in my sleep?"

Alana sighed and stared out the window. This would be her existence if she stayed in Monument. She would forever be placating her mother's paranoia. Whenever the retreat received women with new stories of horror and sadness, Susan Shelton would give herself reason not to let go of her own pain.

It would be a continuous cycle unless help was sought.

"I'm sure they're not doing anything untoward."

"I wish I had your confidence."

It wasn't confidence. It was a lack of care. She had no more left to give. Any empathy had dissolved when the truth came to light. Yes, she should be more concerned with her mother's health. She should be making plans with Patty and ensuring the retreat was in working order, but all she wanted to do was release the pressure of a thousand questions from her chest.

"When was the last time they sedated you?" She turned back to the bed and focused on the coverings, unable to make eye contact.

"Last night."

"I'm sure it was given to help you rest." Alana wouldn't be surprised if it was due to physical assault against the staff. The verbal would've been bad enough. "How about painkillers? Are they giving you meds to make you more comfortable?"

"Not anything that will make me drowsy, I made sure of that." Her mom smiled, her eyes bright with the misguided warmth that showed she thought Alana cared. "Trust me, the injuries aren't all that serious."

"Are you sure?" She was shamed to be asking for reasons other than concern, but not enough to quit her train of thought. If it weren't for the accident, Alana wouldn't be here. They would still be estranged. There had been no plans in her near future to travel to Monument. There hadn't even been a thought to call her mother and mend the broken bridge sitting between them.

"There's no need for the inquisition, sweetheart. I'm fine."

Sweetheart.

Her heart clenched. Mitchell had been the last person to call her that, and the endearment sounded so much sweeter on his lips. She still missed him, still thought of him every night before she fell asleep.

"Actually, there is." Alana opened her handbag and pulled out the bottle she'd purchased at the airport. "Tequila or coffee?"

A deep frown stared back at her. "You know I don't drink."

"For the conversation we're about to have, you might want to start."

Silence.

Alana calmly placed her bag on the floor, nestled the liquor in her lap and stared at her mother without expression. "Would you like to start, or will I?"

Her mother shook her head. "No." She winced and repositioned herself on the bed. "Not here. Not today." She glanced behind her, at the alarm for the nurse's station. "I know what you want to discuss, and I'm too tired to do it now."

Too tired, and apparently willing to contemplate calling a male nurse to get out of it.

"Maybe exhaustion will help to ease the truth out of you." She smiled, hiding her pain. It was hard enough to accept the lies. It was worse to witness the reluctance to give an apology, or even an explanation.

Her mother continued to shake her head. "Can't you see I'm in pain?"

Alana's face fell. Her perspective had changed in a few short days. Her whole life too. There was a selfishness in their relationship she'd never noticed before. It had always been there, looming. She'd just never noticed it because the woman who raised her always liked to back up the narcissism with something that required pity.

"Can't you see *I'm* in pain?" she whispered back.

The room fell silent. Footsteps echoed from the hall, buzzers beeped, patients called out, and through it all, her mother lay there, stubborn.

"I guess I'll grab my belongings from the retreat and be on my way." It wasn't a threat. It was a conviction. There was no way she could return to the place she'd grown up. Not permanently. She'd anticipated being able to help her mother recover while she packed her life into boxes and arranged to move her belongings to Richmond. But she couldn't offer to help without receiving information in return.

The woman who turned fact into fiction had to give her something.

Anything.

"Alana, be reasonable."

That was it? That was all she could say?

"Stop chastising me with my name." *God damn it.* She grabbed her handbag off the floor and pushed to her feet. "There is no blame on these shoulders. I'm free. My heart may be broken from the lies you fed me, but I'll walk from this room with my head high. There's no way you can do the same."

She strode for the door, calm and in control. She already had days to lament how this discussion would conclude. She was far from shocked by the outcome. Merely numbed.

It was time to move on.

To live her own life.

To smile on her own terms.

"Wait."

Alana paused in the doorway.

"I'm sorry. I didn't intend to keep the truth from you forever. That's just the way it turned out." Regret hung heavy in her mother's voice. "Please, Alana, try to understand my perspective."

She swung around. "I've tried doing that since I met the Bowens. I couldn't stop thinking about what it would take to make the decisions you did. I understand it would be hard. That you were protecting me from pain. But then I met my father."

Her mother's lips parted.

"Yes, Mom. Imagine my surprise when I stared into the eyes of a man I thought was dead. Eyes that were exactly the same as mine."

A lone tear blazed a trail down her mother's cheek, followed by another and another.

"Don't cry," Alana grated. "You don't deserve to shed tears over this. Not anymore. You had twenty-seven years to prepare me for that moment, and yet I was alone. I had no one."

No one but Mitchell.

Her mother nodded, finally acquiescing. "I'm sorry." She began to sob. "I'm so sorry."

An invisible force pushed at Alana's back, demanding she provide comfort. Instead, she squared her shoulders and ignored it. She stood there and watched her mother wipe tears on the sling holding up her arm. Not once did she offer support.

"I've never known how to make this right." The sobs came louder. "I don't know how to move on."

"You'll learn." Alana sucked in a deep breath. "You'll learn, or I'll never come back to the retreat again. You need help, Mom, and unless you get it, I don't think I can be a part of your life."

"You don't know what it's like. You don't know what I've been through."

"No." Alana gave a sad smile and shook her head. "I have no idea. I only know what it's like to experience what you put me through. To live in seclusion for my entire life. To be sheltered, not just from men, but from love—"

"You were always surrounded by women who loved you."

She inclined her head. "Yes. But I never knew what it was like to experience love or heartache. I never had anyone to call my own. Not a father, or grandparents. I only had you, and what you gave me were lies."

"I gave you everything I had."

"No, you didn't. The truth would've cost you nothing."

Her mother sniffed. "You don't understand—"

"Make me understand." Her voice rose. She couldn't help it. No matter how loud she became, it seemed like she wasn't being heard. "Explain why you lied to me my whole life."

"The truth was too hard for me to face." A long sigh filled the room. "I know I'm not normal, Alana, but the world I created made me feel safe. I wasn't scared in the life we shared together."

"The world you created wasn't real, Mom, can't you see that?"

"I do now."

Why wasn't that enough? There was no relief from the pain. No understanding. "Like I said, you need to get help."

They'd only scratched the surface on what they needed to discuss. There were years and years of lies to be cleared. But nothing else would be uncovered today. Her mother was searching for pity, and she needed time to understand she would no longer get it from her daughter.

"I hope you recover quickly." She turned and focused down the hall. "I'll be waiting for you at home once you're discharged."

"*No.* Alana. Don't go."

She glanced over her shoulder, unsure what to say.

Her mother's reluctance to see her go inspired a brief flutter of relief. She didn't want to be the only one fighting for them to make things right. She'd lost that battle with Mitchell. She didn't want to acknowledge the same defeat with a woman she would love despite her flaws.

"Don't leave me." Her mom reached out her able arm. "I hyperventilate whenever the male nurse comes to check on me. They'll arrange for me to be sedated again. I need you to tell them I can go home."

Anger stole Alana's relief. She didn't want to acknowledge defeat, but neither would she allow herself to be a doormat.

"You need to face your fears, Mom." She sneered at the guilt banging at her chest. She wasn't going to let it in. Not today. Not ever. She grabbed the handle of her suitcase and started for the door. "Now is a great time to start."

Chapter Eighteen

One week later

MITCH RUBBED HIS eyelids, trying to massage away the tension. His life was hell. Not just a scorching inferno of uncomfortable existence, but a soul jarring, mood altering, fucked up actuality which made him want to crack open his ribcage with his own hands and scoop his own heart out with a spoon.

"We're nearly home." Blake spoke softly from his position next to Mitch on the jet's leather sofa.

Home. He scoffed to himself. The thought of going to his empty Manhattan apartment gave him the chills. He didn't know where home was anymore. Wasn't it meant to be where his heart was? He'd unwittingly given it to Alana before he left Richmond…without getting the bastard back.

"I don't want to go home."

Blake didn't say a word.

Mitch opened his eyes and glanced beside him, not surprised to see his friend staring back with an expression devoid of emotion.

"I'm going to go to Richmond with Mason."

Blake nodded slowly. "Do you want company? I don't have any

plans for our down time."

Mitch nudged his friend's shoulder in the masculine, non-verbal way of showing thanks. "You think you can handle a few more days with me?"

Blake raised an eyebrow and shrugged. "I've already had my daily dose of revenge. I've been cleaning the hotel toilets with your toothbrush every night."

A burst of laughter broke free, and Mitch nudged him again, harder.

"So what's the plan?"

He exhaled a slow breath. "I'm going to drive to Kate's house and stay there until I get what I want." He'd camp out on her front lawn, batting away groupies with a stick if he had to.

"Which is?"

"Alana." He breathed her name and closed his eyes, letting the pussy-whipped sensation crash over him. "She's all I want right now."

"Well let's go get her."

Two hours later they pulled into Kate's driveway. Mitch opened the passenger door and climbed out before the car stopped. Night had firmly set in, and the streets were quiet. Lights were on in the house, but eleven o'clock was still pretty late to show up unannounced.

He pounced up the steps leading to the porch in one jump and knocked loudly on the door. His heart hammered, thumping and pounding behind his rib cage. He couldn't wait to see her, even if she greeted him with hostility. He would be patient. She deserved a thorough apology, and if she didn't accept his words, he would make sure he spent more time to convince her of his sincerity.

Footsteps echoed down the hall, and he glanced over his shoulder to where Blake sat in the car with his arm resting on the driver's side window frame. "Someone's coming."

Blake gave a thumbs-up and turned up the music, his subtle way of telling Mitch he wouldn't listen in on their conversation. Not that

Mitch cared. He wouldn't hide his feelings for Alana again.

The door locks clicked in release and the heavy wood creaked open. The bright light from the hallway pierced his eyes, and he blinked to focus on who stood in front of him.

"Mitch?"

"Hey, Kate." He wiped his palms on his black jeans to remove the sweat. "How are you?" He held no interest in the answer. His chest grew tighter with every passing second.

"Fine." She scrutinized him.

"Can I speak to Alana?" He glanced behind her, hoping to catch a glimpse of long brown hair and light green eyes.

"Umm…no sorry…you can't." Her hesitant words triggered an alarm that sent his nerves into a panic.

"I-Is she out on a date?" He was fucking stuttering. The thought of her alone with another man made him nauseated. "I can come back tomorrow… Or wait around." Yeah, he could wait around for the inevitable kiss at the front door. That would be awesome.

"No. She's not here at all." His stomach roiled. "She went back home." And there went his balls, nose-diving into the porch floor.

"Why? I thought she wanted to start a new life? I-I thought she was happy here?"

Kate raised her eyebrows, and for the first time he noticed the disapproval in her expression.

"Maybe if you called her, she would've told you about it."

He deserved that. "Is she coming back?"

Her frown deepened and she crossed her arms over her chest, ramping up her breasts, even though he tried not to notice. "Not my place to tell, and even if it was, I wouldn't go out of my way to make getting in contact with her easier for you. You. Have. Her. Number." She punctuated every word with a tilt of her head.

"Gotcha. You despise me and don't want to see me back with her." He shook his head in defeat and turned toward the porch stairs.

"Wait." Her command lacked conviction and he contemplated

not turning back at all. "I don't hate you."

He swiveled on his toes and gave a sorry smile. "I didn't mean to hurt her."

"Well, you did. Bad. And that shit isn't fixed with a flash of your famous smile or by leaving a four-word blog comment."

He winced. His regret had doubled every day that Alana hadn't replied to his stupid message.

"What you need are some kneepads to grovel and expensive jewelry. Very expensive, Mitchell Davies."

He chuckled and bowed his head in acceptance. "Duly noted… So does that mean you'll give me her address?"

"Not on your life."

Alana lay on her bed, staring at the flaking white paint on her ceiling. Exhaustion consumed her bones, every muscle ached, and her heart beat with a lazy melancholy. A knock at the door yanked her from the self-pity, and she swiped a rough hand over the stray tear gliding down her cheek.

"Hi, Mom."

Her mother gave a sad smile and strolled into the room. "Everything packed?"

Alana nodded. "Most of it, anyway."

She hadn't planned to stay here this long. Her emotions were still raw from betrayal. Yet, over the last few days her mother tried a little harder to make things right. Glimpses of truth were sprinkled into their conversations, enough for Alana to hang around longer than scheduled. "How's the arm?"

Her mom lifted the wrist covered in plaster and shrugged with a wince. "Not as sore as my chest."

There were still topics that weren't up for discussion. Her mom refused to talk to her about the information the Bowens had shared. She would neither confirm nor deny that her father had paid for the property they currently lived on, or that he'd religiously sent money to them.

But what her mother did do was explain the trauma of the night and how she thought she was doing the right thing, even though she now knew it was wrong. They'd placed new boards on the broken bridge between them, slowly mending it until it resembled something that would hold weight.

"I guess karma is finally coming to claim vengeance." Her mom gave a derisive chuckle and sat down on the end of the bed.

"No," she said softly as sympathy overwhelmed her. Her mother's emotional scars had always been visible to anyone who knew her well enough. Why hadn't Alana noticed how deep they ran? "I don't think that's the case at all."

Over the last few days they'd shared a million tears, discussed a lifetime worth of memories, and came out on the other side somewhat stronger. Her mother needed help and promised to go to counseling. The step in the right direction didn't make up for a childhood full of lies, but it was a start.

"I can't talk you into staying?"

"I'm sorry." Alana shook her head. This wasn't her home anymore. She couldn't even look back on her past without a stab of deceit firing through her soul. She understood the reasons why her mother tried to change history, but it would just take time and space to forgive. "I want to get to know the Bowens and maybe meet my father properly."

Her mother pulled back in shock, then schooled her expression and stared down at the carpeted floor. She released a pained breath, glanced up, opened her mouth, and then focused on the carpet again.

The silence thickened, and Alana gave her mom the time she needed to reply.

"I..." Her mother swallowed hard. "I know you don't understand my fears and that you have your own life to lead. I'm just scared for you. I can't sleep when you're not here. I can't think. I'm worried you'll repeat my mistakes. I'm petrified some man will hurt my baby."

Alana scooted forward on the bed and grabbed her mom's undamaged hand, squeezing tight. "I know you're scared. You're my mom, you're meant to worry about me. But I'm not a child. I need to build my own life and make my own future."

Her mother glanced up with glassy eyes.

"I want to fall in love and get married and have babies. I'd love to work in a city and have my own studio. There are so many things I want, and I've been cut short on the opportunity to get them."

A trail of tears fell down her mom's cheeks as she nodded. "I just want you to be happy."

"I will be. I'm scared too, and I've already been heartbroken by a man, believe it or not." She shrugged. "Feeling heartbroken is better than feeling nothing at all."

Her mother's posture straightened and she frowned. "The musician broke your heart?"

"A little," she lied.

The sharp trill of an incoming call sounded. She grabbed the cell off her pillow and rejected the connection without checking the ID. "Maybe you could come visit me in Richmond."

The blood seeped from her mother's face, turning her skin a shade of white. "I… That will be hard for me, Alana… If you promise to be patient with me, I promise I'll try."

"That's all I ask for."

They stared at each other in silence until her mother patted her hand gently and stood. "I'm going to let you finish packing before I turn into a blubbering mess."

"Sounds like a plan." It was already past nine, and her body wouldn't cooperate much longer without rest.

Her mom strolled to the door and paused in the hall. "I know I told you I'm going to try and change, and I promise to give it my all. Just keep in mind a lot of the women here are still sensitive. I need you to make sure the men coming with the moving truck don't go anywhere near the main house."

Alana nodded. "I've already arranged to meet them at the property's entrance. I'll escort them in myself." She also informed the retreat residents that there would be men on the property tomorrow. With her private cottage situated a couple hundred yards from the main house, nobody else should be disturbed.

"Oh, good." Relief eased the lines of tension on her mother's face. "I'll see you at breakfast, then."

"Yeah, I'll be up early." Hopefully after her body had rested from the pulling, pushing, and packing of the past three days.

Her phone interrupted with another incoming call at the same time her mom waved and then disappeared down the hall. Alana gripped the cell in her hand and glanced down at the screen—*Private Number*. Someone with a private number was calling her after nine at night? The thought of talking to anyone right now made her exhaustion increase, so she rejected the call for a second time.

She planned on spending the next twenty-four hours packing the remainder of her belongings and saying goodbye to the women she considered her family. Switching her phone to silent, she lay back down on the mattress and fought to keep her eyes open. The rest of the world could wait for now.

Alana woke before the sun. As promised, she shared breakfast with her mom, who fidgeted at the table. Her anxiety at having men on the property was clearly visible, and no amount of consoling would calm her nerves.

A little before lunch, Alana met the moving truck at the front gate and led them down the gravel driveway in her mom's car. The men were big and bulky, complete with the most well-defined arms in Colorado and manners her mother would appreciate if she would quit hiding and come to say hello. Interaction with the opposite sex would do the women good. Alana didn't have a psychology degree, but shutting yourself away from men entirely didn't seem healthy. Well, not for as long as her mother had, anyway.

"Ma'am, are you all right?"

She glanced up from cleaning the kitchen sink to see one of the movers frowning at the front door. She followed his gaze and found her mother standing on the outside of the screen, her posture straight, her chin high. "Mom?"

Her mother flashed Alana a quick glance before bringing her focus back to the man standing in the middle of the room with a large box in his hands.

"Sorry," Alana mumbled under her breath. "She isn't used to… strangers." She pushed from the counter and strode from the house, letting the screen door shut with a slap. "What's up?"

"I—" Her mother's focus strayed inside. "Um… Kate rang the house phone."

Alana stepped into her line of vision and claimed her attention. "And?"

She rested a hand on her mom's shoulder to steer her into the front yard. Her mother ignored her, leaned forward, and reached for something propped against the wall.

A gun?

"You brought a damn gun!"

The rifle hung from her mom's good hand. "I have a right to protect myself."

"Jesus." Alana tugged her mother away from the cottage, trying to place distance between her and the men.

"I came to tell you Kate rang. She said she tried to call you last night and wants you to get in contact with her."

Alana's gaze drifted from the gun, to her mother's serious expression, then back to the gun. An armed courier wasn't really necessary to deliver that message. "O…K…"

The door of her cottage squeaked, and both men came toward them carrying boxes. From the corner of her eye, she could see her mother's grip on the rifle tightened, and she feared hell was about to break loose.

"Mom, you need to go back to the house. Everything is fine here. I'll call Kate later."

Her mother gave a jerky nod, her focus remaining on the men until she pivoted on her toes and strode to the main house.

As afternoon fell, the movers left with her belongings, and she sat on the dusty floorboards eating a sandwich she made earlier.

"Oh, shit." She dusted her hands and hobbled to the kitchen, her muscles protesting as she grabbed her phone from the counter. She forgot to turn the ringer back on and found the announcement of eight missed calls on her screen. Clicking on the call log, she read the details of three of Kate's calls and five from a private number. She poised her finger above the icon to return Kate's call, but the far off sounds of hysterical shouting caused her to drop the phone and rush to the door.

The screen closed with a slap and made her jump. She strode out the front of her cottage, toward the main house, and found an unfamiliar white car parked in the driveway. Her mother stood on the porch, rifle poised and ready to fire. She aimed down at the vehicle and the two men standing on either side of it.

"Get off my property!" Her mom's voice was frantic, unfamiliar.

Alana focused back on the men as she began to run, her stomach dropping with each step.

Oh. God.

Mitchell.

Chapter Nineteen

MITCH RAISED HIS hands in surrender. "Ms. Shelton?" Finding Alana had been a group effort. Mitch had the good fortune of catching their pilots before they left Richmond and convinced them to make a flight to Colorado Springs first thing in the morning. Leah had also been kind enough to answer his late night call to help locate the women's retreat.

Now they were here, unwelcomed, and staring down the barrel of a rifle. He should've paid more attention to the *No men allowed unless authorized* sign on the front fence.

"Get off my property!" the woman wailed, her voice shaking with emotion.

"Holy. Shit," Blake whispered over the hood of the car. "I think this is where I punch out on the friendship card and back the fuck away."

"Please, just let me see Alana."

"I won't tell you again, buddy." Her voice rose.

It wasn't as if they arrived unexpected. Mitch had been on the phone to her only minutes earlier. He'd taken the number off the retreat sign at the front gate and called to ask for permission to enter. Not that it mattered. He hadn't planned on taking no for an answer anyway. He knew what the retreat was for, he knew he would be Satan trying to enter heaven, but he had to see Alana. He couldn't turn back now.

"Please, ma'am." Blake skirted the hood with raised arms, his tattoos gleaming in the sunshine. "We've come all the way from New York. We only want a few minutes with her."

She peered down at Blake with disdain. Mitch knew exactly what she saw, a hoodlum with inked skin, spiked hair, and frayed jeans. A door slammed in the distance, followed by footsteps crunching on gravel. The woman glanced to her right, then back at Blake, who still approached.

"Stop!" she yelled.

He took another step. "I'm sorry, I'm—"

A hollow pop blasted the air and Mitch ducked. Blake stumbled in front of him, his hands falling to his hip to clutch tight. Mitch grabbed him around the shoulders before he fell, keeping him upright.

"She shot me!" Blake glanced down at his shaking hands.

Oh, shit. What had Mitch dragged his friend into? Adrenaline kicked in, accelerating his heart, clearing his mind. Loud footsteps echoed from behind them, and Mitch moved to shield Blake with his body before looking over his shoulder.

Alana.

She ran toward him, her wild, brown hair flailing around her shoulders, eyes wide, mouth agape. He stared, shock gripping him by the shrunken balls. She spared him a fleeting glance before glaring back at the porch where her mother clutched at her ribs.

"Mom, get inside!" she screamed as she came up beside him and nudged him out of the way. "Get Patty. Now."

"I-It's only a pellet. It isn't a r-real rifle," her mother replied, fear evident in her voice.

Blake slid to the ground, his back resting against the car tire.

Alana fell to her knees. "Show me." She raised his shirt and hissed in a breath at the blood. Her head snapped to the house, toward her mother, who still waited on the porch, the gun now lowered. "It may not be a *real* rifle but you've caused *real* damage. Now go get Patty." She turned back to Blake. "I'm so sorry."

Mitch retreated and allowed the guilt to take over his body. His head pounded, making his vision swim, and he stumbled sideways. He laid a hand against the cool metal of the car and breathed deep. Red liquid covered Blake's stomach and Alana's hands. Not much at all, just enough to make him giddy.

"It's only a scratch," he heard Alana whisper.

He peered down at her and caught her staring back at him, her eyebrows raised. "What are you doing here?"

The front door slammed, and Mitch moved out of the way as an auburn-haired lady knelt beside Alana with a first aid kit. "Hi. I'm Patty."

Blake shrank back, his gaze flashing from Alana to the other woman. "I'm fine, really." He held up his hands. "It's a scratch."

"Don't be silly." Patty opened her first aid kit and snapped on a pair of gloves.

"It's all right, Blake. Patty's a nurse. She works here." Alana squeezed his shoulder, and he slumped with a deep breath.

"Why don't we get you into the house so I can take a look at you?" Patty gripped his elbow.

"Umm." His gaze went from Patty, to Alana, to Mitch, and back to Alana. "No offense, but your mom is all kinds of crazy. I'd prefer to stay out here if that's OK."

Alana grimaced as the nurse chuckled.

"A big tattooed guy like you is afraid of a little lady with a broken arm and a pellet gun?" Patty raised her brows and stood. "Come on." She held out her hand. "I'll protect you."

Blake moved to his feet with a wince. "I hope so, 'cause those pellets hurt like a bitch."

Alana kept her back to Mitch, her body facing Patty and Blake as they made their way up the front steps and into the main house. Her spine was stiff, her shoulders rigid.

"I'm sorry, Allie."

Her chin rose and she heaved a heavy breath. "Why are you here?"

"I needed to see you. I needed to apologize."

Silence.

He gravitated toward her, closing the distance, and placed his hands on her shoulders. She shuddered at his touch, and he didn't know if he should back away or clutch her tighter. "I'm sorry."

She stepped forward, dislodging his grip. "I better go check on Blake." She walked toward the house, quickly making her way onto the porch.

"Allie."

She paused, the screen door held open in her hand, and glanced over her shoulder. Her eyes were glazed, her lips pressed together in a tight line.

He wished he could wipe away her anguish with a brush of his lips. "Promise you'll give me a chance to explain later?"

She lowered her gaze and shook her head. "There's no need. You made your position clear on the Daybreak breakfast show." She raised her chin. "I'm nobody's distraction, Mitchell. I think it's best if you leave."

Alana strode down the corridor to the first aid room, shaking her hands to dislodge the hold Mitchell had on her. He was under her skin, in her heart, clouding her mind. It was suffocating. Nauseating. It made her throat dry and her eyes burn.

Why show up out of the blue without even a phone call? She'd yearned to hear his voice, or even a text. In friendship or love, it wouldn't have mattered. Now too many days had passed. She deserved a man who had time for her whether they were in or out of town. A man who would love her wholeheartedly and promise fidelity through weeks of separation. Not someone who would turn up when he had a few hours to spare.

She pasted on a smile and entered the small room where Patty had Blake cornered on a hospital gurney. He sat straight, naked from the waist up, the artwork of his body on full display. She admired the definition of finely sculpted muscles and concentrated on what images marked his skin. When her gaze reached his face, he was staring at her, his eyes wide with a silent plea.

"How's the patient?"

Patty scoffed. "For a man covered in ink, he's awfully skittish around needles."

"If I thought your poking was going to leave a cool picture, maybe I wouldn't mind so much," he mumbled.

"He declined my finest scotch, too. Nancy-boy didn't even want a shot of courage."

Alana gave a fake gasp. "Patty! If Mom found out you have liquor, she would go ballistic."

"Don't you go blabbing on me, girl. It's my own secret stash that I keep in a locked cabinet. No need to upset your momma any further. And I don't remember you complaining when I gave you your first taste of alcohol as a teen."

Alana *tsk*'d and shook her head before turning to the patient. "Need me to hold your hand, Blake?"

"I'm sure you could distract me with something better than handholding, sugar." He winked, then winced and sucked in a breath. "Holy f-f-f-f-fire truck. I think you just stitched my kidney."

"Sorry, my hand slipped," Patty clipped out.

"Please be gentle with him." Alana pulled the chair from the office table in the corner and dragged it to sit beside the gurney. "Under the bravado, he's a big softie."

Blake fixed her with a sweet smile and reached for her hand. "Did you speak to Mitch?"

She shook her head and schooled her features, pretending the sound of Mitchell's name didn't clench her heart like a vice.

"Do you plan on speaking to him?"

"Blake." She slumped her shoulders and pleaded with her eyes. She couldn't talk about it. Maybe when the craziness settled she would be able to think straight again. But not now. Not when she had boxes to move, a mother to manage, and her heart firmly lodged in her throat.

He took the hint and changed the subject, sticking to trivial topics like the weather. When Patty finished bandaging the wound, he grabbed his shirt from beside him and scooted off the gurney in a flash.

"Let's blow this popsicle stand before your mom finds the knives." He reached for her hand, placing it in the crook of his elbow, and led her from the room.

Alana sighed and braced herself for the two uncomfortable conversations she had to endure.

Easiest one first.

"Will you press charges?"

He peered down at her as they strolled down the hall. "Against your mom?" He shook his head with a frown. "No. I'm happy to blame Mitch for this one. If I would've known she warned him from driving onto the property in the first place, I would've waited on the highway."

Alana paused, and he took another step before doing the same. Her hand fell from its place on his arm, slapping back to her side. "Mitch spoke to her before you arrived?"

"Yeah. He's been trying to get in contact with you since last night. First we went to Kate's house, but all she told him was that you were back in Colorado. He's been calling in favors from everywhere to try to find you. Then before we drove onto the property, he spoke to your mom on the phone."

"What did she say?"

"Something along the lines of 'you aren't welcome 'cause you broke my daughter's heart. And if she wanted to speak to you she would've answered your calls.'"

"I didn't leave his calls unanswered on purpose," she mumbled. "My phone was on silent." She glanced up at Blake, and he pierced her with his deep brown eyes. "I probably wouldn't have answered anyway."

He nodded. "Yeah, we both thought as much. Mitch didn't plan on giving up, though."

She frowned. "Why?"

"I told you weeks ago, before we left Richmond. He likes you. I warned you he'd push you away, and you didn't fight for him."

She placed her hands on her hips and scowled. "He thinks he knows what's best for me. He tried to tell me what I needed and what I didn't. I will never disrespect myself enough to be with a man like that, no matter how much I lo-like him."

Blake raised a brow. "And why do you think he said those things?"

"Because he's a jerk!" Her heart skipped a thudded beat. She needed to believe he was a chauvinistic pig. Otherwise, she would end up crawling on her knees and asking him to give their relationship another try.

"No, sugar. He said it because he knew it would get you to let him go without a fight. And in case you didn't know, that time we spent together—"

She frowned in confusion and he waggled his brows at her. "Ohh…yes." He meant the time when they were *all* together. Her cheeks heated at the memory.

"—Mitch has never done that before. The whole protective-jealous thing, I mean. He cherishes you, Alana. I've never seen him this way."

"I don't understand. Why did he need me to let him go in the first place?"

Blake stepped toward her and grabbed her hand. "I'm not the person you need to ask." He tugged her toward him. "Come on. Let's go find where he's hiding."

She followed in a daze, her mind mulling possibilities that made her smile. Mitchell was here for her. He flew half way across the country—for her. They turned the corner to the entrance hall and found her mother pacing near the door. Her gaze shot to them, then lowered to their joined hands. Her face paled and her fingers shook as they rose to cover her mouth. "I apologize."

Alana's heart warmed with appreciation. She hadn't expected her mom to atone for her dangerous mistake without the threat of legal action falling into play.

"I-I don't know what happened… I just…there was too much… I didn't mean to… I…I—" She began to sob, big chest heaving cries that echoed off the walls.

Dropping Blake's hand, Alana embraced her mother. She became the rock, holding strong while tears dampened her white camisole. "You need help."

Her mom nodded into her shoulder. "I know. I started looking into it after I left the hospital. I've made plans to see a counselor. It's been too long. I can't go on like this." She squeezed Alana tight. "Is he going to press charges?"

Alana glanced over at Blake and he shook his head. "No, Ma. He's not going to press charges."

"You love him?"

"What?" Alana leaned back. "No. This is *Blake,* not Mitchell."

"You shot the wrong guy." Blake chuckled, then winced and clutched his side.

Her mom stepped away from Alana's embrace and faced Blake. "I hope you can accept my apology."

"No worries." He smiled and opened his arms.

Her mother glanced at him with wide eyes. Alana held her breath waiting for the man hater to run for the hills. Instead she stepped forward, paused, then did it again, and again, until finally she was in Blake's arms.

"Don't hold too tight, she has fractured ribs."

With her mom's stiff posture and the uncomfortable expression on Blake's face, they wouldn't score the world's most comfortable hug, yet those few steps were a lifelong journey for her mother.

Alana sniffed and blinked away tears.

"You want to join in, sugar?"

She rolled her eyes and Blake released his hold.

"Are you ready to go find Mitch?" He held out his hand and she grasped his offering.

"Yeah." Hope would kill her if she didn't speak to him soon.

He led her past the front door and paused on the porch. Mitchell rested against his car, legs crossed at the ankles as he stared at his shoes. He glanced up when the screen slammed shut and frowned when his focus lowered to their entwined hands.

Blake leaned in close, his breath whispering against her cheek as he placed a kiss on her temple. "Just for good measure," he whispered.

She struggled not to laugh. "You're a horrible friend," she scolded.

"Don't worry, he'll thank me for it one day."

She sighed and raised his hand to her mouth. She kissed his knuckles, silently thanking him with her eyes. "Just for good measure," she whispered, and then pressed her lips together to stop from blubbering.

"Now, this time, don't back down. Clamp those delicate hands around his neck if you have to. Don't let go until all your questions are answered."

"I plan on it." She dropped his hand and marched down the stairs, her chest expanding with each step.

She didn't take her gaze off Mitchell, not even to check if Blake followed. Her attention remained on the man who held her heart.

Chapter Twenty

MITCH PUSHED OFF the car and wiped his hands on his jeans. He waited until Alana stopped in front of him and gazed down at the most beautiful shade of light green irises he'd ever seen.

"How's Blake?"

"He's fine." Her voice was gentle, soft and sweet and feminine. "Patty gave him a few stitches. He's lucky the pellet only scraped his side."

Mitch released a relieved breath. He already felt like a heel for dragging his friend here. He should be the one getting stitched up… the one Alana took care of. "That's good."

He wanted to reach for her, to hold her hand just as Blake had.

"I'm not leaving, Allie. Not until you give me a chance to explain." He tried to implore her with his gaze. "I'm opposed to being shot in the ass, but I'll risk it."

"OK." Her lips tilted in the faintest smile.

"OK?"

Her grin widened. "OK."

"Is there somewhere we can go to talk? Preferably out of shooting range?"

"Yeah, I live over there." She glanced over her shoulder and pointed to a small brick cottage. "Well, I used to, anyway."

He turned to Blake on the porch of the main house and threw him the car keys. "We're going over there for a little while." He jerked his head in the direction of the cottage. "Do you want to drive the car out to the highway and wait for me?"

Blake nodded. "No problem. I'll go into Monument and get a coffee."

"Are you guys staying in Colorado Springs?" Alana asked.

He focused on her for a moment, reading the uncertainty in her features. "That depends on you."

She raised her eyebrows. "Let's go talk, then."

He followed a few steps behind as they walked to her cottage. Without a word, she held the screen door open for him and allowed him to lead the way. He strode into what he assumed was the living area with a small kitchen at the back. Everything was bare, no photos, no rugs, not even furniture. The only thing in the room was a handbag on the kitchen counter.

"I…like what you've done with the place."

She chuckled and slapped him gently over the chest as she passed. "The moving truck—"

He grabbed her hand and pulled her back. She gasped and sank into him, her warmth a welcomed sensation he'd never get enough of. He held her wrists to his chest, their bodies joining at the waist.

"I… The movers took my things this morning." Her wide eyes gazed up at him through thick dark lashes.

"You're moving?"

She bit her lip and nodded. "To Richmond."

"I assumed you'd moved back here for good."

"No." The word whispered over his skin. "Mom had a bad fall, and when I found out she was in hospital, I came straight home." She breathed deep and let it out slowly. "I'm not staying. This place isn't for me anymore. It never was."

"Have you ever been to New York?"

She opened her mouth as if to answer, then lowered her gaze to stare at the floor. "Why are you here, Mitchell?"

His heart clenched, burying its way deeper into his chest. "I was stupid to push you away." He released her wrist and cupped her cheek with his palm, drawing her attention back to his face. "You were right. I was scared… The way I feel about you frightens the hell out of me. The time we spent together…" He inhaled deep and measured his exhale, needing each additional second to settle his hypersensitive nerves. "I haven't had a woman treat me the way you did since before I became a part of Reckless. You were blind, yet you could see me better than anyone else. You aren't after my fame, or my money, or my success. You're…" He swallowed hard to clear the discomfort clogging his throat. He cupped her other cheek in his palm and stared deep into her eyes. "You are beyond perfect. And I'm a fool for thinking I could ever let you go."

"So why did you?" she whispered.

"It isn't easy living in the spotlight. I thought letting you go now, while things between us were good, would be better than waiting until you started to resent me. You're the first to admit you've had a sheltered life. I didn't want to ruin your first experience away from home with the drama that follows the band around."

Her eyes filled with moisture, and his own burned in response. "I've watched a never-ending line of relationships crumple around me, with each sordid detail publicized to the world. I couldn't stand to hurt you that way."

She peered up at him, her eyes swimming in unshed tears. "What changed your mind?"

"Letting you go nearly killed me. I saw your blog posts. Each one made me want to throw away my commitments and fly back to you. I dialed your number a thousand times because I missed the sound of your voice. You never left my mind, Allie."

He brushed his lips over hers. The feather light touch ignited a flame that burned his chest. "I won't let us turn into another statistic." He rested his forehead against hers. "I won't. The time we'll spend apart because of work will be torture, but I have plans to make it easier. I can handle it for now, as long as I know I will always be coming home to you."

A single tear streaked over her flawless skin, and he leaned in to kiss it away. "You won't have to worry about my fears again. My only concern now, is that I might scare *you* off."

She moved her arms around his waist so their bodies touched from thigh to stomach. "I wasn't scared in the first place."

"Yeah, I know. But you might be now." He reached into his pocket and pulled out the white gold ring he purchased a week ago. He placed it in the middle of his palm and held it out to her.

She sucked in a breath and stepped back. Her eyes were wide as her hand raised to cover her mouth.

"Don't panic."

Her focus shot from the ring to his face.

"I'm not proposing."

She released a heavy sigh as her shoulders relaxed.

"No need to be so relieved, sweetheart." He chuckled. "It's a commitment ring. I wanted to show you how serious I am about us."

Her hand fell away and she smiled. "You scared me. We haven't known each other long, and although I do love you, a marriage proposal would make me run—"

He grabbed her hand and tugged her back into his body. "You love me?" He scrutinized her face as his heart threatened to explode.

Her smile widened, bringing out two beautiful dimples. "With all my heart."

Grabbing her ass, he lifted her off the ground. She squealed with laughter, circling his waist with her legs.

"God, you don't know how happy that makes me." He kissed her hard, once, twice, the third time swiping her lips with his tongue. He walked her to the kitchen counter, placed her down, and held the ring out for her to take. "Be with me, Allie. Make me the happiest man alive."

She bit her lip and stared at his offering. Her hand shook as it rose to roughly wipe the tears away from her face. "I don't know what to say."

He grabbed her hand and stroked the ring finger on her right hand. "Say you'll be mine."

She nodded, her head bobbing up and down as tears continued to flow. He pushed the ring along her finger and winced at the loose fit.

"Well, even though it doesn't fit, will you still be mine?"

Alana sniffed and leaned forward to place a kiss on his lips. "I will…Always."

Epilogue

ALANA HELD UP her camera and captured the shot of the three women smiling at her.

"Thanks, ladies. I hope you enjoyed the concert. The photo will be uploaded to the Reckless Beat website within the week, if you want to check it out."

The women paid her little attention. They were too hyped, the adrenaline pulsing from them in waves as they spoke loud and fast about their favorite aspects of the show. Tonight marked the last night of their U.S. tour. The fans had been wild, the screaming continuing well after the second encore.

Alana turned away and strolled to the staff entrance that led back stage. As she walked, she scrolled through the images she'd taken via the camera's display screen.

A strong set of hands encased her waist and she screamed when they began to tickle. "I've been looking for you."

"Mitchell, stop it!" She gripped her camera tight in one hand and whacked him with the other. "People will see you."

He stopped tickling and turned her into his body.

"Oh, boy. Who picked this disguise?" she asked.

He wore a long black wig and a patch over his left eye.

"Blake dared me to wear it." He shrugged. "It's a man code thing."

"Of course it is." She smiled and placed a soft kiss on his lips.

"Take any good photos?" He glanced down at her camera, then back into her eyes. Admiration was in his gaze, and she had to fight the emotions that always hit her when in his arms.

He eased the gaping hole that had formed once she left the retreat for good. She knew she no longer had a place in Monument; it was no longer her home. Moving on with Mitchell made it all the more worthwhile.

"I have some great images of you on stage, and a lot from fans as they left the arena." Since the start of their latest tour, Mitchell had arranged for the band's private jet to pick her up every weekend so they could spend time together.

When he was busy setting up, or practicing, or on stage, she used the time to take photos. Some were of cities, with many of the better images already under contract at boutique art galleries back in Richmond. Others were of the band and their fans, which Mason had shown an immediate interest in. He used her shots as promotional material on their website and insisted on paying her for her services.

"You were awesome tonight."

"Mmm?" He kissed her back. "The awesomeness isn't over, sweetheart. I plan on getting you back to the hotel and being even more awesome."

"Even more awesome? Is that even possible?" She chuckled. She would miss him like crazy once he left for their world tour in a few weeks. It would mean months apart, with his love confined to the restraints of communication via the internet or phone.

"I've gotta keep improving my bedroom skills, otherwise my gorgeous girlfriend might start looking for someone else to do the job."

She nodded. "True."

He retaliated by lifting her off the ground and carrying her in a fireman's hold over his shoulder. She squealed and squirmed, clutching tight to her camera as he tickled her waist.

"Oh, you break my heart. And just when I had a special surprise for you." He clucked his tongue.

"A surprise?"

He quit torturing her while he waited for their security guard to open the staff door leading to the backstage dressing rooms. When the door closed behind them, he started again, running the fingers of one hand up the back of her thighs, causing heat to burn in her belly.

"Unless the surprise is a vacant supply room, you really need to stop touching me like that."

He released his grip and let her slide down his body and back onto her feet.

"And why is that?" He gave her a one sided grin and backed her into the corridor wall, caging her between his arms.

She licked her lips without thought then bit down hard to stop encouraging him. Ignoring his question, she wrapped her hands around his neck and batted her lashes. "What's my surprise?"

He chuckled and leaned in to smash his lips against hers for a quick kiss. "Let's go find out."

He grabbed her hand and led her down the corridor and into the backstage rooms. The rest of the band was there, lounging with beer bottles in their hands, except Blake and Leah, who nursed sodas. Tony grinned at her from the arm of one of the couches, and a few of the stage crew nodded and smiled to her in greeting.

"Hey, Alana."

"Hey, Mason. Great show."

The face of Reckless Beat strode toward her. "I've got a proposition for you."

She raised an eyebrow. Her mind ran wild with possibilities, so she kept her mouth shut to remain composed.

"How do you feel about being our official photographer?"

The room went quiet, waiting for her response.

Alana smiled and nodded. "Of course." She turned to Mitchell. "Whatever you guys want, I'm happy to do."

She already felt like their official photographer. Where possible, she attended their concerts and even tagged along to promotional events to take additional snaps for their website.

"So you can be ready in ten days to come on the world tour with us?"

Her gaze snapped back to Mason, and Mitchell squeezed her hand.

"You want me to come with you on tour?" Her stomach filled with butterflies.

"I never want you to leave my side," Mitchell whispered into her ear.

Her chest expanded with too many emotions to name. "I…" Traveling around the world would be a dream come true. Getting paid to do it was unimaginable. "I… Really? You really want me to come with you?"

"Of course," Blake announced from the sofa.

"Your photos are great," Mason continued. "The fans can't get enough on the website, and there's always the scope for you to place the images on merchandise and sell them. I have a heap of ideas I want to run by you, not only with your images, but in running a band blog as well…"

Alana rubbed her chest trying to dislodge the excitement building to the point of pain.

"And bringing you along with us will also ensure we don't have to deal with a grumpy-ass lead guitarist." Mason turned his gaze to Mitchell and smirked.

"Ha ha, you're so funny," Mitchell bit back.

She glanced around the faces in the room, needing to make sure everyone agreed. They all smiled back at her, making warmth take over her chest. She turned to her man and swallowed over the happiness in his expression.

"Are you sure you want me to tag along?"

"Sweetheart, I always want you with me." He stroked his fingers through the loose hair at her cheek and ran it behind her ear. "And when we get home in a few months, I'm hoping you will move in with me."

Her insides burned with overwhelming elation. "All right." She nodded and wrapped her arms around his waist.

"'All right,' you'll come on tour, or 'all right,' you'll move in with me?"

"Both." Her face hurt from smiling as the room filled with words of enthusiasm and encouragement.

"And how about if I asked you to marry—"

Alana leaned back and slapped a hand over his mouth. "Mitchell Davies, don't you dare propose to me backstage while dressed like a pirate."

"Classy, bro," Sean called from his position beside Blake on the sofa.

Leah *tsk*'d in disapproval.

Mitchell chuckled, his heated breath warming her palm. "All right, all right. I'll work on it."

Alana dropped her hand and stared into the hazel eyes of the man she loved. "Work on it," she whispered, "and maybe next time I'll say yes."

THE END

~ Please consider leaving a review on your ebook retailer website or Goodreads ~

~ Look for these titles from Eden Summers ~

Reckless Beat Series
Blind Attraction (Reckless Beat #1)
Passionate Addiction (Reckless Beat #2)
Reckless Weekend (Reckless Beat #2.5)
Undesired Lust (Reckless Beat #3)
Sultry Groove (Reckless Beat #4)
Reckless Rendezvous (Reckless Beat #4.5)

Vault of Sin Series
A Shot of Sin (Vault of Sin #1)
Union of Sin (Vault of Sin #2)

Concealed Desire
Sneaking a Peek
"Phantom Pleasure" Halloween Heat V
Ravenous

~~ Keep reading for a sneak preview of ~~

Passionate Addiction

Sneak Peek

Passionate Addiction

Prologue

Lost: Is anyone there? I need help.

Blake Kennedy typed with shaky hands, hoping one of the four people in the online chat room would respond. There hadn't been any talk amongst them since he signed on five minutes ago, and he'd begun to worry they wouldn't reply.

This was his last option. His *only* option. He didn't know what else to do. He had no one to turn to. No one to trust. And if he didn't pull his shit together soon, his life wouldn't be worth living.

Modaroo: I'm here. How can I help?

He rested his fingers against the keypad. The tattoo marking his right-hand knuckles mocked him in thick black, broken text—*Reckless*. No shit. He should get "moronic" splayed across the other hand.

Lost: I need a distraction. I can't go back again. I just want someone to keep me company until the burn wears off.

The demons were overtaking him, clawing, enticing—almost succeeding at dragging him back to the dark side. He huffed out a breath and wiped the sweat of exhaustion from his forehead.

The anonymity of the internet was his only solace. Support meetings weren't an option, neither was rehab. If the paparazzi or anyone in the public found out about his problem, he would be booted from Reckless Beat and disgraced in front of a worldwide crowd.

Modaroo: I can do that. I'm quite adept at chatting about inconsequential things until I put people to sleep. It's a female thing.

He gave a half-hearted laugh, and the noise came out stuttered, maniacal. This was good, though. It was a start. The pounding agitation in his chest even wavered, igniting a spark of hope.

Lost: So you're a female and enjoy staying up late chatting in drug addiction support groups? Are you a moderator or an abuser?

Modaroo: Yes, I'm female. One of, if not the most, stunningly brilliant females you will ever encounter. But no, I'm not a late night person. I love my sleep. I assume I'm on the other side of the world to you. I live down under ;) And yes, I'm a moderator.

Blake's cell phone vibrated on the couch cushion beside him with an incoming call. He rushed to grab it, to smother the miniscule noise. The laptop teetered on his thighs, threatening to fall.

"Shit." Clutching the phone in one hand and the laptop in the other, he closed his eyes, breathed deep, and waited for the buzzing to stop. Each passing second tempted him, pulled at him, demanding he answer. His demons knew who was calling. He didn't need to glimpse the screen to verify.

Seconds later, sweet relief rushed through his veins. He passed the first test. If he could ignore the calls, maybe he could overcome everything else. First thing in the morning, he would change his phone number. For now, though, he would turn the damn thing off.

He glanced across the hotel suite toward Mitchell Davies' open bedroom door. The lead guitarist must have sensed Blake's restlessness after tonight's performance and had started asking questions.

Questions Blake didn't want to answer, or couldn't answer, if he wanted to keep his position in the band. He'd only been part of the team for eight months, and already he'd fucked up. Big time.

Lost: Yeah, I'm in the States. It's three a.m. here, and I'm so fucking tired. I just want to sleep, but the crazy-ass nightmares won't quit.

So tell me about Australia. What's it like down under?

He needed to stop thinking about it. To stop turning every thought process into something that related to the white powder destroying his life.

Modaroo: Withdrawal can be nasty on your mind and body. Just remember, it's all temporary, and it WILL get better. Do you have someone locally you can depend on?

And what's it like down under? Pretty darn awesome. At the moment, the weather is hot, the air con is cold, and the beach is looking mighty fine.

Blake ignored her question. He had no one. Not a single soul, and he refused to tell her why.

Lost: You surf?

Modaroo: A little. I can stay on a board for about as long as I can hold my breath.

He let out another laugh. This time it came easier, more natural, less hysterical.

Lost: Lol. So in other words, you kinda suck.

Modaroo: Now, now. No need to point out my failings. I prefer to think of it as a balance imperfection.

Blake snickered and ran a lazy hand through the tangled spikes at the front of his hair. A total stranger, on the other side of the world, had made him laugh for the first time in months.

She was his savior.

Lost: Your failings are nothing in comparison to mine, honey. I'm going to lose the best thing that ever happened to me if I don't control my cravings for cocaine.

Modaroo: Sorry, Lost, but please don't use specific drug names in the open chat rooms. The reminder can be harmful to others.

Shit. The last thing he wanted to do was make things harder for another addict.

Lost: Sorry.

Modaroo: Not a problem. So is it a woman?

Lost: A woman?

He rotated his shoulders, cracked his neck, and stretched his arms above his head. The state of relaxation was miles away. However, each second chatting with this woman brought him closer.

Modaroo: The "best thing" you will lose.

He clenched his fists. Disgust and self-loathing were his companions, and he was too weak to do anything about it. All of this pain, suffering, and craziness because of one simple little thing—beauty.

Oh, and lust.

Lost: No. A woman is what got me into this mess in the first place.

Chapter One

GABRIELLE SMITH GLANCED at the text message from her colleague, Tammy. *Getting old, Gab. I hope those fragile bones are prepared for a big night out.*

She smiled and tossed the phone onto her bed. Tammy needn't worry. Now twenty-nine years of age, Gabi had a lot of experience with alcohol. She could even drink her father under the table on a good night. Tonight, she'd be putting those skills to use. It was a case of drink to celebrate or stay sober and drown in her sorrows. She chose the former. She always did on her birthday.

Her phone trilled, this time with an incoming email. Instead of jumping to the bed like her excitement demanded, she continued to towel dry her hair and lazily stretched over the mattress to pick it up. At her age, she should've outgrown this overexcitement at the possibility of male communication. Must be her biological clock and all that other hormonal crap.

Oh, who was she kidding? She'd been experiencing the same thrill for the last four years. All because of one man.

When Blake's name came up on the display screen, her heart clawed its way into her throat.

Hey angel, if u r free, turn on Skype.

She scoffed. As if denying him was even an option. She could be in the arms of another man and still find the time to pull away and chat with Blake.

With a click, she turned the application on…and watched…and waited. After ten life-long seconds, a voice call came through from his account. Blood rushed through her veins, the same way it always did when he called, even after all this time. She pressed the button to connect, placed the phone to her ear, and tried to contain her smile.

"If I remember correctly, I think it's a special someone's birthday today," he purred.

God, he had such a smooth, seductive voice. And that accent. She closed her eyes and let the sound sink under her skin. American guys seemed to have sexy cockiness down pat. Or maybe it was just world famous rock stars.

"Hey, Blake."

"Hey, angel. Have you had a great day?"

She thought it over—easy day at work, great weather, presents, coffee, upcoming ladies' night, and a phone call from the man she adored. "It's been awesome."

"You think everything is awesome."

She laughed. "True. I'm just lucky, I guess."

"So, are you having a party?"

She shook her head, even though he wouldn't see. For the last five years, she'd felt guilty at the thought of making big plans on her birthday. It didn't seem right to formally celebrate the night her brother had been placed on life support. God knew her parents wouldn't show up for any kind of celebration.

"I'm going out with the girls." She padded to her wardrobe and picked out a pair of comfortable skinny jeans. Going to a club and keeping herself occupied was what she did every year. The drinking helped to numb the pain and guilt.

Blake cleared his throat. "Where's my invitation? Hmm?"

She held the phone to her ear with her shoulder and removed

the pink silk halter-top from a coat hanger. "Umm, I'm sorry. I didn't even think, seeing as though you're on the other side of the world and all… You also have a penis. You did hear me say 'ladies' night,' right?"

He chuckled, and her chest tightened. Fate was cruel. She'd always been picky with men, yet with a click of her fingers, she falls in love with a guy on the other side of the world. A celebrity, no less.

"Yes, last time I checked, I did have that appendage. It's fully functional, too. So I guess that means I don't get an invite."

Ouch. The reminder of his revolving door woman policy wasn't appreciated. Jealousy turned her stomach, and the more she tried to ignore it, the more persistent it became.

"Thanks for the visual, but just in case you were wondering, I do occasionally read the tabloids, and the reminder of how well that part of your anatomy works is always pointed out in black and white." Maybe "occasionally" was an understatement. She had his hashtags saved on Twitter, Google alerts of his name subscribed to her email, and a daily habit of checking the gossip on the Reckless Beat website. Stalking wasn't a term Gabi liked to ponder. Blake just lived on the other side of the world, and the internet was a great tool for her to keep up to date with his life.

Walking back to the bed, she threw down her clothes. Her mood had changed, now hovering far from the previous "let's go dance and have fun" frame of mind. The green-eyed monster demanded she sex it up. Stuff the comfy shoes more appropriate for dancing. She needed shiny, black, three-inch heels, with straps that wove around her ankles and tied in a bow at the front. Not that Blake would ever see their awesomeness. She would have to take her frustrations and heartache out on another unsuspecting bachelor.

"So, is that a 'no' on the invitation?"

"What?" She frowned. "Why do you keep bringing that up?"

"Aren't we besties? How come I didn't get an invite?"

She shook her head in frustration and growled into the phone.

If only he knew what she would sacrifice to see him tonight. Maybe then he wouldn't taunt her with his crazy-ass questions.

"Oh, you know I love when you make that noise," he cooed.

Damn it. She was laughing again. "Fine, Blake. I would love if you came along to my ladies' night tonight." She rolled her eyes and moved to her hands and knees to retrieve the sexy shoes from underneath her bed.

"OK, I'll see you soon."

She paused, her hands embedded in the carpet, her eyes on the shoebox. "What do you mean?"

Silence.

"Blake?"

She sat back on her haunches, retrieved the phone from her shoulder, and stared at the screen. He hung up. What the hell?

Gabi pressed his name on the Skype application and selected a voice call.

No answer. The bastard changed his status to "offline."

Climbing to her feet, Gabi sat on the edge of her bed and started typing an email.

What's going on? Why would you say that?

After the years of emails, internet chats, and voice calls, they'd never met. She was pretty sure Blake didn't even know what she looked like. It had been a stipulation she made months after their communications had turned from occasional chat sessions into a natural part of their everyday life. The same day he entrusted her with the knowledge that he was the world-famous bass guitarist for Reckless Beat.

She had a decent amount of confidence, and still her ego had crumpled under the thought of his scrutiny. It had been bad enough when he was a nameless, recovering addict who effortlessly brightened her day and made her smile with every written sentence. Add to that the sexy bad-boy appearance, those talented fingers, and an enviable lifestyle… Yeah, she'd decided to hide behind the internet for a little longer.

Gabi stared at the phone screen, her heart a wild bird under her ribs. She wouldn't be ready when Tammy came to pick her up, and for once, being late didn't faze her. She was preoccupied with an insane idea that her brain knew would never happen, but pulled at her emotions nonetheless.

Why would he tease her like that? It didn't make sense. He was meant to be finishing up the UK leg of Reckless Beat's worldwide tour.

Damn him for making her contemplate the possibility. And on her birthday! He knew his friendship meant everything to her.

Her phone vibrated and trilled with the arrival of an email.

Sorry. Bad service. Hope you have a great night. ;)

Her heart slid south, lodging itself in the pit of her stomach. She was stupid. Stupid. Stupid. Stupid. Of course he wasn't in Australia. Reckless Beat weren't scheduled to play in Melbourne until Friday—six days away. And even then, Blake already told her he wouldn't have time to catch up. Between tour performances and promo obligations, he would barely get a lick of sleep. *"We're better off meeting for the first time when things won't be so insane for me. I want to see you when I'm not delusional from lack of sleep and running on caffeine."*

With a huff of frustration, she threw the phone back on the bed and continued getting ready. Bye, bye, laid back, comfy jeans. Her grumpiness demanded one-hundred-percent femme fatale. She stormed to her closet and pulled out her skin-tight, black lace, thigh-high dress. She may need to wear her best underwear and be cautious of giving unintentional glimpses to strangers, but she didn't care. If Blake's attention was unobtainable, she would get it from somewhere else.

She could close her eyes and pretend as well as any woman.

Blake strode down Cavill Avenue, Surfers Paradise, trying to find the nightclub Gabi's friend had emailed him about. The night was clear, the air warm and thick around him. Jetlag weighed down his mind, making his head heavy, and his body reeled from the abrupt change from the brutally cold weather of London, to the heat and humidity of Queensland, Australia.

Things wouldn't be as bad if he'd caught the private jet across the globe, but he'd wanted to see Gabi, which meant he had to leave earlier than the rest of the band and slum it on a commercial airline. Not that first class was lacking, he just couldn't sleep when people were staring at him. And there had been many people staring, all of them curious and eager for the opportunity to speak to him.

He could deal, though. He could deal with anything right about now. For years, he'd held a flame for a woman he'd never seen. Almost fifteen-hundred days in which he'd fallen head over heels for someone who may likely be a five-hundred pound yeti.

Four fucking years.

When Blake finally sucked up the guts to tell her who he was, not just a weak, drug addicted asshole from the US, but all of the above plus the bass guitarist for a world famous band, Gabi had taken a step back, openly telling him she wanted to remain anonymous.

For the most part, she had.

It took over a year to learn her full name. Then another to determine what part of Australia she lived in. He still didn't know what she looked like, and her reluctance to share a photo of herself spoke louder than words. Only he wasn't listening.

Gabi was his best friend. His savior. His angel.

Yeti or not, he would always love her. Although, his interest may change from the sexually charged emotions that kept him hard at night to a brotherly affection, if she resembled an NFL linebacker. He just needed to see her once and for all. To stop his imagination from running wild every time they spoke. Or emailed. Or chatted online.

She had the sweetest, most playful voice he'd ever heard. And her laugh. It drove him senseless.

He shook his head and continued down the street, ignoring the curious glances from people who strode by. If he stopped, even paused, they'd be on him like groupies on gig night. For once in his life, Lady Luck shined down on him and nobody paid him more than an inquisitive stare. That would all change if he slowed his pace. The people he passed would have more chance to scrutinize his appearance and figure out who the hell he was. So he kept walking, pounding out the pavement, his heart thrumming in anticipation.

Vibrations from dance music surrounded him, and up ahead, he read the name of a familiar club. He paused in front of the windows, double checked the business name in his cell, and then glanced back at the blue neon sign on the front of the building—Pink Ox.

This was the place.

He'd been anxious for the last month, knowing what the end of the UK part of the tour would bring. Women had never fazed him before. Yeah, he loved to enjoy them as much as the next guy, to talk to the ones with half a brain and get between the thighs of the attractive ones who were less fortunate. He didn't *do* the whole nervous thing. Yet, right now, standing a few feet away from the bouncer of the Pink Ox nightclub, his hands tingled with something akin to terror.

No backing out now.

He stepped up to the guy who had a chest the size of a fridge and jerked his head in greeting. "Hey."

The man raised a brow and looked Blake over. The reaction wasn't new. With Blake's preference for dark clothes, the black spiked hair, leather wrist cuffs, and all visible skin on his arms inked, he was trouble personified. The fuck-you expression he currently sported wouldn't help.

"You got I.D.?"

Blake suppressed a scoff. He didn't look a day under his thirty years. Obviously the guy wasn't a Reckless fan.

"No problem." He reached into the back pocket of his charcoal stone-washed jeans, contemplated pulling out a middle finger salute, and showed the bouncer his identification.

The man grunted and Blake stepped past, assuming the caveman reaction meant he was allowed entry. Inside, the noise grew. The main bass beat came from upstairs, vibrating through the walls and muffling the lyrics. Couples sat in booths and along the bar. None of them paid him any attention, all of them engrossed in their conversations. He took his time scrutinizing every female, his heart in his throat, and so far he couldn't find the cluster of partying women he was looking for.

He headed for the stairs, taking them two at a time. The music became louder with every step, pulsing through his chest, as if he needed it to pound harder. When he reached the top, he paused and surveyed the room.

The bar glowed in dark purple light, bathing the rest of the club in shadow. A mass of people danced in the far corner, strobe lights and lasers slicing over the crowd. More booths lined the floor to ceiling windows facing a balcony. A man approached him, ramming Blake's shoulder in an effort to drunkenly get down the stairs. He ignored it, too caught up in finding Gabi to give a shit about some jerk who couldn't figure out the basic fundamentals of walking.

His gaze raked every seated group of people, every person sitting on a stool by the bar. When he reached the middle booth, with its table of laughing women, he paused. Swallowed. They were well into their night of drinking—at the easy-to-get-their-panties-off stage. Empty glasses covered the table, along with more half full. He scanned each face, waiting for a buzz, a connection, some sign of familiarity.

Nothing came.

One lady caught his eye and her gaze brightened. Oh, fuck, was that his angel? He stopped breathing. She was tall, big enough to make him feel like a midget, with broad swimmer shoulders and a healthy tan.

Gabi swam. She loved to surf. This could easily be her.

She slid from the booth, stumbled a little, then righted herself, her expression now alight with a goofy grin. His heart beat harder as she approached. He tried to convince himself it came from nervousness, but he couldn't lie to himself. There was no spark, none of the fairytale love at first sight bullshit he'd hoped for. Instead of moping, he concentrated on being the best friend he was supposed to be and plastered a smile on his face.

"Gabi?" he called over the music.

The woman raised her eyebrows and tilted her head back with a snort. At least he thought that's what that animalistic sound was.

"No, I'm Tammy." She placed a hand on her chest, over a huge amount of exposed cleavage.

Ahh, Gabi's friend. Thank fuck for that.

"Gabi's out there." She pointed to the corner behind him.

He sucked in a breath, let it out, and slowly turned toward the dancefloor. The group of people bounced to an unfamiliar song. Most were men, all vying for the few pieces of ass to grind against.

"She's requesting a song," Tammy's voice yelled over his shoulder.

His attention shot to the D.J. and the woman bent over the speakers. Her toned legs were lit up from the surrounding lights—on full display—the lace material at the bottom of her dress riding up her thighs as she leaned in to speak to the guy.

Blake gravitated forward, stopping at a stomach-high table close to the edge of the dancefloor. He rested his elbows on the cool wood and stared.

"I'll leave you to it," Tammy yelled.

He should've replied, at least thanked Gabi's friend for all her help in setting up tonight, only he couldn't function. His mind had drowned in awe and deprived him of speech. He stood fascinated, his greedy gaze eating up the woman his heart had claimed as his own.

She was blonde, just like he imagined, with short, wavy hair cut above her shoulders. Her body, from the back view, showed off mouthwatering curves. The black dress she wore hugged her ass and tightened over a lean waist and delicate shoulders.

She was flawless. It didn't take much for a guy with a healthy sexual appetite to imagine those delicious legs wrapped around his hips—or face for that matter.

He shook his head, dislodging the depravity. She had to have a coyote-ugly face. He believed in karma and knew he didn't deserve the front side of her body to match the spank bank material of the back.

She nodded at the D.J. The fucker flashed his teeth in a heated smile like he was getting his pole smoked by a supermodel. Jealousy reared its ugly head, and Blake fought hard to contain it. He gripped the side of the table, and for the first time in a damn long time, he wished he had a stiff drink in his hands. A little something to take away his nerves, his jealousy, his obsession.

She turned.

"Fuck. Me." The words whispered from his lips. He snapped his mouth shut and kept his fingers busy by wiping the sweat from his palms onto his T-shirt.

His angel was gorgeous. A mix of sweet beauty and confident sexuality. Her blonde hair framed a face he itched to see close up, and her lips were tilted in a man-eater grin as she maneuvered into the center of the dancing crowd, her arms above her head, swaying to the beat.

The song finished and another began. One he knew by heart. It was her song—*Angel of Mine*. The one he wrote with Mason Lynch, the lead singer of Reckless Beat, and Sidney Higgins, a world famous songwriter with a knack for brutally raw and heartbreaking lyrics.

It spoke of Blake's savior. His angel. The woman who pulled him from the cliff's edge and gave him strength to live. The one and only song he had contributed to lyrically meant more to him than any other career achievement. During his dark days, when Gabi was on the other side of the world, fast asleep, this song gave him the will to carry on. It reminded him of where he'd been and how he'd survived. Only he hadn't told his bandmates that the lyrics were his reality. He'd lied, again, telling them that his emotions came from the experiences of an old friend.

You saved my soul. Gave me new meaning.
Fought against my demons, while I lay sleeping.

Did she know this was her song? He'd never mentioned it. Couldn't. The cryptic lyrics held too much significance. They laid out his soul for the world to see, and although Gabi knew she was important to him, she wouldn't have a clue how much he cherished her. He'd hidden that behind a computer screen and a cocky persona for the duration of their friendship.

He smiled, watching her dance, trying not to blink. Every second that passed made him want to be out there with her, beside her, against her soft body. If only he could move. His legs were glued to the spot, and he doubted his brain would work to string together a coherent sentence, let alone the monumental words he should've prepared for the first time they met.

He admired her as men brushed against her, devouring her body with their gaze. Not once did she pay them attention. She thrust her arms about to the hard beat, shook her hips in time, and became one with the music. It was like he was in a dream. His angel dancing to the music of his soul.

My savior with a heart of gold.

The song ended and she squeezed her way through the crowd, smiling at men who grinned at her and apologizing to others she bumped into. When she reached the edge of the dancefloor, her gaze skimmed past him, toward the bar. She faltered, then paused, stiffening her posture as her attention snapped back to where he stood.

Her mouth slowly opened and time stood still.

He was done for. Completely and utterly lost in her eyes. His mind yelled at him to move closer to determine the color. And he would've if he knew how to walk. The club was too dark, the techno lights flashing too quickly to give him the confirmation he craved.

A man bumped into her from behind, and she stumbled on her sexy black heels. Blake jerked to attention, ready to run to her. Unaided, she righted herself and moved forward, her attention never leaving him. With each step, her facial features gained more clarity—the curve of her petite nose, the soft lips, the tanned skin. Each characteristic held beauty, and together they made his mouth dry.

She walked up to him, stopping a foot away. The smoothness of her forehead wrinkled in a frown as her gaze scanned his face.

Blue. Her irises were a light shade of sky-blue, cool and calm and completely intoxicating.

His nervousness faded under her confusion. Gabi was made for him. There was no question. No doubt. Fate had pushed them together, and now, he only needed to prove that he deserved to keep the gift.

He grinned at her, trying to show all the heated emotion he'd kept bottled inside for years. "Hello, angel."

About the Author

Eden Summers is a true blue Aussie, living in regional New South Wales with her two energetic young boys and a quick witted husband.

In late 2010, Eden's romance obsession could no longer be sated by reading alone, so she decided to give voice to the sexy men and sassy women in her mind.

Eden can't resist alpha dominance, dark features and sarcasm in her fictional heroes and loves a strong heroine who knows when to bite her tongue but also serves retribution with a feminine smile on her face.

www.edensummers.com
eden@edensummers.com
http://www.facebook.com/authoredensummers
https://twitter.com/EdenSummers1

Printed in Great Britain
by Amazon